"*Nick Fisher knows the Jurassic Coast inside out: his compelling, salty slice of Dorset noir is full of secrets and betrayals that will keep you reading all through the night.*"

Chris Chibnall, writer and creator of *Broadchurch*

"*Nick Fisher's highly original crime caper delves into the deeply fishy underbelly of Weymouth Harbour. Among the stinky bait buckets, raggedy nets and battered lobster pots, drugs are being smuggled, old friendships stretched to breaking point, and someone's clearly about to make a killing... There's a nice whiff of Carl Hiaasen here, but with the unmistakable tang of the British seaside standing in for the Florida Everglades. Funny, dark, surprising and altogether highly entertaining.*"

Hugh Fearnley-Whittingstall, author, broadcaster, chef

"*A brutal but brilliantly witty tale of life on the sea. One that illustrates with painful truthfulness the reality of how tough life can be for commercial fishermen these days. To the point that these two dysfunctional brothers are driven to do some very desperate stuff to survive. I loved it.*"

Mark Hix, chef, restaurateur

### Author's acknowledgements

Thanks to the town of Weymouth and its charter skippers, commercial
fishermen, anglers and divers who have been my inspiration. Thanks
to Pat Carlin, who introduced me to this world. To David Huggins
for reading an early draft and encouraging me to finish. To Adrian
Cooper of Little Toller Books for telling me to keep going. And to
James Rudge at Peridot for pouncing on my early draft like a big
bass finding a peeler crab. To Jonathan Barnes and Alex Sharratt
at Peridot for making it all happen from that moment forward.

# POT LUCK

**NICK FISHER**

*To my fish-eaters Rory, Rex, Patrick, Kitty.*
*And to Helen who makes everything possible.*

Adrian looks down at the Kitty K and feels a familiar wave of nausea. Thirty-six feet of rusty steel and chipped blue paint. A fat herring gull sitting on the front of the wheelhouse shits a squirt of green-grey ooze down the portside screen. Adrian knows if he doesn't wipe it off soon, it'll harden and sit square in his vision, all day long, as he steers to the potting grounds, 20 miles south. Another day staring through a film of shit.

The deck's littered with tourist debris from the night before. Polystyrene chip trays in balls of paper that gulls have ripped apart in the early dawn, searching for cold chips and ragged chunks of batter. A crushed can of Stella and a smashed brown cider bottle lie on deck among the crab-stinking coils of rope, and half dozen pots that still need mending, two weeks after the last storm trashed them against Dogleg Reef.

The mess depresses him. The smell bores him – for far too long he's breathed the sweet-sour fumes of rotting pot bait and diesel. But what really fucks him off more than anything this morning is once again he's alone. No sign of Matty.

On every other crabber tied to the harbour wall, at least two men go through the morning ritual of tossing out the tourist crap, cranking up the engine, topping up the live well, untying ropes and stowing away spare pots to stop them skittering across the deck as they steam out through the chop on Weymouth Bay. Every other crabber has a skipper and a crewman, to perform the same daily rituals of preparing to cast off. Only Adrian, on the Kitty K, does everything single-handed. Waiting until his shithead little brother finally makes an appearance. Today is no exception.

Every potter working out of Weymouth; Nicola B, Salsette, October Morning, Dawn Mist, and others who fish the grounds to the far south-east, want to be underway by five-thirty, at the latest. There's a small spring tide flooding eastwards for another hour, and every skipper wants to use the last rush of tide – pushing up their boat's heavy, gear-laden arse – to get to the grounds quicker and cheaper. The five knots of eastward-flowing flood tide will shave a chunk off the day's fuel bill. Cost of diesel already squeezing everyone's operating margins tighter than a mullet's arsehole. So, getting the morning tide to help push the boats to the grounds will save skippers like 'Damp' Dougie, Pete The Worm and Leaky enough wedge to get half-pissed in The Sailors this afternoon.

Adrian doesn't want to get drunk this afternoon. Nor does he want to throw away fuel money, just because his fucking brother's incapable of getting out of whoever's bed he's in, in time to make the flood tide.

All the ten-metre-plus crabbers are tied up, side-by-side, gunwale-to-gunwale, sitting two-deep out from the harbour's west wall. Kitty K on the outside of her pair, furthest from the wall, because she was last to unload last night. Not last because she'd such a huge catch of crab to unload at the fish dock. Nope. Last because the brothers were late getting back to port, because they pushed *against* the tide coming home. They pushed nose down against the outgoing tide, burning extra diesel, because they'd been late heading out in the first place. Just like today.

Ruby J is tied on the inside of Kitty K. Ruby J's motor's already running. She's ready to swing her stern out to catch the flow of the out-pouring River Wey and head south out the harbour. Cuttle, the skipper on Ruby J, looking over at Adrian, with a roll-up sticking to his lips, eyebrows raised – expectantly. Ruby ready to go. But she can't cast off until Kitty K drops back to give her room. One of the deck crew on Ruby J, a ginger-haired, pimply lad is already untying the stern line that'll set Kitty adrift. Adrian has no choice but to start her engine. The pre-heater light on the dashboard blinks off to tell him the engine's ready to fire. Adrian turns the key, and the huge ancient Cummings chugs and coughs into life.

Witnessing Kitty K come to life is like watching a lung cancer victim fight off death. A rattle of hollow bones is followed by a gritty cloud of black smoke, erupting from her exhaust. Kitty K is sick. Somewhere in her confused oil-guzzling heart is a problem that is terminal, yet remains untreated. Adrian can hear Kitty's engine is slowly dying. So can Cuttle. And as Ruby J pulls away from the harbour wall, leaving Kitty still waiting to head for sea, Adrian recognises pity in Cuttle's eyes.

The pity might be for the chronic state of Adrian's boat, but more likely the pity's because Adrian, once again, is left in the harbour, holding water, engine running, burning over-priced diesel, waiting for his pisshead, waster brother, Matty.

Adrian holds Kitty K's nose upstream into the current that pushes down through the harbour from the river. He slips her in and out of gear, holding water. Waiting. He could tie her up to the harbour wall again, there's more than enough room now every other crabber and whelker has left. He doesn't; because he hopes against hope that Matty is about to arrive, stumble down the harbour steps and slide, groaning, onto the stern of their boat.

He stares through the film of seagull shit that the worn screen wiper is smearing from side to side, weakly lubricated by a thin drizzle. The oil pressure light flickers on, then off again. A blink. A warning. A sign of the sickness eating away at Kitty's innards. Adrian ignores it. His shitty morning is shitty enough without accepting the boat his father bought brand new in 1982 – when Adrian was five and Matty was three – and fitted out himself, over the winter, working 18 hours a day, cracking ice off the tarpaulin every morning, is dying in his sons' hands.

The tragedy of Kitty K's slow, painful mechanical demise was preceded three years ago by her financial death. Adrian and Matty failed to keep Kitty K afloat financially and were forced to sell her to Paulie West, the landlord of The Sailors. Paulie gradually buying up all manner of property, boats and businesses in Weymouth, over the last few years. He's well placed – like a pint-pulling parasite – to cash in on every scrap of bad luck that hits his customers. So, when Adrian and Matty sank into debt, Paulie bought the mortgaged boat out from under them. Now they work for Paulie. The brothers on a third share of the daily catch. They don't catch, they don't earn. All running costs and pot repairs split between the shares. The more diesel they burn, the more pots they lose, the less they earn. Today so far, it's costing Adrian to go to work.

Matty might appear from one of three directions. From the east, through Museum Lane, from the north over Harbour Square, or from the west, down Helen Street. East is best. East usually means Matty's climbed out his own pit and walked to the quayside from his raggedy bedsit. North, the route that leads from the biggest portion of town, means that Matty's slept in another bed, either Megan, Dom, Lisa, Talia or another new addition to his ever-evolving list of girlfriends. For a little while Matty liked to use the term 'fuck buddies' to describe the various and varied women in his life.

He'd heard the phrase on some American TV show and adopted it. Thinking it sounded funny and cool. Even Matty eventually dropped it, realising with a very rare glimmer of self-awareness, that it made him sound like a prick.

West is the worst direction Matty can appear from – west is the seafront. West means Matty hasn't been to bed at all. West means he's stayed up all night, drinking, snorting, pilling or huffing in the clubs and pubs along the prom. West means Matty will still be off his face. Stinking. Wild-eyed. Hyperactive. A danger to himself, to the running of the boat and to his brother. West means Matty will be asleep on a coil of rope on the wheelhouse floor by two o'clock, leaving Adrian to haul the last ten or more shanks alone. West means Adrian will have to use every ounce of self-control to stop himself picking up the scallop-shucking knife and sticking it up to the handle into his lazy, selfish, fucked up brother's snoring face.

As he lays his forehead against the wheel of Kitty K and closes his eyes, Adrian can feel the uneven hunting vibrations of her ailing engine, pulsing against the tight muscle around his temples and jaw. His life wasn't meant to be like this. Adrian was the clever one.

Head Boy at Podimore Comprehensive. A Levels. Technical college. Qualifications. Once, he made his dad proud. Now, he's reduced to hauling pots for Paulie West – a man his father hated. All the while standing by, rubber-necking, as his fuckwit younger brother drives his own life at full throttle straight towards a concrete wall.

The saddest thing of all is that his brother's slow motion train wreck of a life looks, from the outside, to be way more fun than Adrian's married, mortgaged, dad-of-two-toddlers existence. Which, for all its security and convention, seems to make the muscles around his temples pull tighter each and every day.

A loud crack against the screen a few inches away from Adrian's bowed head makes him jump. His heart jolts with a shot of adrenalin as he snaps up to see an empty can of Stella roll off the anchor hatch, where it bounced after hitting the screen.

Adrian now sees Matty on the edge of the quay. Grinning like a turbot. Swaying. Two full cans of Scrumpy Jack hanging from the plastic rings of a four-pack in one hand. A spliff, half-smoked, hangs from his lips. His right arm slung around the shoulders of Lila, a South Korean girl, whose father owns the Chinese takeaway on Preston Road.

Even by Matty's standards Lila is one of his wildest and weirdest. Wears biker boots, snagged ripped tights, hair shaved at both sides and two chrome barbells piercing one eyebrow.

"Nipples and clit," Matty told Adrian one day – as if making small talk on their steam home from the Hurds. "Pierced," he said with a leer. "Clit's like a little cockle, stuck with a kebab skewer."

Matty did this thing. Like some ritual, designed to induce envy and humiliation in Adrian. He'd turn up late for the tide, at the dock, parading his conquest of the night before. Get her to walk him to the harbour where Matty'd climb on the stern of Kitty K, under the watchful, angry eye of his brother. Always, just before he'd get on board, Matty would snog the girl one last time, in front of Adrian. Pulling up a skirt. Cupping a buttock. Or squeezing a breast. Performing some moderately sexual act in front of him, as if to say, "See bro... See what I'm getting, and you're *not*." Then

Matty'd bounce on the boat with a shit-eating grin, enjoying every morsel of his brother's squirm.

True to form, Matty was pressing his face hard against Lila's lips, arching her back and slipping his fingers into one of the ragged holes in the tights, just beneath her tiny round arse.

Adrian looks away. His eyes settle on the other figure with them on the quayside. The teenage boy, staring hard at their mouths as they slurp against each other, then looking down to Matty's hand, fingers reaching inside the ripped tights, feeling, fondling... The boy practically starting to drool.

Adrian feels the heat of raw anger, about to burn a hole in his brain, as he now stares full on at teenage Tim, with unveiled contempt. Adrian can't help it. He fucking hates Tim.

"Today's a 'Tim day'," Matty would always say when he turned up at the dock with the lad. "My apprentice," he'd say, turning to Tim pointing his outstretched finger and saying, "Be good or... You're fired." Matty laughing like a drain at his own joke. Like it's the first time he's said it. Like it's the funniest thing. And inside, another crumb of Adrian's soul would die.

Tim is the son of a woman Matty used to fuck, but doesn't any more – on account of the fact that her ex-bloke, Rich, is currently out of Portland Prison on an early release scheme. And they're back together. Sort of. And also because Rich is as mean as a shite-snake, so Matty in turn is currently giving Carole a wide berth. But Matty still likes to hire Tim to help on the Kitty. In fact, Matty thinks Adrian and him should hire Tim, full-time, like a proper apprentice deckhand. Split Tim's wages between them, and get Tim to do all the shit jobs, while they get their feet up in the wheelhouse.

Adrian says no. They can't afford to run the boat as it is. Season's earnings are crap. So why would they increase their overhead? Matty wants a deck hand because Matty is lazy and would rather shave a few quid off of his take, to pay Tim, than have to bust his own balls day in, day out. Especially on the days when he's hungover or still pissed. Which is most days.

Adrian wants no part of Tim. He needs every penny he can make out of Kitty K and more. He's even looking for other jobs, for evenings and on days when the blow's too rough to get out to sea. Plus there's another issue, in that Tim is a retard. A lippy-mouthed prick who drives Adrian mad. Having him on board is so not what Adrian needs.

Adrian's made it clear: if Matty wants to employ Tim to help out on deck, it's his shout. No way is Adrian sharing that wage bill. Because of this, Tim's not a permanent fixture. Only on days when Matty is either too wasted, or else feeling flush – because he made a few extra quid, doing the sort of stuff Matty does when he isn't aboard Kitty K. Like selling a little spliff, growing a few heads of skunk, or middleman-ing a bit of knock-off gear. He will then bang on Tim's mum's door at Sparrow's Fart, or call her mobile, and get the little prick to come down the quay for a day's graft.

Also, Matty likes to have an audience for whatever it is he's doing. An audience dumb enough and young enough to think Matty's a bit of a player and a 'dude'. Unlike his big brother Adie, who Tim thinks is just a moody old prick.

Adrian clamps his mouth shut in a thin straight-lipped line and says nothing. Not a word. Not a greeting. Nothing. He reverses the transom to the harbour steps. Matty and Tim climb aboard and Adrian slips Kitty into forward gear, aiming her seagull shit-splattered prow towards the harbour mouth.

On deck, Matty regales Tim with a story. Adrian can't hear the details. Thank God. What with the consumptive growl of Kitty's 80-horse Cummings inboard diesel and the wheelhouse door being half closed, means Adrian's spared the details that Tim is now drinking up with teenage glee. Details of the night before. Of how twatted Matty got. Where. Who with. And what he ended up doing to the Korean Chinese chip shop owner's daughter, nearly half his age.

This morning Adrian hates his brother – his only sibling – with a hate that makes his face hot and stingy. His jaw is clamped shut, cheek muscles bulging, stewing in his own passive aggression. Believing his silent sulk will communicate to Matty just how monumentally fucked off he is. At the same time, his sulk makes Adrian feel pathetic. He knows he's behaving like a child. Nothing about Adrian's relationship with his brother makes him feel good.

Adrian's hate for Matty runs deep like the layer of brown fat in a mackerel. Deep inside. Hugging the spine. Laid down year on year, like a seam of geological hate that runs through to his core.

Adrian's hate for Tim is like a cod worm. Anisakis. Burrowing into his flesh, near the surface, in the muscle. Most of the time he can bear it. Overlook it. Pick the orange-bodied nematodes out of the meat and move on. Extract Tim from his mind in the knowledge that Tim and Matty will one day have some infantile bust up, probably throw fists and shout 'cunt!' in each other's faces. Then the little prick will never put a stinky trainer-shod foot on the Kitty ever again.

Adrian can let the parasitic hate he harbours for Tim wash over him, most days. But there are days, times, when the toxins that those worms of hate leach out into his bloodstream start to affect his brain. Times when his hate for Tim is so close to causing an eruption of earth-scorching proportions. Close to making Adrian do something that he will wish he hadn't.

Times, like with Tim's gun.

Tim's *fucking* gun.

One morning, after he stepped over the transom and lit a Lambert and Butler, he lifted the front of his crusty, stained fleece, in an imitation of some south Los Angeles gangbanger, to show Matty what he had hidden in the waistband of his tatty, low-slung jeans.

"What the fuck?" says Matty staring at the grey metal.

"Heckler and Koch," says Tim in a conspiratorial whisper. "Heckler and Koch P30 FDE."

Adrian seeing the pistol grip of a gun pressed against Tim's puppy fat belly.

"Anodised aluminium finish with an Ambrose Dexter grip."

"The fuck," says Matty, getting hot for a nano second, at the notion that Tim was packing a real shooter.

Of course he wasn't. It was a replica of the Heckler and Koch P30, as supplied as standard issue to the US military and Police Departments, which was fitted with a magazine capable of firing ten rounds of .45 duty grade ammo. Tim's Heckler and Koch fired .177 air gun pellets, or little silver BB balls. And was powered by a little metal gas canister of $CO_2$. The sort that gets used in SodaStreams, racing bike tyres, nail guns and self-inflating automatic life jackets.

"Can kill a man," says Tim, taking it out of his waistband with squinty-toothed pride. "If you know just where to hit him."

Matty saying this was bollocks. Tim saying he saw it on YouTube. Fact. The rest of that day and other days spent firing at seagulls and arguing about where anatomically you need to shoot a man with an air gun pellet in order to kill him. Until the thing finally jammed solid and Tim swapped it for a bottle of shoplifted Irish whisky and a replica samurai sword. No seagull ever died. The gas canisters always running out, or the mechanism jamming. Which usually meant Tim had to take it apart, putting the gun pieces one by one

14

on top of the engine box. Telling Matty he'd been practising taking it apart blindfold – "like in Vietnam".

Adrian wanting to jam the barrel of the Heckler and Koch P30 in Tim's ear. Right in the hole. Pull the trigger. Over and over again. See if that would kill a man. Or a prick of a boy, at least. But it'd probably just jam or the gas bottle would run out. Like it always did.

"Know much those cost?" whines Tim about the gas canisters as another pellet fails to be propelled in a fatal fashion towards a blissfully unawares shitehawk.

Tim slipping the spent gas canister out of the guts of the pistol grip.

"Read the comments on the forums," says Tim. "All the military guys and the Feds rate the P30's grip. Feel it."

Tim passing the fake pistol to Adrian. And for the first time Adrian taking it in his hand. Feeling the comfortable weight, lifting it, pointing it at Tim's head. No gas. No bullets. Tim not even flinching.

"It's an Ambrose Dexter grip," says Tim.

"*Ambidextrous*," says Adrian.

"What?"

"Ambidextrous."

"It's Ambrose Dexter."

"It's ambi-fucking-dextrous. You twat," says Adrian, the bile rising in his throat. "It fucking means… it can be used in either…"

Adrian stops. Catches himself. Lets the bile subside. Drops the gun on the engine box. And walks back into the wheelhouse. Closes the door. And starts the hard job of packing his anger away again. Damping it down. Deep. Forcing it into corners. Stuffing it. Trying to make it fit back inside him. Safely. So it didn't spill out. He closes his eyes and tries to breathe.

The wheelhouse door slides open and Matty walks in acting like there's no question of tension. Just-another-lovely-day-on-the-boat. He plonks the two cans of Scrumpy Jack on the bulkhead in front of Adrian. "Present," he says. The two cans of cider skidding on the cheap Formica their dad bought in an under-the-counter deal to fit out the wheelhouse surfaces, and most of the kitchen at home. Adrian looks from the cans to his brother with cold eyes. Matty oblivious, too busy watching the flame of his Zippo lighter, as he teases it swaying towards the half-smoked joint between his lips.

Adrian began attending AA meetings 14 months ago. He'd been clean and sober almost ever since. He'd had a couple… well, three… 'slips' since his first meeting. Two had been proper full-on binges. Three days, back-to-back: vodka, cider, beer, pub, shed, boat, coke, more pub, cider, collapse… Twice… Then home. Home to Helen. Recriminations. Tears.

His pregnant, scared wife crying with fear and confusion. This followed by several nights sleeping on the sofa. Or lying *awake* on the sofa, feeling the cold jelly fingers of depression and self-loathing tearing at his soul. Feeling like he's moving backwards with his life – turning into his father – repeating a terrible mistake, over and over again, even though he knows exactly where it will all end.

It was hard for Adrian to accept he was an alcoholic. Hardest of all to know what being an alcoholic meant, in terms of drinking or not drinking. The men and women at AA talking of 'total abstinence'. A life free of alcohol, drugs and all mood-altering chemicals. He'd achieved this state in bursts. In spurts. A few weeks. A few months at a time. But after a while it would fall apart. Often for no good reason.

No big event. No catastrophe. Sometimes it'd happen when he was feeling very good about life. When there was hope and happiness and a future to look forward to. Sometimes it was exactly that tiny moment of joy that threw a spanner in the works, by making him think that a couple of beers, a pill, a toke, a tiny line, would just make this joyful glimpse of sunlight, feel even better. Needless to say, that thought was invariably the prelude to shit meeting fan.

Matty looks up from his now glowing joint straight into Adrian's cold stare. "Oh yeah… forgot," he says, lying. "I'll leave one in the sink. Case you change your mind." Matty tugging a can out the plastic handcuffs and cracking the ring pull, filling the wheelhouse with the tangy chemical scent of industrial cider. He sucks deep. Burps. Burps again. This time with a little laugh, leaving the wheelhouse sliding door half open as he goes back out on deck.

Adrian's anger now cranked up two more notches. If he thought he was pissed off when Matty first came on board, now his fantasy is taking the conger eel gaff down from the peg in the wheelhouse, stepping out on deck and jamming the stainless steel hook deep into Matty's neck.

Adrian has to take deep breaths. Count them in and out. And say the Serenity Prayer to himself over and over and over again. "God grant me the serenity to accept the things I cannot change…"

Fourteen miles out into the English Channel, heading south by south-east at a bearing of 135 degrees, in a sea that hid some choppy short swells, the Kitty K pushes across the tide at eight knots. It feels pathetically slow. The other, bigger crab boats from Weymouth harbour can cruise at 16 or 18 knots, in comfort. Slow or not, the Kitty K sounds like she's straining near to breaking point. Something deep within her bowels grinding and clanking. So, Adrian winds up the volume on the VHF radio to mask the pain that makes her growl.

He catches the tail end of the forecast from the Portland Coastguard station. A low-pressure front is edging across the Atlantic, pushing in towards the Western Approaches of the Channel, down to the south-west of Cornwall. The front would be bowling along the Channel by mid to late afternoon, bringing thick rain and big seas. Adrian looks out of the seagull shit-smeared screen, now with the officially-confirmed knowledge that this is as good as it's going to get. From now on, it's only going to get worse.

He glances at the can of Scrumpy Jack cider, rolling back and forth along the inside edge of the grimy steel sink. '6% alcohol by volume' reads the label on the side… Even from this distance Adrian can see it. One of the many reasons he knows he's an alcoholic is that he can quote the alcohol-by-volume percentage of any drink. Stella Artois, 5.2%. Carlsberg Special Brew (an old favourite), 9%. White Lightning, 7.5%. Britannia Ruby Sherry, 15%. Smirnoff Vodka, 37.5%…

When he drank, Adrian would drink anything. Didn't matter what it was made from, what it tasted like, or how many times it was filtered, fermented, casked or corked. Only thing that interested him was that percentage number on the side. Alcohol-by-volume. He shudders. Like a goose walks over his grave. He checks the GPS co-ordinates and stares out at the grey moody sea. Twenty-six nautical miles due south by south-west from Weymouth lies a chunk of the English Channel called the Hurd's Deep. It's a shelf. The edge of a tectonic plate that crashed into another plate, pushing up from continental Europe – and the English side won. The English side of the plate romping over the top of the continental plate, like a wrestler getting his opponent in a headlock and climbing on top, to body slam him to the mat.

The geological body slam left a huge deep valley of broken-topped underwater hills. Between the hills lies a carpet of hard boulders strewn across the seabed, which is in turn etched with a spider's web of fissures.

The mixture of the sudden depth and the broken, craggy, landscape of the seabed makes it a safe haven for crabs and lobsters. It's dark. It's cold. There's so many places to hide, and very few predators brave enough to venture into such inhospitable terrain. At the same time, the Channel's huge tides relentlessly convey endless amounts of food down into the Deeps. So, if you're a crab or lobster, Hurd's Deep is a righteous place to grow fat.

Very few of the crabbers from Weymouth bother to set their pots across the Hurd's. It's too far away, too deep and too fucking snaggy. Get part of a shank of 20 pots wedged under one of those big boulders, and try to jag it out with the boat winch in a big sea, and shit will happen. The Deeps are infamous as a graveyard of First and Second World War naval ships and merchant cargo vessels. These ships sunk by mines, torpedoes and four-and-a-half inch armour piercing shells. Apart from the 19 military wrecks that litter the subterranean landscape of the Hurds, there are another dozen or more crabbers and whelkers that sunk in the same waters.

The French crabbing fleet working out of Cherbourg and St. Maxime took a fancy to fishing Hurd's Deep in the early 1990s, when crab prices hit a record high. They came north from their home ports and scattered pots around the Deeps, like a fat farmer's wife tossing corn for her chickens.

The French crabbers investing in longer downlines, heavier, steel-based pots to counteract the stronger currents, with bigger marker buoys to indicate the position of their 50-plus pot shanks. And then they went to work, trying to remove as much big crab from the Deeps and get it down to market in St Malo as quickly as possible, to ride the price hike.

Three French crabbers were sunk in the first month of fishing Hurd's Deep. Two more were sunk a month later. And the last one, Allouette, was sunk six weeks after, with all hands lost. The Allouette was lost – like all the others – while trying to free her trapped pot gear from the seabed. Since the Allouette went down, no French boat has ever potted the Deeps again.

The Channel Islands' crabbing fleet, whose home port lies closer to the Hurds than either the English or the French fleets, have never tried to pot the Deeps. The islander fleet work smaller boats and, living where they do, in the second fastest tidal stream in the world, they've grown up with a deep respect for the sea, and for the Hurds in particular. None of the Channel Islanders would even consider wetting their gear across that terrain. Far too dangerous.

Adrian and Matty on the Kitty K sometimes shoot their pots around the edge of the Deeps. And in desperate times they'll shoot gear across the middle too. It's a fuck of a long way to steam. It's the most dangerous shoot. But if the gear does go down well-baited, and comes up again without having to be cut loose from snags, the haul is guaranteed to be a fuck sight better than from pots shot on shallower, safer ground.

A hundred pots shot in the Hurds will reap more crab than 200 pots shot above the shelf. It's a simple choice – take a risk with less gear, for bigger reward, or play safe and work your tits off, doing shank after shank for a mediocre return.

Commercial fishing's the most dangerous profession. Statistically, a commercial fisherman is more likely to die at work than a soldier fighting in Afghanistan. Most of the time, the pay is shite too. So for Adrian and Matty there is no real question. If the weather allows them to get out as far as the Hurds, then they go. Simple as that.

More risk. More money.

According to Adrian's scribbled notes in his little black book of pot marks, the Kitty K is currently fishing 430 pots in total. Mostly in shanks of 20 pots, daisy-chained with an anchor at one or both ends of the line and a pot buoy and flag on a post to mark the down-tide end of the shank. Some of the shanks just have a pot buoy. The flag posts get broken, and maintenance is something that happens infrequently on board the K. The steam out and steam back to port is supposed to be the time when deck hands do pot maintenance. Not on the Kitty. Not today. Not any day lately.

Adrian always takes the wheel – it's a big brother thing. While Matty sleeps off whatever's coursing through his veins, and Tim picks his nose and stares out to sea. Adrian always amazed at how complex a job Tim can make of nose picking. Hours pass with Tim's crooked finger searching, swivelling, and hooking up inside his nostrils, one after the other. Every day Tim seems more dim-witted – only coming alive when Matty's entertaining him with another tale of 'How-fucking-smashed-did-I-get-last-night?' Seems like he's gradually picking his brains away.

To pull, re-bait and reshoot all 430 pots in one day would be a suicide mission of blood, sweat, tears and sulks. None of them are in the right state of mind or body for that kind of work. So, Adrian has to make mental calculations, based on his pages of black book scribbles, of which shanks need to be pulled, because all their bait will have been eaten up. And which ones can wet for a couple more days. Hoping those left to soak will still have enough rank-smelling fish clamped inside their bait bands to keep on calling to crab.

On the far western edge of his Furuno plotter is an X with the number 076 above it. It marks a shank of 30 pots they shot over a week ago. These pots lying along the edge of the Kidney Bank. Normally they wouldn't shoot pots on the edge of a sandbank. Edible brown crabs don't live on sand. They live in crags and ledges, reefs and wrecks. They like structure and cover, places to hide from predators, and places from which to ambush their prey.

The day the brothers shot on the Kidney was a bad day. Big winds, a hydraulic fluid leak on the pipe to the hauling winch and a massive 'Fuck you. No. Fuck YOU!' argument that grew to a peak during the afternoon, and reached its climax on the journey home to port. It was about money. Of course. And so Adrian, out of teeth-gritting frustration, had to shoot the baited pots, single-handed, across the southern edge of the Kidney, while Matty sat in the wheelhouse, sulking, throwing acid-bitter glances astern at Adrian, while he struggled to lob the pots, one at a time, over the aluminium shoot-plate.

Adrian thinking the pots might as well lie on the seabed, rather than stink up the boat overnight. And who knows, there might just be a crab or a lobster, lost enough or suicidal enough, to crawl into a pot. God knows, Adrian is. Adrian making a note to himself to bring Kitty back over the Kidney Bank on their run home tonight to pull the rogue shank. The empty pots could be rebaited in the morning and shot again on the way out to the Deeps tomorrow. Never hurts to have a shank or two within five miles of port. Means if the weather's too rough to get far out, there's always something nearby to pull. During long spells of storms, those close-in shanks provide a little tick-over cash to last until the weather breaks.

This is the way Adrian's mind works. Planning. Looking ahead. Making decisions. Trying to make the best out of what little they've got, before they lose it all. This is *not* the way Matty's mind works. "Live fast. Die young. Leave a beautiful corpse," is one of those annoying fucking phrases Matty trots out with his signature cheeky grin – usually to some girl he's trying to impress – as he buys another round, or gram or over-priced restaurant meal. Chucking money around. Trying to act like Bertie Big Bollocks.

As he nudges the throttle back a few clicks with the heel of his right hand, Adrian bangs on the wheelhouse window with his left fist. "Coming up on one," he shouts. Loud. Making sure to wake Matty with a jump, and make Tim yank his finger out his nose.

The first haul of the day is like an omen. A premonition for the day to come. A first good haul should be a smooth pick-up of the marker buoy off the sea with the boat hook, two neat loops of line tossed around the capstan, to crank up a clean, weedless pot from the seabed, in one snag-free run.

Ideally, in the pot there'll be a clattering, skittering, snapping, half-dozen keeper crabs, and maybe a bonus lobster. That kind of first haul is mustard. Any skipper sees that on his first pot, of his first shank of the day, and his heart will fill with hope for the next 30 shanks that lie ahead.

Adrian angles the Kitty to meet the first pot buoy, on her starboard bow. The hauling jib – a right angle of rusty iron box section, with a stainless steel loop on one end of the boom and a hydraulic winch on the other – is located on the starboard side, behind the wheelhouse.

"Haul from midships and shoot from the stern," their dad used to say. Like it was some noble code of conduct that could never and should never be broken. In truth, doesn't matter if you haul from starboard or port. Modern crabbers with drum haulers even pull from the stern. But most of those are catamarans, with twin hulls to spread their load. If you haul from the stern of the K, a biggish wave could easily breach her transom, and she'd go arse-down quicker than a weighted sack of kittens.

On the Kitty the brothers haul from starboard midships, because that way Adrian can monitor each lift from his ripped and sticky captain's chair. Also, it makes it easier to haul single-handed, on the days when Matty is missing, or too fucked up to be trusted to operate a winch.

To haul a shank of 30 pots quickly, crabbers lift the uptide pot buoy first and use the flow of the tide to propel the boat down along the line of the shank. In a big tide the boat will move fast. Hauling pots at speed only works if the deck crew are co-ordinated, executing every movement like well-oiled clockwork.

If you don't haul pots as the boat drifts with the tide, you have to haul *against* the tide, which means running the engines against the current and churning the winch harder and faster, hauling pots up against the drag of the sucking sea. Adrian is fucked if he's going to waste more fuel pulling against the tide, just because Matty and Tim are in a raggedy-arse state.

The buoy floats past below the wheelhouse window while Tim is still trying to wrestle the boat hook from the pile of broken pots heaped in the stern. Hook jammed in the nylon mesh of a knackered pot. "The fuck you doing?" says Matty.

"It's stuck," Tim whines. Matty grabs the handle and shoulders him out the way. "Give."

Matty now yanks hard on the shaft of the hook, ripping it through the mesh as he catches a glimpse of his brother's face, staring sanctimoniously out the wheelhouse door, expecting, maybe even *willing*, Matty to fuck up at hooking the first buoy of the day. If he misses, then the K will run broadsides over the buoy. Once a buoy has gone under the keel, the boat has to go round 360 degrees, back up the tide to start all over again. Burning diesel.

Which of course will give righteous Adie something to piss and whine about, and make Matty look bad. Like the dumb-fuck little brother he can so often be. But not today.

Matty hooks the buoy, yanks it over the gunwale, throws the boat hook at Tim – who fails to catch it – and loops the rope into the V groove of the winch wheel, in one smooth fast motion – even before the boat hook has stopped clattering on the grey steel deck. Matty jabs the drive button of the winch, which turns, biting on the rope as it snakes through the stainless loop at the end of the boom. Below the loop, the rope runs straight down, under tension, into the murk. Water pings off the nylon fibres as they creak and stretch between the growling winch and a heavy metal crab pot, 125 feet beneath the lumpy sea.

Even half-stoned, half-pissed, half-awake, Matty's reactions can be fast, if he put his mind to it. For all his endless abuse, he's still strong and swift and dangerous. Something which impresses and annoys Adrian in equal measure, as he watches his little brother handle himself surprisingly well, and haul the first shank in a manner that would've made even their father proud.

There's two ways to go when you haul a shank of pots. You can either haul and store. Or haul and drop. Hauling and storing means pulling the 20 or more pots on board one at a time, emptying the crabs out, chucking away bait scraps and stashing the pots on deck. Each metal-framed pot takes up the same amount of space as a pair of beer crates. So, chances are, on a ten-metre crabber there'll only be space to store one shank, beyond that they start to get in the way of business.

And then there's the rope. A hundred-and-fifty foot of down-rope, leading from the floating pot buoy to the first anchor. Fifty foot more to the first pot. Fifty to the next. And the next… and so on, all the way along the shank. Another 50 foot from the last pot to the down-tide anchor. Finally another 150, up again to the down-tide buoy. All in all, a shit-load of rope to store on an already overcrowded deck. And, laying coils of rope on deck is just an accident waiting to happen.

Sensible alternative is haul and drop. Haul the pots one at a time. Empty out the crabs by opening the 'parlour' door, held shut by two bungee chords with hooks, chuck out the old bait and stuff in new bait, before shutting the parlour door and then hefting the pot back on to the gunwale, just before the next pot breaks surface beneath the winch. And so on.

A good crab pot crew works like a conveyor belt. Pot up. Swing off jib. Heft onto table. Open door. Empty crabs. Empty bait bands. Load bait bands. Close door. Heft onto gunwale. Drop. Turn to quickly sort crabs into boxes, just in time to swing the next pot off the jib. It's like a mechanical ballet. A rhythm. A dance to the music of whining gears, crashing pots, scuttling crabs, twanging elastic, the dull splat of bait and hoarse roar of sea.

Against all odds, the brothers' first shank goes well. There's shouting and swearing and Matty throws a blue velvet swimmer crab at Tim's head, for going too slow and not clearing the baited pots quickly enough to leave room for newly-hauled pots on the work table. The small furry blue crab bounces off the back of Tim's head and over the gunwale to freedom. Lucky crab. Blue velvet swimmers, unlike brown, edible crabs have no market value and no regulated minimum landing size limit, so most potters chuck them in a fish box, where eventually they get stamped on, when the box is half full. Stamped and stomped by a dim lad like Tim, in a pair of white steel toe-capped wellies, until they're just a sickly sludge of guts-and-shell.

The sludge is frozen and kept until winter, for whelk pot bait. By the time the dying crabs have been left in the sun for a few days, starving and suffocating to death, then mushed with a boot, they'll stink worse than a week-old dead badger. And there's nothing a whelk likes better than putrid stinking bait. Lobsters too. For all their culinary class and high-end fan club, lobsters are carrion-loving, bottom-feeders of the lowest kind.

Baiting the pots is a mug's game. As a task, it's always delegated to the lowest crewman on any crab boat's well-defined ladder of hierarchy. It's a horrible job. Once the pot hauler has tipped out the trapped crabs, the baiter uses both hands to stretch open the thick rubber bait bands and remove the chewed remains of the now gag-inducing old bait. He then lobs it over the side, and replaces it with new, slightly less stinky, fleshier bait.

Big rotting fish heads still attached to a few inches of spine are the easiest baits to handle. They're the easiest to fit in position under the band, because it snaps down on the backbone and holds the head in place. But *nothing* is easy with both hands stuck in a pot, using one to stretch the rubber and the other to insert the bait. Nothing is easy when the boat is lurching, the bait is soft and covered in thick grey slime, your hands are freezing and the guy hauling pots is threatening to dump the next one on your head, if you don't hurry the fuck up.

The most common mistake a baiter can make in his fumbling hurry is to forget to close the parlour door properly. On a commercial potter, if a pot's hauled and the door is found open, so the bait's been wasted and any crab has been able to escape, it's the baiter who gets a kicking from the skipper. Or the hauler. Or both.

If a run of pots is hauled, empty of catch and empty of bait, the pot-baiter always gets the blame. Badly banded bait will fall out as the pot drops to the seabed. And if the bait's fallen out and so the pots have fished a wet without bait, then everyone's wasted their time. Once again, it'll be the pot-baiter who gets the shit.

Skippers want to see baits tight, clinched by the band. But getting baits to sit tight is fraught with complications. Bait is slippery, mushy, impossible stuff to handle with or without gloves. And if you do wear gloves on a crab boat, the rest of the crew will mercilessly take the piss, at best. More likely they'll sneak a treble hook or a cod's gall bladder down a couple of the fingers – just for a laugh.

Tim is an annoying, mouthy twat. And yet he's wise enough to know wearing a pair of gloves working on the Kitty will only put him in line for a heap of crap. A blue velvet swimmer to the back of the head is nothing compared to some of the abuse he's taken from Matty as part of this daily routine.

"Fuck you," is all he mutters, as he struggles to loop his fish-gizz-slimed fingers under the next bait band, and pull it open to insert a pollack head that's already way too fetid to handle. The rotted cheeks pop off in his fingers as he squeezes the head under the band leaving him a handful of mushy fish flesh and a pot that's now only baited with bones. But there's no time to stop. Certainly no time to replace the heads. So he hauls the pot to the gunwale and sneakily drops the fetid cheeks into the sea, before launching the pot, and turning back around to the table, where two more pots already wait, as Adrian eyes him accusingly from the wheelhouse.

Adrian heard a film actress talking on the FM radio – back in the days when it worked. Matty cracked it with a wooden-handled bass descaler because the cassette bit ate up his Bob Marley tape.

This woman had won an Oscar or something for her part in some big costume history movie, and she was explaining how much of an up and down rollercoaster her working day was. Said it was hours and hours of mind-numbing boredom; make-up, costume-fitting, standing around waiting for the 'right light' or something – interspersed with concentrated short bursts of intense, adrenalin-rushing drama, which was then followed by more hours of tedium.

Adrian thought how she could've been describing crab-potting. Steaming to and from the crab grounds is like a time warp of tedium. The hours stretch out in some bizarre continuum. Seconds last for minutes, as the boat seems to stand stock-still in the middle of the sea, even though the engine is flat out, rattling its main bearings like a biscuit tin full of masonry nails.

But then, haul a shank of 30 pots in a five-knot ebb tide with the wind on your port side and suddenly you don't have enough hands, enough space, enough crab boxes, enough time to do anything but haul, tip, sort, bait and shoot. Until finally the last pot in the shank is back in the water, with the down tide anchor tossed in after.

Some shanks, especially in the Hurd's Deep are shot close together, maximising the coverage on the good deep rocky ground. Especially if there's a plot with enough rocks and fissures to hold crab, but not so many to make pot-hauling a snaggy, suicidal affair.

Shanks that are too close together do cause more chaos up on the deck. There's just no recovery time between each shank. No time to catch up from the last shank, with a pile of crab that need to be sorted by size and lobsters that need to be separated from the crab, and each other. Lobsters' claws have to be banded with thick rubber straps to stop them cutting and chopping and crushing the fuck out of each other, or the crabs.

Lobsters are psychotic cannibalistic mother-fucking baby-eating sociopaths, who cannot be left alone together without being neutralised. As Adrian's dad always said – as a way of teaching the necessity of hauling all pots within 48 hours of shooting – "Leave two lobsters in a pot together overnight, and in the morning you'll only have one".

It's a good lesson, but one which these days Matty and Adrian struggle to abide by. Sometimes they shoot pots that soak for up to a week or more. It's because they shoot too many pots, too far away from harbour, in some of the ugliest seas anywhere in the Channel. They spread themselves thin and wide, so some shanks soak for much longer than they ever should. The result is a lot of damaged lobster and crab, because a big lobster who finds himself stuck amongst his brethren for too long, soon turns violent and hungry and cannibal.

Adrian points Kitty's nose towards the next of their pot buoys, which he can't actually make out yet because of the size of the chop and swell of the grim sea over the Deeps. The craters, reefs and peaks of the boulder-strewn hills that litter the bottom of the Deeps cause up-welling seas that affect the surface even 200 feet above. The heavy swell means Adrian can't see either a buoy or a flag, but the note in his black book and the corresponding waypoint on his frizzing GPS plotter tell him that the next shank lies just over half a mile to the north-west. They've come as far south, the furthest from port, as they need to go. Now all the shanks left to haul are dotted to the north and west. The way back home.

There was a time he would have just set the autopilot, to hold the course to the next waypoint. It even had an alarm, a high-pitched whine that would yell when the Kitty got within 100 yards of the next shank. But like everything else on this miserable fucking boat, the autopilot was broken, long ago. So now, instead, Adrian points Kitty's nose roughly to where the GPS says the next pot buoy is located, and stretches two bungee chords, one on either side of the wheel, and hooks them in position. It is rough. A guesstimate. Kitty will veer off east or west of where they want to go by several degrees. But the bungees will steer her in the general direction, and give Adrian ten minutes without his hands on the wheel. Ten minutes to go out on deck to help Matty and Tim catch up with themselves.

Matty is sorting crabs between the worktable, various boxes cluttering the deck, and the live well – a 600-litre tank of circulated seawater beneath their feet. The hatch is open. Water from the brimming well slopping on deck with every pitch of the short waves that shoulder Kitty's starboard bow. Waves fuelled by the growing, growling wind that funnels up the Channel, the weight of the east Atlantic at its back, giving it more guts than it deserves. It's a snotty wind that promises worse to come.

European Marine Directive says all hands working on deck on a commercial fishing vessel must wear life jackets. Three self-inflating CrewSaver jackets hang on a cup-hook screwed in the plywood at the back of Kitty's wheelhouse. No one ever wears them. Like gloves, they're objects of derision. A piss-take opportunity.

After an obligatory Sea Fish Industry 'Safety At Sea' course, where he and eight other Weymouth skippers spent the day in a Scout hut, watching a Powerpoint presentation by a retired Welsh miner on accidents at sea, Adrian took to wearing his. The big Welsh lump of a man told them every year one in 14 commercial fishermen dies at sea. After the day, and the slides and the presentation and the statistics, Adrian wore his inflatable CrewSaver for a week. All that week Matty sneered and took the piss, with the unrelenting repetition of a five-year-old. Eventually, Adrian gave up wearing the CrewSaver, not just cause of Matty's bitching, but because it got in the way and made his neck ache.

Now the jackets hang on the hook. Nobody wears them.

Matty and Tim, crabs and boxes, ropes and pots, water and bait, knives, bands, velvet swimmers, half a lobster and a short metal baseball bat, slop from side to side, gunwale to gunwale, as Kitty rolls from the short punchy waves.

Adrian wades in to the chaos, picking crabs off the table and the deck, checking them quickly against a metal measure. All the undersized brown crabs are thrown overboard. Matty in his messy frenzy will chuck small crabs over his shoulder. Some crack against the wheelhouse frame, bouncing off on their way to the sea. Some hit the steel jib bar, shells shatter, legs get smashed off. Matty couldn't give a shit. He treats undersized crabs like hateful little bastards that deserve to be mutilated, because they aren't big enough to be of value to him. They're too small to translate into booze or drugs or fags, or lock-ins in The Sailors. They have no conversion-to-Matty's-life value. So they might as well die.

Other crab men are careful with undersized crabs, seeing them as the future. Small crabs become big crabs. It only takes a matter of time. You work the same grounds month after month, year after year, you catch the same little crabs again and again. Little crabs become big crabs. Treat them well and they'll go back, grow fat and you can catch them again once they're sellable. This kind of forward planning doesn't work for Matty. If the little fuckers aren't worth having now, they aren't worth having.

Ten minutes of Adrian's time on deck, with the wheel lashed, makes a difference. The downside of lashing the wheel is the passage is made rougher and uglier, so it's harder to keep a decent footing on deck. When Adrian is steering, he can feel Kitty's path; subtle shifts of the wheel help her ride up or down or slide across aggressive waves. Steering helps the boat work with the swell. A good skipper can help keep the working platform stable, even in the messiest sea.

Two bungee cords, strapping the wheel rigid in one locked-off position, do fuck all to keep the deck stable or safe. Bungee cords only steer one course, in one direction, which means the hull smashes into waves. No deviation. No finesse. No pitch-and-roll.

Just bang, crash, bang. And the shocks and vibrations make the deck a dangerous, unpredictable place to be.

It took ten minutes of rough riding and lurching, but between them, wordlessly, without ever meeting each other's gaze, the three men caught up with the four shanks already pulled. One hundred and six pots have so far been hauled, emptied and re-baited. Crabs are stored: keepers in the live well, velvets in the whelk bait box. Lobsters banded and separated. Stored in shallow fish boxes, two layers deep with a cloth laid in between the layers.

In total the catch is 58 brown crabs over the legal minimum landing size limit and nine lobsters. Not bad. Still, at Brixham Fish Market – given that the Spanish, Italians and French, the biggest buyers of Weymouth-landed crustaceans, are fucked to Friday and back, because of the Euro bullshit – today's crab price is pants. Haulage fees to Brixham are hiked, because of fuel prices and so, so far Kitty K hasn't even washed her own back yet this morning. She's drunk more diesel than the catch will fetch. Four shanks in. Four fairly good, disaster-free shanks hauled, but still no one on board has earned a single Euro of their own.

The upside is, if the weather holds and they haul another 15 or so shanks of the same quality as the first four, without snagging on a big boulder, or wrapping a warp rope around Kitty's propeller, or killing each other, they should head home with a decent enough catch. Even though the shipping forecast and the squally gusts barrelling down the Channel suggest the ride home is going to be long and spine-jarringly rough, today might just yet be worth the grief.

As he unlashes the bungees from the wheel, checks the position on the chart plotter and corrects Kitty's course to the next pot buoy – only a couple of minutes away – Adrian almost immediately begins to regret having moved so fast, when he was out on deck. A quick glance over his shoulder confirms his fears. The deck crew's heads are up. Matty and Tim have caught up with themselves. Everything is stowed and stashed and ready for the next haul. Just a little too soon.

They have time now, to stop working and look around. Their hands empty, everything in its place, more or less, and like toddlers with Attention Deficit Disorder, instant boredom, need and want, sets in.

Just the way Matty is wiping his hands down the front of his bait-splattered fleece – a promotional gift from Kenny's Tackle Shop that says 'Team Diawa' across the chest – tells Adrian he's helped his crew too much. Matty finishes cleaning his hands by wiping them up and down the seams of his Dickies, before stepping into the wheelhouse and saying exactly what Adrian knows he'll say.

"Just time to skin up, Skip."

Fuck. Too soon, thinks Adrian. Too fucking soon.

Matty peels a king-size Rizla out a broad red packet, and lays the packet on the sink drainer, to rest the cigarette paper in the right angle between the pack and its cardboard cover. The angle creating the perfect cradle to hold a fag paper. From a battered packet, fished from deep within his fleece, Matty produces a Dorchester Menthol cigarette and proceeds to lick it along one side. Using his thumb, he teases the cigarette open along the wet line of spittle. The compressed tobacco bulging out as he tips the whole length into the open Rizla.

As Matty ferrets around with one hand, inside his fleece jacket, searching into the lining to locate his knotted bag of spliff, his other hand snakes its way towards the unopened can of Scrumpy Jack in the steel sink. One hand pops the ring pull on the top of the can, while the other produces half an ounce of Bristol's best Vietnamese-grown skunk. Matty is ambidextrous when it comes to consuming drugs.

Too fucking soon, thinks Adrian. He should've left them to do their own deck work or just helped them for five minutes. Kept them busy right up until they reached the next shank. Not let Matty get a moment. Get his head up. And do what Matty always does – have a smoke, toke, drink, pill, or anything else that'll get him wasted.

It is 18 minutes past ten in the morning. Way too soon to let Matty get much of a buzz on. His mind will wander. His co-ordination will falter. His hands will fumble. And sooner or later his mood and his temper will turn to shit.

Fuck, it's like running a fucking kindergarten, thinks Adrian. Like being an unpaid child minder, looking after Matty and Tim. Fact it's easier looking after his two tiny sons, Jack and Josh, than keeping tabs on Matty's mood swings. Exactly the same mindset though. Knowing when they're hungry, when they need a nap, when they need a crap, and when they should or shouldn't smoke a finger-thick spliff. Or neck half a litre of industrial cider. And now, before they've hauled a third of what they need to haul to make today even a passable punt at earning a living, is not a good time.

"Coming up on it now," says Adrian through gritted teeth, nodding at the pot buoy 60 yards off the starboard bow.

Matty says nothing, his tongue between his teeth as his filthy fingers roll and knead and smooth the joint into shape. He's already sprinkled a mammoth heap of dry skunk along the back of the baccy and is squeezing, squashing and rolling it to fit inside the king-size skin. His tongue sliding along the gummed edge. His forefingers smoothing the sticky seam shut, before he upends it and puts a twist in the bottom of the joint, to stop any precious mixture spilling out.

"The fuck, Matty," says Adrian, annoyed as much with himself, for letting this moment happen, as he's annoyed with Matty for skinning up, right in the middle of a series of pot hauls.

"Not the fucking *tide table*!" whines Adrian. Hating himself for sounding like a little bitch. But, it's too late anyway. Matty's already torn a square hunk out the cardboard cover of the tide table. Adrian only bought a new tide table book three days ago, from Kenny's, as the last one'd fallen to pieces because Matty'd torn off the covers to make roaches for spliffs.

"I just *bought* that!"

"Good man," says Matty, as he sucks a pull from the Scrumpy Jack can and burps a gassy, cider-stinking burp in Adrian's face.

Matty holds up the nearly-finished can in front of Adrian and raises his eyebrows in a question – You want this?

Adrian turns away and watches the pot buoy as Kitty drifts closer and closer. Now only ten yards away. He doesn't look back at Matty. Can't. Too angry and too scared of his own boiling hate for his little brother, but he does hear the click and spark of his Zippo as Matty lights the spliff.

A waft of acrid skunk smoke and menthol baccy rolls over Adrian's shoulder. The smell partly disgusting him, but also making him angry and jealous and sad and frustrated. Adrian doesn't want to get off his face most of his life, like his brother does, because Adrian has dependants and responsibilities and even ambition. But he does *sometimes* want to be stoned and pissed. *Some* of the time. *Any* of the time. At times. At hard times. At good times. At bored times. At *this* fucking time, for God's sake!

And so Adrian fights it. If nothing else, if not for his wife, his boys, his faint little hopes for the future, if nothing else, to just be different from his head-case of a brother. If nothing else, just to not be like Matty.

Five yards before the pot goes under the keel. Four. Three. Matty out on deck now. Two yards. Like a miracle Tim is already waiting, leaning against the starboard gunwale, holding the boat hook, ready to give it to Matty.

Was a miracle that Tim, little shithead Tim, should actually think ahead, and be ready for Matty. Adrian knows why. Isn't some amazing revelation of learning and forethought. No, simply that Tim'd seen Matty get a spliff on the go. And Tim thought if he does something useful to help, then Matty'll give him a tug.

Adrian knows Tim and Matty getting stoned will just slow down and complicate the rest of the day and cause him more grief. And yet, weirdly, at this precise moment the spliff is a positive thing, because it encourages sneaky Tim to suck up to Matty, by having the boat hook ready. Which means with one yard left to go before the pot buff gets sucked under the keel, Matty snares it with the boat hook and drags it over the gunwale.

He flicks the rope up through the jib hook, winds it into the hauler and draws in a lung-busting toke, holding the chest-full of skunk and menthol inside him as long as is humanly possible. Then he passes the burning joint to Tim, who with his blackhead-pocked

15-year-old face, grins like a fucking retard, exactly mimicking Matty, and sucks on that thing like tomorrow was cancelled.

Fuck, thinks Adrian. Way too soon for this shit.

First eight pots of the shank went well. Adrian nudges the throttle and corrects the angle of the Kitty so she drifts perfectly on the line of the pots. The swell growing from the west, whipped up by the south-westerly winds that push her just a little too fast into the drift. Gusts hitting the wheelhouse, making her lean over into the drift. She leans, as a wave sneaks up on her port side pushing her even further over, into the drift.

A boat that's leaning while being wave-bumped from behind during a haul makes a hard job harder. As the winch bites into the lift, the side with the pot-hauler is pulled down towards the sea. Sometimes so far, the top of a swell rides over the gunwale.

Matty's boots are getting wet as sea surges up through the starboard scuppers. He's leaning forward, hand outstretched, holding the swinging jib that guides the rope up out of the sea to the winch wheel, where its V-shaped profile pinches on the rope. Kitty is leaning over, practically as far as she safely can, Matty leaning with her, riding her. Stopping himself from falling into the sea, just by his one hand on the jib. Adrian's shoulder is squashed hard against the pitching starboard wheelhouse window. Even Tim is struggling to stand upright at the bait table, when suddenly the rope jams.

So many potters have been sunk by winching on a jammed rope or snagged pot. If a pot's being hauled by an electric or hydraulic winch and the rope is unexpectedly caught underwater, in rocks or a wreck, hauling has to be stopped, immediately. Otherwise a meaty winch can pull a small boat right on over. If the sea's swelling on the opposite beam of the boat, a crabber can flop right over on its side, and then over on its back – keel stuck up in the air, fisherman trapped underneath – in a heartbeat.

And still the winch will keep on winding and pulling downwards, causing a small crab boat to flip over again. Only this time it's spinning *under* the surface, being pulled deeper down. Down until the winch finally stops pulling. Which in the case of an hydraulic winch is when the engine is engulfed with seawater, and coughs and splutters to a stop. But in the case of an electric winch, powered from the boat's batteries, it can go on turning and pulling until the boat's been winched down to the seabed. Either way, hydraulic or electric, doesn't make much difference to the crew, when they're trapped underneath, getting sucked into the winding gear or tangled in the deck ropes, fighting to hold their breath. Until eventually they're forced to suck in a lungful of seawater and call it a day.

When a small boat like Kitty is already leaning right over and then the rope jams, it might not be enough to hit the kill switch and stop the winch. Stopping winching only stops the pulling. If the boat is pitched over, and being held tight at an angle, one more wave – which might be only a second or two away – could be enough to kick her on her side.

To stop her breaching, the pulling needs to be stopped, and the rope needs to be yanked out the V-trough on the winch wheel and made slack. Only when there's no tension yanking down on the pot rope, is the boat safe.

If ever there was a moment when Matty's drug-addled reactions and sloppy sense of safety was a threat to Adrian and Tim's life, this is it. If Matty's slow to kill the winch, or fumbles getting the rope out of the V-groove, they could all be sucking seawater.

Being inside the wheelhouse means Adrian would get longer to breath than Tim. Matty and Tim would be flipped over the gunwale in a blink, with the boat rolling on top of them. But Adrian would be stuck inside the wheelhouse when Kitty's keel went tits up. Sea crashing in through the wheelhouse door, making it impossible for him to get to the winch controls, or swim free of the sinking boat.

For all his fucked-upness, Matty still has the ability to surprise Adrian. Before Kitty is tipped more than half way over, with the winch growling and the rope singing with tension, Matty punches the kill switch and whips the rope out the winch wheel.

"Jam up!" he shouts as he hangs on the wheelhouse window. As if Adrian needed to be told.

Most shanks of pots are shot with two anchors. One on each end of the shank, with a rope and buoy attached above each anchor. Anchor at each end is the safest way to shoot pots. Means both ends of the shank are fixed to the seabed. Otherwise the end that doesn't have an anchor can move, if tides are big. A powerful tide pushing the line of pots for six hours and then swinging round and pushing from the opposite direction for another six can roll the end that's not anchored. This can start a slow tide-powered wag. Like the tail of some gnarly big dog. If the end of the shank furthest from the anchor begins to wag, with 50 foot of polyprop rope attaching each pot to the next, the potential for snagging on sunken rocks is high. This is exactly the reason most boats, especially those shooting pots on snaggy ground, or in big tides, shoot with an anchor on each end.

Trouble with anchors is they cost best part of 20 quid each. Sure, you can make your own, a lot of crabbers do. All it takes is a few scrap steel reinforcement rods and an hour or two in the workshop every week, wielding an arc welder and an angle grinder. Which is definitely something you might do, if you own your own crab boat. If you haven't sold it already. And of course, if you *give* a shit.

Anchors cost money. Anchors also take up a lot of room on a small boat like the Kitty K. If you shoot 20 or 30 shanks of pots, that adds up to 60 anchors. Fuck of a lot of dead weight to be shifting across the Channel on overpriced diesel.

The most important function of an anchor is that it's designed to get snagged into the seabed or caught between, behind or under rocks. If it didn't get caught up to the seabed somehow, wouldn't be much of an anchor. Trouble with anchors is sometimes they don't know when to give up hooking themselves into the seabed. They get themselves so involved with underwater structure, they don't want to come out. Even when the man on the other end of the anchor rope dearly fucking *wants* that anchor to give up with the anchoring shit and come back on board without any more struggle.

Anchors get stuck. Anchor ropes get cut in frustration. So boats like the Kitty K end up with fewer anchors than they really need, if they intend to shoot their shanks of pots with an anchor on each end. And so some shanks, like the one now jammed under the bucking, tossing Kitty K, only have an anchor at *one* end.

To haul this kind of a shank, you need to haul up the end with the anchor first. Which means if you hit a snag half way along the shank, there's every possibility of losing all the other pots from the snagged one down the line. Because without an anchor and marker buoy on the far end, there's no way of telling where the end of the line of pots lies. If you don't know where the far end of the line is, you can't haul it. So, if you cut through a snagged line, especially in a big sea, on a shank with just one anchor, you probably have to wave goodbye to the rest of the pots in the shank.

To lose 20 pots today would be a major fucker. Matty and Adrian's deal with Paulie is a share in profits as well as running costs, including diesel and gear. If they lose pots, they lose money. And today, so far they've barely broken into profit. New pots, off the shelf, are best part of 40 quid a pop. No fucking way Adrian and Matty can afford to lose one or two pots, let alone 20. So snagged or not, this shank is coming to the surface, no argument.

First thing Matty does is walk the rope around the stern of the boat and up the port side. They should be able to drift down past the snagged pot and use the force of the tide, straining in the opposite direction, to try and dislodge it. But the weight of the boat isn't enough, and the pot doesn't shift. So Matty loops the rope back up through the hook and roller of the jib and tries to winch the pot with the rope running across the deck of the boat, rather than straight down. It's safer, because it pulls the boat flat, instead of tipping it over. The rope bites into the port gunwale gouging a groove into the wooden rail. Adrian slips a length of nylon drainpipe over the gunwale to protect the wood. Still the pot doesn't shift.

Those are the two safe options to try and shift a snagged pot. The only choices left are more dangerous ones, like tying the pot rope around a cleat on the stern of Kitty K and using her engine to yank on the rope. Tugging with the tide and using her propeller to force her whole weight down on the line. It's a shit-or-bust alternative. The pot could pop out, or the rope could snap. Or worse, if Adrian misjudges the lumpy sea and the heaving swell, he could pull the stern of the boat down under a rear-ending wave, flood the engine compartment and sink Kitty arse-end first.

Matty winds the rope twice around the stern cleat and Adrian pushes the throttle forward, gently at first, increasing the load until finally he's gunning the engine. All the time keeping an eye on the transom for a big wave that might swamp them from the rear. With every power surge of the engine, the back of the boat dips down lower and lower. As the engine howls the rope stretches so tight it changes colour as the fibres stress and straighten, almost to breaking point.

Suddenly the K jolts forward, as something gives. Adrian yanks back on the throttle and shoots a quick wary look at Matty, who stands staring down over the transom…

"What was that?" shouts Adrian, once the engine roar dies.

"Not the rope."

"It free?" asks Adrian. Matty leans over and hauls on the rope to check.

"Hey fuck-face!" he shouts at Tim, who realises *he* should be hauling too. They both heave together, making a few yards of rope back in the boat, until they can't make any more. Both straining. Matty puts his boot up on the transom to get more leverage. But they can't make any more line. Matty winds the rope back around the cleat, to hold the boat, as Adrian slips the gearbox into neutral and walks to the stern, where he joins them, all staring over the stern at the rope, disappearing into the deep.

"Something shifted. Now, it's snagged again," says Matty.

"Maybe we pulled off a rock into another rock."

"S'a fuck," says Matty spitting.

"Could go round, pull uptide."

"Take fucking ages."

"What's the choice?" says Adrian, staring at the line where it disappears beneath them. "Still ten, maybe 12 pots down there."

"Buoy it off. Leave it. Do some other shanks. Come back when it's calmer."

Adrian says, "When's it *ever* calm out here?"

"Buoy it off. Least we can haul some of the other gear," Matty says. "We spend an hour trying to get this unjammed, we'll *never* get to haul the other gear."

"'Less we work into the dark."

"Bollocks," says Matty. "I'll tie a buff on it. We leave it. Pull rest of the gear. Come back tomorrow."

"Then we've got exactly the same problem, this time tomorrow," says his brother.

"*Fuck* it."

"No."

"Come on," says Matty. "Don't be a dick."

"We give it one more go."

Matty considers it. *"One* more," he says.

"One more *proper* go. It doesn't shift we buoy it off."

Matty nods agreement.

Adrian swings the Kitty around again. Matty tightening the rope to the starboard sternpost. Adrian pushes the throttle forward, this time running with the tide a few yards, when the rope jams tight again, straining against the post. The transom flexing scarily as the force of the propeller churns the sea into creamy foam. Nothing shifts. The engine howls. Adrian looks back to see Matty's hanging over the transom again, peering down at the rope where it disappears into the foam. Matty now beckoning to Tim, and shouts something in his ear over the roar of the engines. Tim comes trotting up the deck to the wheelhouse, with a message for Adrian, "He says, stick her in neutral. Come and look." Over Tim's shoulder, Adrian can see Matty's gesturing.

"What the fuck's *that?*" says Matty, pointing down the rope as Adrian leans across the transom beside him.

With the propeller at rest, the sea is clear and down the rope three or four yards below, Adrian can just make out the outline of another rope.

"Whose rope's that?"

"Not ours. S'a Joseph," says Matty.

"It tight?"

"Fuck yeah. Look at the angle."

The strange rope, known commercially as a 'Joseph' because it's weaved with multi-coloured fibres, is twisted at an angle around the rope that links some of Kitty's pots in the middle of the shank. The clean, new, expensive-looking rope veers off at an angle to the east, in the direction of the running tide. But the upper section of the smart rope seemed to have a little slack in it.

"The fuck's *that* doing here?"

"Someone else shooting gear out here?" suggests Adrian, like he already doesn't believe it. They both look around, scanning the sea for more pot markers, but see none.

"One shank?" shrugs Adrian. "No one comes out here to shoot *one* shank."

"Could be pots rolled out from further in," says Matty, trying to make sense of it. "Busted up stuff."

"Rope's too clean," says Adrian. "Too new. Not been in the water long."

"Yeah…" They shake their heads. Some kind of mystery.

"If I gun it some more. Take up the slack," says Adrian. "And you can reach it with the hook. Cut it off. Then maybe our shank'll come free."

"Uh huh," shrugs Matty.

"Could be it's the Joseph's snagged. And, *we're* not. Cut us free, and maybe we're back in business," says Adrian, not believing the words coming out his own mouth. But living in hope.

"Don't you want to know what's on the other rope?" asks Tim.

"Just be loose warp being dragged around by the tide," says Adrian. "Some yachtie's stern-line, fallen off his deck and got looped around our pot rope."

Adrian pushes Kitty hard down-tide. Matty leans over with the boat hook, fighting to get a glimpse of the Joseph through the foam. Leaning right over, Tim grabbing the back of his waistband with both hands, as Matty manages to snag the shiny rope and pull hard. Trying to pull it up out of the water within knife-cutting range. Tim taking the filleting knife out his belt sheath, passing it to Matty, who strains, pulling, fit to fucking burst. When suddenly, he jerks backwards, canonballing into Tim, throwing them both back, crashing into the worktable. Tim rolls and falls on deck, knife clattering from his hand, Matty managing to stay upright, by grabbing the edge of the table.

"Motherfucker!"

The boat hook lies on the deck, Joseph rope still caught in its crook.

Adrian is out of the wheelhouse now, Kitty in neutral. As he picks up the new rope, he can see now it's torn free from Kitty's pot rope. One end of the Joseph still angled down into the deep, the other end of the rope waving in the tide, behind the stern of the boat.

Hand-over-hand Adrian pulls the loose end of the rope to the boat. He coils it at his feet until, in the tide-wake behind the transom, all three men see a small green plastic fender bob up on the surface. Sort of little plastic fender you'd use to protect the side of a sailing dinghy. It too looks brand new, although deflated. All crumpled up, because the air bung that keeps it sealed is missing.

Adrian turns it over in his hands. Apart from being wet, it looks like it could've just been plucked off the shelf in some posh yacht chandlery. Is even a sticky square on one side where a price tag was once stuck.

The knot that had been tied to fix the green fender onto the line is an over-complicated thing, with way too many turns and tucks. Like whoever tied it wanted to make very sure it didn't come apart, but knew fuck all about what was really needed to secure a buoy to a rope.

"Fucking yachtie knot," says Matty, studying the rope where it meets the buoy.

"We going to see what's on it?" asks Tim again, grinning like an idiot, half-smashed on the spliff and just glad to be getting a break from baiting pots with week-old pollack heads.

"Be a fucking anchor. Some yachtie twat got his hook stuck and then tied his tender buff on the end of his rope to mark it," says Matty. "Prob'ly thinking he'll waypoint it on his plotter. Then ask the Navy or the Coastguard to come retrieve it for him."

"Who anchors out here?" says Adrian, his tone serious. Scanning the horizon. Not a boat, a ship, a yacht in sight. Fair point, thought Matty.

"It's 200 feet deep. Middle of the shipping lane. There's no shelter, no clubhouse, nowhere to buy a Pink Gin," says Adrian, thinking it through. "*No one* anchors on the edge of the Hurds. Not even a yachtie twat. Wouldn't probably have enough anchor rope, anyway."

"S'not *really* yachtie rope, anyway," he adds. Like he's Sherlock Holmes all of a sudden. Turning it over in his fingers. "More like expensive *commercial* rope."

"S'a yachtie buff though," argues Matty, picking up the lime green fender.

"Why don't we pull it?" asks Tim.

"We still got half the shank down there," says Adrian, getting his priorities straight.

"Fuck it. Give it a pull. If it *is* a yachtie anchor and we get it off the bottom, gotta be worth a few quid," says Matty. "Some of them yacht anchors is a fucking fortune."

"Alright."

"And, if there's a few yards of anchor chain on too, we could–"

"*OK!*" says Adrian sharply. Worrying about the time and the worsening weather. "Cleat it. We'll give it one tug."

A part of Adrian can't believe he's about to mess around yanking on a length of mystery rope in the middle of the Hurds, in the middle of a snotty sea, when they already have a full day's pot-hauling ahead of them. It's coming up to noon. And one of their longest shanks is still stuck to the seabed. Another part of him is a little curious too. He could see the sense in hauling up a free anchor to make a little cash. Something for nothing is always a tease. First they'd have to get the fucking thing off the bottom though.

The engine rattles and growls as thick black sooty smoke pours out the exhaust. The strain on Kitty's engine, making her pump more fuel oil than she can burn, so it's expelled as thick black smoke.

With the Joseph wrapped around the sternpost, the strain of pulling on the stuck rope holds Kitty rigid in the water, foam churning out her arse. Frustrated, Adrian pushes the throttle hard against the furthest stop, the rattle of her bearings is sharp and clanging. Tim, closest to the engine box, covers his ears and takes a pace backwards, like he expects the whole thing to blow.

Adrian shuts his eyes, now lost in the roar and rattle of this miserable tub's fucking sick, fucking engine. Adrian almost willing her to blow. At least then there'd be an end to it. When suddenly Kitty hoofs forward with a lurch, the rope still fixed to the sternpost. Something somewhere gived.

Adrian flings her into neutral and walks back down the deck where Matty's already hand-hauling the line. He's making rope, but it's hard going. Obviously, something still attached to the far end.

"You fucking beauty!" he says as he pulls.

"Still on?" asks Adrian, thinking of the anchor.

"Fucking right, bro. We got ourselves a yachtie hook!"

Matty looking a mixture of elated and wild-eye stone-baked, as he hauls a few more arm lengths. Then changes his mind.

"Let's winch it," he says.

The Joseph rope is looped over the jib's hauling hook and rollers, and wound onto the pot-hauler wheel.

All three men leaning over the starboard gunwale to look down into the sea, as the winch pulls on the fancy-coloured rope. Two hundred feet later, out of the gloomy depths there appears... a crab pot.

Matty sucks his teeth in bitter disappointment.

"Bastard. S'a fucking pot," he says, bummed out, at seeing what he sees every day of every week. Just another crab pot appearing out the sea on the end of a rope.

He kills the winch and the pot swings on the end of the jib. They all look at it. Nothing unusual about the pot. Except, once again it's a brand new piece of kit. Rubber lashings all still shiny and even the metal frame still showing blue enamel paint, instead of layers of brown gritty rust. On first glance it looks like the entrance funnel-tube's been removed, as has the parlour separator mesh, and instead of there being bait or crabs or lobsters inside, there is nothing. Nothing except a weird big dark bulge that fills the pot.

Matty swings the pot off the jib and rests it on the gunwale. They all stare at it. Inside, through the nylon netting mesh, is the dark shape. Adrian sticks his finger through the net to touch it. The coating of the thing gritty, like roofing felt.

Adrian looks at Matty. "The fuck?" he says.

Matty hefting the pot onto the worktable, straining. It's heavy. Much heavier than a normal pot. Even one full of crabs. Heavy as a crab pot with a big conger eel inside. One of those mean-eyed fuckers that climbs in, to eat the bait and then the lobsters, and then gets stuck. It's because of congers and big bull huss that Matty keeps the metal baseball bat handy. For slugging the fuckers when he finds them in his pots.

Matty tries to unhook the parlour door but it's locked shut. All around the door rim are thick black cable ties. At least a dozen of them spaced around the edge of the parlour door.

"Someone *really* didn't want this to fall open," says Matty. As he flips the lid on the rust-encrusted toolbox under the worktable and takes out a pair of wire cutters, jammed open, from a mixture of long-term corrosion and fish scales. With both his hands he manages to close the cutters and open them again, four or five times, freeing the pivot enough to start cutting through the cable ties, one by one.

Adrian and Tim watch, fascinated to see what's inside the pot. Instinctively, Adrian also taking time to look up and scan the sea, 360 degrees, all around the horizon. Something making him wary.

With the door open, Matty grabs at the black thing inside and tries to pull it out. Looks like a bag made of roofing felt. Some sort of thick waterproof coating stuff for construction or ship building. Something heavy duty that's been folded and sealed into a shape, like a duffel bag.

He pulls on the top seam, the lipped edge where the felt stuff's been heat-sealed by melting the two sides of the felt stuff together in a waterproof weld. The felt rough and gritty, scraping skin off Matty's fingers, as he grunts and tugs, pulling at the thing.

Eventually, it comes out. He stands it on the worktable. The exact size and shape of the inside of the crab pot. Even has the mark of the pot's metal hoop-braces imprinted into the felt.

Using the scallop-shucking knife, with its short wedge-shaped blade, made for prying open shells, Matty stabs into the gritty felt just below the sealed edge. With the thick blade inside, he cuts an opening six inches long and prises the felt apart, to peer inside.

Adrian wants to look. But first he feels compelled to scan the horizon again. His hackles up. Without knowing why, Adrian feels exposed. Even though he's in the middle of the English Channel miles from any eyes. Still he scopes the water. Nothing visible, apart from the large dark shape of a container ship, four or five miles to the west making a good pace along the shipping lane, moving away from the Kitty, heading towards the Atlantic.

All Matty can see inside is more blackness. So he works the blade along the front edge and up along one long side. Before moving back to his first incision and cutting up the opposite long side, so he can peel the felt back, like the lid on a sardine can.

Under the felt is thick black plastic. So thick it's almost rubberised. Like inner tubing rubber's been used to wrap up the bundle. Whoever did this is taking waterproofing to a whole new level.

The more complex the packaging gets, the more layers they unveil, the more nervous Adrian feels. A queasy feeling. Layer by layer the feeling gets worse. The evidence of just how much time and effort someone's spent creating this parcel, giving him a chill.

"This's someone's fucking stash," says Matty, sucking through his teeth as he cuts into another layer of plastic and peels it off. "Fucking *got* to be." Layers of rubber-plastic now strewn across the deck, beside the empty pot and the roofing felt bag.

"Of what?" says Tim, almost wetting himself. "Stash of what?"

"S'what I'm trying to fucking find out."

Under four layers of black heat-sealed rubber-plastic is a mass of cling film. Like suitcases that gets wrapped at one of those airport concessions, to stop them being tampered with by light-fingered baggage handlers. The inner shape, inside the rubber-plastic, inside the roofing felt, sheathed in layer upon layer of heavy grade clear plastic.

Matty tearing into the layers. Ripping and slashing with the short knife, pulling the plastic off in hunks and handfuls. Everywhere around him now, folds of plastic. The deck practically knee-deep in packaging, and still he hasn't got to the inside.

"It's like pass the parcel," says Tim, stooping over, to get a look in.

Again Adrian scanning the horizon. As Matty pulls the last wrap of cling film off a grey polythene-covered block, about half the size of the original shape. This new layer, thick and grey. A heavy duty bag. Like something used to line a recycling bin. All taped shut with silver duct tape. Matty cutting through the tape along the top seam, then tips the bag forward, as a bundle of plastic wrapped slabs fall out on the deck.

Matty picks one up. About the size of a bar of cooking chocolate. It's also wreathed in cling film, which peels off easily to reveal a slab of black shiny sticky material, like a slab of pressed figs. On top, embossed into the tacky surface is the image of a camel, coloured in gold. Beneath the gold camel is a small cream label with three squiggles of some Arabic-type lettering.

"That heroin?" asks Tim.

"Heroin's a powder, you dick."

"Opium?" says Adrian.

Matty presses the block to his nose and breaths deep.

"Hash. Black hash! Fucking, black hash!" he says. "Afghani … or Paki or something. Black fucking hash!"

Matty throws his head back and howls. Like a hyena. Whooping and yowling and hollering.

Tim watching him, with an open mouth at first, and then trying a few whoops of his own. Adrian just staring down at the slabs on the deck, and then kneeling to peer inside the grey bag. Inside another 15 or 20 bars, maybe more, still neatly stacked.

"This is someone's stash!" says Matty, clapping his brother on the back and grabbing the scruff of his neck through the collar. Turning Adrian's face towards his. "This is *it*. We are fucking minted!"

"Whose?" says Adrian.

"Who gives a shit?"

"Who put it out here?"

"Probably a drop off from some freighter. For some wide boys with a speedboat to come and collect, from Bournemouth. Or Brighton. Who cares? *Ours* now."

"Don't think we want to hang about," says Adrian, scanning the sea.

"When was the last time you saw black dope?"

Adrian shrugged.

"I've not seen any in ten, maybe 15 years," says Matty. "Long before the Iraq war and shit. And then, piece I saw was about as big as a postage stamp. And thin. Like wafer fucking thin."

"We shouldn't be here."

"We should smoke some," says Matty. Tim nods, enthusiastically.

"No!" says Adrian. "Not now. Not here."

"Fuck, *yeah*."

"No."

But Matty is already walking to the wheelhouse, fishing his Rizlas out of the depths of his fleece.

"Bring them in. Let's count them," he says to Tim. Tim bends and picks up the four slabs lying on the deck amidst the layers of packaging. He drops three into the grey bag and holds the other to his nose. Breathing deep. Trying to smell it through the plastic.

Tim's eyes meet Adrian's. Adrian's stare is cold and hard as he looks back at this boy-man face. Spotty. Scrawny. With a scraggle of fluff on his top lip. Tim holds the grey bag under one arm and presses the slab of black hash to his nose.

"Fucking great, eh?" he says to Adrian, like it's a real question. Tim all excited. Like he's just seen his first pair of boobs.

Adrian, staring back, says nothing. Thinking. Suddenly, what this boy-man thinks or says or does is relevant to Adrian's life. This little mouthy shit that hangs out with Matty and could normally be ignored or abused, without any glimmer of concern, has all of a sudden become a relevant and complex factor in Adrian's future.

Adrian watches Tim's back as he walks into the wheelhouse, then he turns around again and looks to all points of the horizon.

Through the window he can see Matty skinning up on the sink drainer, warming the edge of the block of hash over the same Calor gas ring they infrequently use to boil a kettle, to make a brew, or wet the contents of a Pot Noodle. Already Adrian can smell the sweet tarry scent of the black hash as it warms in the flame. Matty pinching lumps of the crumbly hash from the block and sprinkling it in a long thick layer over the tobacco.

Matty grinning at Tim. Tim hopping on the spot, his hand raised like he wants to high five Matty, while inside Adrian's heart sinks another whole layer into doom. The sight of these two jiggling with joy as they roll a spliff with some of fuck-knows-how-many thousand of pounds' worth of someone else's hash doesn't make him feel warm and fuzzy for the future. It makes him feel fear.

Adrian walks to the back of the boat where the rope still attached to the rest of the shank of crab pots is tied around the sternpost. He picks up the scallop knife from the edge of the worktable and, with one swift sawing motion, slices through the rope. It sinks out of sight beneath the surface. The stuck shank of pots will have to stay stuck. Adrian isn't hanging around. He bangs his way into the wheelhouse and slams Kitty in gear, ramming the throttle forward. Matty caught off balance as he sucks hard on the joint he'd rolled with the black hash. Tim stumbles against Adrian, who bounces him away with a hard shoulder barge.

"We don't want to be here," says Adrian.

"The pots?" asks Matty holding his breath, lungs full.

"I cut them."

"No fucking way," says Matty in a cloud of smoke. Then smiles. "Don't want to leave any evidence. Smart thinking."

"Get the packaging bundled up before it gets blown over," Adrian says to Tim. Tim points at the joint.

"I haven't had a toke on–"

"*Do*. It." Adrian's eyes full of hate.

Tim slouches out the door. Shooting a look at Adrian and starts gathering up packaging as it whirls around the deck.

Matty exhales a huge lungful of smoke and sighs.

"Well. *Is* it?" asks Adrian.

"Fucking amazing," says Matty.

He holds the joint in front of Adrian's face. "You *got* to, man."

Adrian looks at it. Smouldering, smoking, dropping little nuggets of burning hash crumbs onto the deck beneath his captain's chair. He looks. A hesitation, a moment of mounting weakness. And then.

"I don't need to get fucked up and paranoid. Believe me, I'm paranoid enough already."

"Why you paranoid?"

"Why you think?"

"Should be creaming your pants, bruv. This. Just. Happened." Matty grinning now. "To us. Not anyone else. To *us*. We just hauled up a pot-full of black hash. What the *fuck!*"

Adrian not sharing his brother's ecstasy. His face serious. Matty oblivious. Matty holding bars of black up to the light, studying them like they were antique works of art.

"We smoke some," he says. "Well, *I* smoke some, anyway. Sell the rest, and then we are pig-rich and pretty. We can stop doing this shit-arse job day after day."

"You not worried whose dope it is?"

"Couldn't give a toss. 'Fact, that's a lie," says Matty. "Cause, it's *our* dope now."

"Don't worry someone's looking for it?" says Adrian. "Maybe someone's been out in the Hurds already, searching for a green buoy and all they seen is our buoy. A Kitty K buoy."

"Maybe no one's looked yet."

"Ours the only buoy for miles."

"If they was looking. They'd be out here. Looking." Matty indicates the horizon now.

"The only pot buoys showing anywhere in the whole Hurds is ours."

"So what? We're talking about drug smugglers," says Matty. "Not crabbers. Look at the fucking knot they tied." His thumb crooked out towards the deck where the shiny green buff and rope is still lying. "They don't know one buff from another. And definitely don't know ours."

"No?"

"Wasn't even marked. The 'K' was long washed off. Only we know that was our buff."

"Except no other boat from anywhere has any pots in the area."

"So?"

"So anyone asking around would know Kitty K's about the only crew stupid enough to work these grounds."

"Anyone asking *who*?" says Matty. "Who's this doing this asking? And who're they asking? Fucking Drug Smuggling Information Bureau?"

"You don't think whoever dropped that is going to come looking for it?"

"Too bad."

Tim walks up to the wheelhouse door, his arms straining to hug a huge ball of plastic packaging. "Want me to chuck this over the side?"

"Yes," says Matty.

"No!" shouts Adrian. Tim freezes, a step towards the gunwale. Matty looks at Adrian.

"Got your fingerprints all over it. You really want it just floating around out here?" he says to Matty.

Matty blinks a beat and turns to Tim. "No," he says. "Ball it up. Stash it under the hatch. Forward, below the wheelhouse.

Tim looks pissed off. A moment ago he thought he was just going to lob it over the side. Now he's got a whole lot of faffing and sorting to do. He looks at Matty, knitting his brows, pouting.

"Sort it out, and I'll skin one up for you," Matty says, seeing the disappointment in Tim's puppy dog face. Tim grins. Happy again.

"This is going to curl your fucking toes!"

Adrian steers the boat in as fast and as clean a line directly away from the grounds. Engine roaring in his haste. While Matty skins up another joint.

"What about *him*?" asks Adrian flatly.

"What about him?"

"You're not worried whose dope it is. I suppose you're not worried a 15-year-old boy knows exactly where we got it."

"Tim's cool. Leave him to me."

"He's 15. He's got a mouth on him like a rabbit."

Matty prickly now. "Like I said. Tim's cool."

Outside they hear the sound of the fore hatch slamming shut. Tim appears in the doorway holding up the digital fish scales. The ones they used for weighing cod and bags of cuttlefish in the days when they're long lining and setting cuttle traps. Which is practically never, on account of the cod quota and the big slump in the cuttle price, since the Euro started to eat itself.

Tim holding up the digital scales, grinning like he just discovered a gold seam running through the heart of the Kitty K.

"Good thinking, Batman," says Matty, as he hands Tim the joint and takes the scales.

As Tim sparks up his own fake Zippo lighter, Matty jabs the hook of the digital fish balance through a section around the neck of the thick grey plastic bag that still has duct tape stuck to it. The duct tape stopping the hook tearing through the plastic. The T-shaped handle at the top of the balance is designed to be lifted with two hands. And it takes two hands for Matty to lift it off the wheelhouse floor.

He lifts it in front of his face, arms vibrating from the strain of holding it steady. Adrian moving out his seat to stand behind Matty and read the LCD screen. The numbers fluctuating between 21 and 22 kilos. Matty sucks his teeth.

"Fuck," whispers Adrian.

"You said it," says Matty.

"What's it worth?" asks Tim. "What's the street value?"

"Street value?" says Matty.

"When we sell it?"

Matty now catching Adrian's eye, a quick cautious beat.

"How much does Afghani black make an ounce?" Adrian asks Matty.

"Can't say. No one ever got black. Always all skunk. Or brown hash. Moroccan. Lebanese. Shitty stuff."

"What d'you reckon?"

"Hundred quid an ounce?" Matty guesses. "More maybe. People love this shit. Ounce lasts forever. Not like weed."

"So what? Hundred and fifty?"

"Easy. No prob," says Matty. "People bite your arm off."

As if on cue, Tim coughs up a lung of smoke and wobbles. Reaching his hand out to steady himself against the back of Adrian's chair. Colour draining from Tim's face, as his eyes droop.

"See what I'm saying? One toke and he's fucked." Tim reaches out a wobbly hand to pass the joint to Matty. Like he can't take another hit. Hand wobbling, eyes rolling up behind his eyelids. Matty watching him. "See what I'm saying. This shit is fucked!"

Tim slumps in the corner of the wheelhouse, collapsing into a pile of waterproofs. Stupid stoned grin on his face, skin the colour of a turbot's belly.

Matty is doing the math. "Kilo is a thousand grams. Twenty-eight grams is an ounce."

"How many ounces in a kilo?" asks Adrian.

"Don't know. Never had a kilo hash before. Or skunk," says Matty.

"Twenty-eights into a thousand?" asks Adrian.

"Come on, man. *You* was teacher's pet. Not me."

Adrian flips over a page of his black book of pot shank shoots and picks up the small stubby red biro with 'Betfred' embossed around the chewed lid. He scribbles out the sum. His own brain rusty from years of neglect. He scribbles his answer out twice. And swears to himself. Matty holding out his mobile phone to Adrian.

"It's got a calculator." Adrian doesn't take it.

"Just over 32 ounces in a kilo," he says. "Twenty-one kilos. That's… 672 ounces. Thereabouts. At 350 a pop? One-hundred-and-one-thousand pounds, total. Give or take."

"We. Are. *Minted*," says Matty. Teeth clenched.

"Fucking A," says Tim weakly, his eyes still shut.

"Someone loses over a hundred-thousand quid's worth of top quality hash, and you still don't think they'll come looking?"

"Adie, man. Don't spoil the moment," says Matty. "Don't piss all over the bonfire. Think positive."

"Bollocks. I just–"

"No. *You* bollocks," says Matty sharply. "This a once in a lifetime event, big brother. Never going to happen again. Single best thing that's ever going to happen to us. And you're going to piss and whine it away? All worried up about someone who doesn't fucking *exist*."

"They do exist."

"No they fucking don't. Do *you* know them? Do you know their name? What fucking *country* they even come from? Come *on!*"

"I know no one walks away from a stash like that, without hunting for it," says Adrian. "*Seriously* hunting."

"There's a hundred-thousand fucking miles of sea out here. Let them hunt all they want."

"There's all this sea out here. But whoever dropped it, dropped it near, in *sight* of, a pot buoy. *Our* pot buoy. No one else's pot buoy out here, 'cos no one else is ever dumb enough to fish the Hurds."

"So *what*?" says Matty. "You keep saying 'our buoy'. I don't think they even seen our marker buoy. They prob'ly dropped at night. Pinged it as a waypoint. Texted the lat-long co-ordinates to the boys picking it up. Some numpties with a little 50 horse fucking day-fisher thing. They punched in the numbers, bounced the waves for 20 miles and come up empty-handed. End of story."

"They come all the way out here and they didn't notice our pot buoy?" Adrian asks. "Only thing on the surface of the sea for miles around?"

"Maybe they haven't even been out to pick up yet," says Matty, thinking aloud. "Maybe we beat them to it."

"If it was dropped last night, they'd be out to get it soon as it was light," says Adrian. "Even if they come from Bournemouth, or even Cherbourg, they'd be here by now".

"Maybe they're waiting for a weather window."

"You got a hundred grand sunk in a pot on the bottom of the Channel. Would *you* wait for a weather window? Would you fuck," says Adrian. "That kind of money, you'd head out in a force nine in a fucking rowboat, to make sure you got here first."

"Maybe they had mechanicals. Maybe they couldn't find it. We only found it 'cos it snagged on our gear."

"But they'd be looking. They'd be out here, circling round, searching the shit out of the area. D'you see them?" says Adrian.

"So they came yesterday. Found fuck all and went back home to shout at the geezers were supposed to make the drop," explains Matty. "Now they think they been stiffed."

Seemed to Adrian he was the only one taking the trouble to look around. Check round 360, just to make sure wasn't some wide boy speedboat, or a Customs' patrol boat, bearing down on them.

"Like I said, I don't care, who's it is. It's mine now," says Matty.

"Yours?"

"*Ours.*"

Adrian checks the screen on the plotter. Just over two miles from the location where they found the pot. Jesus, why is the Kitty so slow! He wanted to put at least five miles between them and the mark. Five miles. Just get a bit more inshore. Bit more in range of Weymouth. Back to where some of the other potters are working. Back around where the whelkers are working the mud grounds and the dredgers are dragging for scallops. Let other boats see them. Kind of give the impression they'd been around the inshore grounds all day. If no one's seen them all day, they'll assume the Kitty K was out fishing the Hurds. But if other boats see them a couple of times through the afternoon, it'll give the impression they'd been working the near grounds today.

Unlike Matty, Adrian did care. Did care whose drugs they'd just hauled. And *really* did care if those people were ever likely to find out who it was hauled them. Was one thing having a couple of pissed off bad boys out looking for Matty. Matty could melt. Matty could run away. Matty could get out of Weymouth at any given moment, if he had the money. No one would give a shit. For Adrian, with Helen and Jack and Josh to look out for, skipping town would be complicated. Explaining to Helen *why* they were skipping town. That was a whole other thing entirely.

On the horizon, to the north, Adrian can see the shape of two boats. They're moving from the east, heading north. From their profile he can tell one is a dredger. Can see the big square gantry sitting like an arch over the deck at midships, where the steel basket dredges are hauled up before being emptied onto the deck.

From under the control panel fuse board, he takes a small pair of greasy, fish-slime-smeared binoculars out a filthy carry case. They are Tasco, a good make, so he's been told by Pete the Carpet. Pete being a bit of a twitcher at weekends. Adrian had bought them off Chris who'd found them left on his charter boat, Tiger Lily, by a punter who used them when they'd been fishing a competition. Used them to spy on competitors on other charter boats, see what end-tackle they were fishing. Said it gave him 'the edge'.

One of the lenses was fucked. Something inside wiggled around when he lifted them and one side wouldn't focus properly. It focuses well enough for Adrian to make out the other boat on the horizon was a crabber, a Cygnus, with a rear mounted pot cage. It was the Nicola B. Adrian thought about radioing the skipper, Lyall, under some pretext. Ask his advice on something. Ask if he's heard the latest Met shipping forecast maybe. Just something, just so he'd register in Lyall's head, that the Kitty had been around in the vicinity of the near grounds. In case they needed an alibi. *Alibi?* What the fuck? Now he's slipping into the world of *CSI Miami*. Jesus. Why was he so paranoid? *Should* he be paranoid? Should he just do like Matty says and thank God and start thinking about how he was going to spend his share?

He glances over at Tim who's still slumped against the oilskins, eyes shut, a snail-trail of drool leaking out one corner of his mouth.

Then he looks across at Matty. Matty with an unlit half-smoked joint in his mouth and his phone in his right hand. In his left hand, Matty holding up one of the unopened slabs of black hash. Gold camel stamp and Arabic squiggle label facing upwards. Holding it at arm's length, against the backdrop of the metal sink drainer, littered with the king size Rizlas and Dorchester Menthols. Now pointing the phone's built-in camera.

"The fuck you doing?" says Adrian.

"Documenting the moment, bro. Moment our lives changed un-fucking-recognisably." The phone camera snapping as it flashes its tiny flash. Adrian's jaw drops. Can't believe his eyes.

"You mad, or stupid, or taking the piss, or *what*?"

"Relax. It's only a photo," says Matty.

"Exactly. It's a *photo!*"says Adrian.

"Could be fake. No one can prove nothing from a photo. This could be cardboard." He waves the hash block.

"You're messing with me, right?" Adrian not believing his ears either. Was his brother really this stupid?

"You look on Facebook," argues Matty. "You see all kinds of shit. Yardie gangbangers posing with AK47s and nine-mil Glocks and shit. You think them are real guns? Huh? No one believes nothing they see in photos no more. Here…" Matty holds the slab of dope up to Adrian's chest.

"I'll do one of you. Mr Big Time Drug Smuggler."

Adrian snatches the slab from Matty's hand and stands to face him. "You really thinking of posting photos of this on Facebook?"

"Course I'm fucking not," says Matty. "I'm only messing with you." But Adrian could feel sweat gathering at the base of his neck and a shiver chilling down his spine. His safety. Helen's safety. The safety of his two sweet, innocent snot-picking boys now rested partly in the hands of his brain-fried little brother. Matty was right what he said about their lives having just changed – in so many ways. Adrian backing his face out of Matty's face and sitting back down, now pointing the Kitty towards the other two boats, the throb of her engines keeping rhythm with the throb of blood in his temples.

After another two miles steaming, Adrian sees a few more Weymouth boats, and they see him. He radioes Lyall, first on Channel 16, the official Coastguard-monitored channel, then on Channel 72. And tells him the impellor on Kitty's water pump is cracking up and asks Lyall if he's carrying a spare impellor. Lyall isn't. Or if he is, he isn't about to give it to Adrian and Matty. Lyall hates Matty. Has done for years because Matty sold him a 10-horse Honda outboard, what was nicked. And when Lyall found out it was nicked, he asked Matty for his money back, in exchange for the motor back. Lyall didn't want to own a stolen engine. Even if it was cheap. Lyall being a very straight sort of guy.

Matty told him not to be a pussy and refused point blank to reimburse Lyall. Matty hadn't stolen the motor. But he knew it was stolen when he sold it to Lyall. In the end Lyall dropped the motor in the sea off Portland Bill, a couple of miles out, on purpose. Just couldn't live with it. Couldn't even bring himself to try and sell it on eBay. Not his thing. So Lyall chucked away 210 quid. Just spunked away on account of Matty, who of course told everyone what a pussy Lyall was to do such a stupid thing. Lyall was happier losing the money than living with something on the back of his boat that by rights wasn't his. Just the way Lyall's mind works. Not Matty's.

Anyway, it made boat-to-boat relations prickly. Lyall had nothing against Adrian. But where Matty was involved Lyall wouldn't piss in his mouth if his teeth was on fire. And Adrian knew it. Which was why Lyall was the perfect one to ask a favour of, 'cause Adrian knew he'd refuse. Tactfully. On principle. The call would've been recorded on Channel 16, and Lyall would have seen the Kitty off his stern when answering the call. All Adrian wanted was to be firmly put in the near-grounds by an official recording and a dependable witness. Just in case anyone wanted to know if the Kitty K had been in the Hurds today.

OK it wasn't exactly bulletproof evidence. Just because they were logged in the near grounds at, Adrian checks the clock on his phone – shit, it's ten minutes past two. All the other boats heading into port now, to unload their catch. If Adrian wants to make it look like they fished the near grounds too, then they couldn't be back in port much later than the others. They had fuck all catch to unload, which would need some sort of explanation to the Kitty's owner Paulie. And there was the situation with the dope. No way they were going to steam into port with a hundred grand's worth of black hash in the wheelhouse and a 15-year-old so smashed he could hardly stand.

Adrian's mind churning like a washing machine. Matty just staring blindly out the portside window, so stoned his eyes were glazed over and his mouth hung open, half a joint still stuck to his lower lip.

"Selling this dope, right?" begins Adrian. Matty breaking out of his far away stoner daydream. Adrian thinking through the logic. "When we sell this hash …"

"*We?*" Matty snorts. "Who do you know to sell hash to? Fucking Portland Allotment Association?"

Adrian's jaw tightens. "OK … when *you* start to sell this hash. There isn't going to be any other black like it on the market?"

"You kidding? Never any black. Hasn't been black hash about, in quantity for donkey's."

"So, you … will be the only guy out there selling top quality black Afghan?"

"Fuck yeah?" says Matty already feeling the buzz he'll get from being The Man.

"Then, we *can't* sell it."

"I'm, *selling* it,"

"You can't."

"Watch me."

"No. Not local. Not even South-West." says Adrian. His voice firm.

"Why not?"

"Have to be London, or up north or something."

"You want me to take a train, like to Leeds or Yorkshire or some fuck place," says Matty incredulous. "Get out in Bradford and set up a market stall? You're talking shit."

"If this is the only decent black hash for ever, it's going to be noticed. Don't you think?" says Adrian.

"Fucking right it is!"

"And if you were the people went to all the trouble to bring the hash in, and knew it would be the first black on the market for ages. You'd be kind of interested to talk to the geezer was selling a load of decent black hash, just like the stuff you ordered – but didn't get. Am I right?"

"So?"

"So you going out selling makes us into sitting ducks," says Adrian. "Stuff isn't like other stuff, said it yourself. So the guys who're missing stuff so special as this, is going to notice if someone else is selling it."

"How they going to find out?"

"Because there's 22 kilos of it!" shouts Adrian. "Whole fucking country is going to be awash with the stuff."

Matty now beginning to see a little of what Adrian said had a ring of reason to it. "OK, so we sell 20 kilos in one single sale. Take a little bit of a hit on the street price, for wholesale rates. Save the rest for–"

"So what, 80, 90 grand? In one sale?"

"Exactly."

"Who do *you* know got the cash to do a wholesale deal that size?"

"I know guys," says Matty, hunching his shoulders, looking away, feeling this body language might add a little air of mystery.

"*What* guys?"

"Guys you don't know."

"Bullshit!" says Adrian. Pulling back the throttle as the Kitty slows down quickly, a wave from the following sea curling up around her stern. Pushing her forward in a lurch that flings Tim off the pile of oilskins. For the first time in nearly an hour, Tim opens his eyes. Blinking. Still stoned. Trying to get his bearings, his mouth dry. He struggles with his tongue, sticky in his mouth.

"I'm hungry," he says. And then looks up at the two men, who stare angrily at each other.

"We can't land this now," says Adrian.

"Why not?"

"Because we don't know who might be waiting when we dock."

"You're being paranoid," says Matty. "No one knows we got it."

"You're right," says Adrian. "But just say, for whatever reason, the guys whose gear it is, or the Old Bill, or Customs, is waiting when we dock. Then we're bolloxed. Bang to rights. They search the Kitty, we're fucked."

"No one's going to be waiting."

"If we stash it, before we dock," explains Adrian. "And clear every speck of evidence that anything ever happened, out the boat, then no one can touch us."

Matty says, "You think I'm dumping this back in the sea again, you're fucking psycho."

"That's exactly what we're going to do."

"Fuck off."

"Matty, think it through. You said it yourself, maybe the geezers whose blow it is have been out already. Couldn't find it. Maybe they did know it had been dropped near some crab pot buoys out in the Hurds," says Adrian. "You don't think they'd do a bit of research? Watch a few local boats landing? See if anyone's acting weird. Like off their faces planning to hold an all-nighter to celebrate?"

"I don't care. They can walk up to me and say 'give us our hash back' and I'd say what I'm saying to you right now. Fuck off."

"And then they follow you home. They follow *me* home. They follow this little prick home," Adrian says, cocking his thumb at

Tim. "How long before one of us has a can of petrol poured through their letterbox? You really want to look over your shoulder every time you stagger out The Sailors, shuffling your way home? Me, I don't want to live like that. Don't want anyone else to know what went on here today," says Adrian. "I want to live to spend that." He waves his hand at the dope.

Matty for once didn't open his mouth. Which was a good thing, a sign he was letting his brain tick over without talking. One thing at a time. One thought at a time.

"Where you thinking of dropping it?" says Matty. Thank Jesus for the love of Christ, thought Adrian. At last, he was getting through.

"Off the back of the Kidney Bank," says Adrian, quickly, already working it out in his head. "We've got two shanks out there from Tuesday. Ones we shot late 'cos we'd no room left to stow the gear."

Adrian was being kind, in order to massage his plan into Matty's head. In truth, the reason they'd shot those pots on the Kidney Bank was because they were so late steaming in, on account of starting out so late. On account of Matty not showing 'till after the flood tide flowed. On account of him being so hungover and strung out he could hardly function.

"We pull up one end of the shank. Stick the dope in the first pot," says Adrian. "Drop it again. Maybe lash the bag of packaging to the anchor. Keep any sign, anything, off the boat. So we steam home, clean as a whistle. Nothing to fear."

Matty chews his thumbnail. Running it through his computer.

"I need to take a lump of personal," he says, pawing at the unwrapped slab.

"Me too!" says Tim, looking at Matty first, then Adrian.

"No way," says Adrian.

"I'm only talking about half an ounce, max. Just personal."

"*And* me."

This time Matty rounds on Tim. "Shut the fuck up!"

"It's my dope too!" whines Tim in retaliation, sounding like he's eight years old.

"Makes no sense, Matty," says Adrian, his voice now with a pleading, be-reasonable pitch. "You got any of the black stuff on you, you risk us losing the whole lot. Few joints worth is as incriminating as the whole 22 keys. Said it yourself: 'There's nothing else like this out there. It's unique.' You get caught with just a little bit – it says you know where the rest is. It's not worth the risk."

"You can't be serious?"

"Like you said, this is a once in a lifetime event. Life changing. Best thing that will ever happen."

"Fuck, yeah."

"So let's not fuck it up by being careless. Let's be serious. Do it right."

Matty sneers and shakes his head. Like hearing rational sensible logic causes a pain between his ears.

"Roll another joint. Roll *two*," says Adrian. "But just don't take any into port with us tonight."

"We pick it up tomorrow?"

"If the coast is clear. If nothing smells bad in town. Then sure … Although …"

"What?" says Matty, getting annoyed

"Although, if we're going to stash it anywhere, while we wait to make one big sale… Bottom of the sea's as good a place as any."

The Kidney Bank is basically an underwater sand dune. A two-mile long, gently sloping hill of sand built up from west to east by the force of the big flood tides that get funnelled and pinched into a race of fast current, by the long thin rock finger of Portland Bill. Portland tidal race is a rush of tide that curves around the jagged rocks of Portland Bill and violently crashes into the underwater and reefs and boulders that lie just offshore. Portland Race is the most dangerous tidal race in Britain, arguably one of the most dangerous in any shipping channel in the world. More ships have been sunk in a five-mile radius of Portland Race than in any one patch of sea around the whole of the British Isles.

Granted, German U-boats and the Spanish Armada were responsible for a fair portion of the shipwrecks across Weymouth Bay, but the Portland Race itself has caused chaos to shipping for centuries. The force of the tide, accelerated by the funnelling effect of the nine-mile long promontory of solid Portland stone, is so powerful it picks up hundreds of tons of sand from Lyme Bay and carries it in suspension, every time it roars east. Twice every day it transports sand from the west side of the Bill, then dumps on the east side, in two places, the Shambles Bank and the Kidney Bank.

Kitty K's rogue pots were shot on the leeward south eastern edge of the Kidney, where the sand begins to thin out and the rocky bed starts to show through, like scabs on a bald head. Setting crab pots on sand is like trying to grow leeks in concrete. Brown edible crabs don't live in sand. They live amongst rocks and ledges. So, the edge of the Kidney is not a great place to shoot gear, but it's convenient. It's close to the harbour. No more than an hour's steam in most seas.

The only other upside to potting on the southern rocky edge of the Kidney is that none of the other boats would bother. Their working practices aren't as haphazard as the Kitty K, so they're not always trying to make the best of a bad job. Something which is pretty much the daily mantra of Adrian's working life.

Every single morsel of the black dope, apart from two joints, one on the sink drainer and one in Matty's mouth, is in the grey plastic bag, which has been resealed with a roll of duct tape taken from under the sink. Several layers of the thick commercial cling film have been wrapped back around it too. Of course, it's now doing nothing near as good a waterproofing job as the original packaging did, but it'll do, at least for a day or two.

The tide on the leeward edge of the Kidney is much slacker than in the Hurds, which is the reason why all the sand settles on the bank. The Race pushes the sand around the Bill, then as it flows a couple of miles further away from the rocky point which causes the pinching and acceleration, the tide slackens and the sand drops to the seabed. So, on the Kidney, the stash won't have to stand anything like the physical punishment it would out in the Deeps.

The first pot of this rogue shank that's pulled up has a huge brown cock crab and two lobsters inside, all intact. All in prime condition. In fact, they are such good specimens it's tempting for the boys to take time and pull the whole shank. A few more crabs and lobsters would make it look like they'd actually done a day's work, but rather than deviate from the plan and confuse the issue, Adrian settles for pulling the first pot, emptying out the crabs and lobster and replacing them with the grey plastic parcel.

Matty holds the dope-packed crab pot on the gunwale, his fingers curled through the mesh, hooking around the steel brace bars, like he is never going to let it go.

Adrian doesn't say anything. He just waits for Matty to make up his own mind. He knows if he opens his mouth at the wrong moment and says the wrong thing, Matty could easily U-turn, refuse to drop the pot and they'd be right back to square one. Tim is easily distracted with lighting the last joint, and finally, as if saying goodbye to a dead relation, Matty lets the pot fall from the gunwale into the sea. Where it spirals away to its resting place. Matty then heaving the anchor and pot buoy in after it, to mark the precious spot.

Adrian automatically reaches for the 'create waypoint' button on the Furuno GPS plotter. Normally, every shot of pots is marked with a numbered waypoint and the number is written down in Adrian's book. But, because this is a shank they shot three days ago, it already has a waypoint number, 0746. And there's a corresponding note in Adrian's little black book, to remind him how many pots in the shank.

Adrian highlights the waypoint number and then selects 'erase waypoint' from the GPS menu. He knows exactly where it is. It lies on the eastern edge of the Kidney two-thirds of the way south along the leeward edge. He wouldn't say he could find it in the dark exactly, but he doesn't need a waypoint marked in the boat's GPS to tell him how to find it. More importantly, nor does anybody else. No point leaving evidence in the plotter, which could lead to the stash. Better off the location is recorded mentally, not electronically.

Steaming in to harbour after the last haul of the day is normally a time for a skipper to do his calculations. To estimate how much fuel has been used and be able to judge if the tanks are low enough to need refilling before setting out the next day. The Kitty can do about three or four Hurds runs before her levels are so low she's sucking crud and emulsion and rust from the bottom of her ancient corroded tanks. It's when she starts to suck this evil brew into her filters and injectors that everything clogs up. Then she starts to run so rough she can be seen five miles away at sea, by the pall of black diesel smoke that hangs above her.

Steaming in is a time for the skipper to estimate the weight of his catch against market price. There's not a single load of crab landed by a commercial potter anywhere around the coast that hasn't had its cash value calculated, re-calculated, guesstimated and predicted, before unloading begins. And not just by the skipper. Calculating their individual share of the day's earnings in pounds and pence and pints is the daily arithmetic of a crabber's life. He might not be able to add up the cost of two items on a shopping list, but he'll be able to tell you to the nearest 50p what his share of 86 kilos of brown crab and 19 kilos of lobster is, once he's been told the day's market price. A fact which the skipper always finds out, by phone or ship-to-shore radio on the steam in.

A skipper also checks his fluids, his engine oil pressure, his coolant level, and his hydraulic reservoir levels. He finishes off mechanicals for the day and preps for the day ahead.

Steaming in is also a time for the deck crew to clear and prepare the deck, to stash broken pots, to lash down loose gear, to clear and rinse the bait bins, to store the bands, the tools and the rope. Simple sensible safety stuff. This is certainly the stuff other crews do. But not Adrian's. Not today. Instead, Adrian's crew, Matty and Tim, are smoking their last joint of black, passing it back and forth in sticky turns, as they prepare to play their favourite steaming in game: Fish Head Baseball.

It always fucks Adrian off, not just because when they play, they're slacking off work, but also because it was a game originally created by their dad. A game Adrian and Matty played as boys, riding home on the small, 21 foot, Plymouth Pilot their dad used to work his nets and pots, long before he bought the Kitty K.

In those days they didn't have a metal baseball bat. They had a thick turned oak 'priest' about the size of a riot truncheon. This was the weapon their dad used for cracking congers, bull huss and dog fish over the head before he hung them on a nail hammered in the back of his cuddy wheelhouse and skinned them with a pair of rusty pliers.

In those days the brothers always used mackerel heads as their baseballs. Mackerel was the only bait their dad ever really used. Mainly because mackerel was free – so long as you could manage to catch it. Dad wouldn't ever consider *buying* pot bait. He used to say he'd rather chop off his own foot to bait a crab pot than part with good money for something that was going to be thrown away anyway. Some of the netters who snagged by-catch fish, like smooth hound and pouting, would sling dad a bucket of the dead worthless fish for his pot bait now and again. They'd do it in the vain hope that one day he'd stand them a pint-and-chaser in return. That day would be a long time coming. Dad was famous for being tight.

These days, crabbers routinely buy their pot bait. Either fresh from the processors – a by-product of the filleting tables – or frozen in net bags, or in ice blocks the size of a hotel mini bar fridge. No one had the time to catch and sort pot bait anymore, much as everyone hated paying good money for the fish processors' garbage.

It was precisely because Adrian had forked out his good money and bought today's pot bait, and because they'd only used a fraction of it, pulling only four-and-a-half shanks, that there was still a whole box and a half of pollack heads lying under the bait table.

The game of Fish Head Baseball, as invented by their dad, when they were just tiny bright-eyed boys, desperately competing to impress the man they both thought was the greatest living man on earth, is very simple. Heading homewards at a gentle steam of around four to five knots, with the wheel lashed in position. The first part of the game involves preparation, chucking a few handfuls of fish guts over the stern. The fish guts soon attract the seagulls, also known to the Fish Head Baseball players as 'fielders'. The seagulls, big black-backed bastards and scary wide-winged herring gulls, being an integral and entertaining part of the game. Seagulls were happy to play the game too because, if they're quick, they get a belly full of rotting fish to gobble down.

The rest of the field should include one batter – standing with his back to the wheelhouse, facing towards the stern. One pitcher, chucking pitches from around the transom. And with a bit of luck, about 40 sky-soaring shite-hawk 'fielders'. Fish Head Baseball is the opposite of conventional baseball in that in Fish Head the batter's main *intention* is to be caught out. Being caught out by a shite-hawker gull constitutes a 'run'.

To be fair, as a game, it's more of a team effort than an individual sport. The perfect 'over' involves a pitcher tossing a mackerel head at just the right pace and height for the batsman to get his swing to come up under the spinning fish head and thwack it hard enough to launch it in a trajectory that takes it up high above the transom in a smooth arc. The trick is maximising the fish head's time in flight, and so allowing the gulls time to swoop down. If a hit is big enough to give a seagull time to catch the head in its hard dirty-yellow beak, a run is scored. No catch, no run. If the head spirals down to the sea without being caught by a gull, the batsman is disqualified and has to swap with the bowler. Batting is no easy feat considering a perfect strike has to be achieved on the deck of a rocking boat steering itself across the waves.

Fish Head Baseball is a messy game too. Slugging rotting fish parts with a heavy baseball bat creates a huge amount of spatter. Pieces of rotting fish spray from the bat across the deck and the transom and the engine box. For their father to allow them to play such a messy game back then was a big deal. A big treat. A baseball game would increase dad's workload; create a shit-load of extra hosing down for him to do, when he eventually tied up on the quay. So, for the brothers, when they were little, to be allowed to have a game of Fish Head Baseball, swinging at mackerel heads tossed from the leathery work-worn hands of their dad, was very special thing. Something to cherish. Didn't matter one bit who scored the most runs, it was exciting enough just to have had the opportunity to play. A game of Fish Head Baseball on the steam in made for a big fucking red letter day for little Adrian and Matty. Big day.

So, now for Adrian to look behind him through the half-open door of the wheelhouse and watch Matty, spliff clamped between his teeth, lob a huge rotting pollack head, fresh from the bait box, at fuckwit Tim, really sucked. To see the game, that once meant something quite sweet and special and innocent to Adrian, played now in such an ugly way, gnawed away at something deep inside.

A flock of gulls swooped and jeered and dived and shat. Fighting amongst themselves jostling for position, as Tim swings at a spinning pollack head. Adrian can see Tim's swing is late and snatched, bringing the bat around too fast and way too flat.

In Fish Head Baseball the strike is all about lift. Hitting the tossed fish head from underneath with the bat moving through, accelerating upwards. Instead, Tim came across the pollack head, his swing all cramped and spazzy, skidding the bat over the top and sending the pollack head off at an angle, clipping the edge of the gunwale, leaving a huge deposit of glutinous slime. Then the head just slid pathetically off the gunwale into the wake behind the boat.

Gulls aren't called 'shitehawks' for nothing. They have no pride. No manners. No sense of sportsmanship. And so, accidentally dropping a fish head so close into the wake of the boat means half the fielders automatically bale out of the sky above the playing field to go and squabble over the floating debris. They peck and scream and dive-bomb each other for a turn at pecking on the pollack's soft grey weeping eyes, while the few that are left flying above the boat have to regroup into a tight fielding pattern. The ones that have baled out to fight over the badly struck pollack head will eventually return when the last morsel has been devoured. But an important part of Fish Head Baseball is keeping fish heads ascending into the air for fielders to catch, which maximises the number of seagulls attracted to the boat and so keeps the greatest number of fielders 'in play' at any one time.

By dropping a short crappy strike into the sea, Tim just blew the field open. Far as Matty's concerned, he's had enough of pitching good balls to Tim's shitty batting. Tim had now flat-hit three on the trot and cost them at least half the available sky fielders. So Matty took the bat from Tim and told him to go pitch instead. Matty wanting to show him once again how to properly swing at a fish head.

Adrian wants to look away. He doesn't want to see spotty fucking prick-wad Tim do the thing his dad used to do for them. Doesn't want to see Tim bowl a fish head at Matty. It made him feel sad. At the same time, Adrian found it hard to look away.

Matty has broad muscular shoulders, thick-knotted biceps and when his brains aren't too sizzled, he can really swing the bat like a fucking pro. When they were boys, even though Matty was two years Adrian's junior, Matty was always the big hitter. Adrian had a good eye. Adrian had tight hand/eye co-ordination. But he could never swing with the explosive muscle power that Matty could muster.

And so Adrian watches Matty prepare to swing. Sees him suck on the joint, inhale a thick wreath of smoke up the side of his mouth and then wind the metal bat back high over his right shoulder.

The pollack head leaves Tim's hand at waist height, spinning end over end. And for a few moments, it seems to Adrian that everything now goes in slow motion. It's all glorious Technicolor slo-mo from the nano-second the fish head leaves Tim's sticky teenage paw.

Later, Adrian would play the pollack head-toss over and over in his mind. Remembering it in every detail. The head reaches Matty slightly too high and too close to his right arm. But Matty's footwork is swift. He brings his right leg in, to give his body more height, as the bat – already on its way – accelerates in a low back swing. Reaching its lowest point and then, turning upwards, faster, all the while gaining pace, increased by the swivel of Matty's hips as he seamlessly throws his weight behind the bat. The swing powering forward until it finally makes hefty contact with the lemon-sized pollack head. The meat of the bat – the sweet spot – making a solid connection with the bottom half of the spinning head. The head is upside down when the bat rips into it. The top of the skull where it's struck being the most solid part of the head and so the part able to give Matty's powerful strike the biggest amount of lift. A squashier part of the head would have caved and crushed absorbing too much of the force and so decreasing its potential to climb.

It saddened Adrian, but he had to admit it was the perfect Matty slug. Big crunch with a beautiful follow through, the bat's finishing point being perched high over his left shoulder in a perfect symmetrical ending to the swing.

The pollack head climbed on up, spinning as it lifted, 50, 60, 70 feet above the deck, with a long high graceful arc, curving way behind Kitty's stern.

Just like Matty, Tim also looked up to watch the spinning head. Adrian now catching a glimpse of Tim's throat, white and spotty topped with a ring of grime, from the collar of his grubby fleece. Tim turning around now as he watches the head of pollack, still climbing, while the gulls swoop and dive into position, jostling to intercept the head.

One huge herring gull, half as big again as all the black-backed gulls, bullying his way in, wings outstretched, to exactly where he calculates the head will stall in mid-air, before it starts its descent. The stall being the easiest stage of the curve to catch the whole head cleanly in the hacksaw-like jaws of his beak.

Tim watches the big herring gull. Tim's body all turned around now, his back to the wheelhouse, his front pointing out towards the propellers with his face angled upwards to watch the big gull as it checks its flight-path, angles its wings, its red eyes all the while focussed on the twirling prize. Tim's mouth hangs open. His jaw slack, watching, waiting, following the spinning head, as Adrian now becomes aware of Matty, stepping forward towards the stern. Towards Tim, the baseball bat still in his hands. Only now he's cranking it back again over his right shoulder.

As the big herring gull's beak opens in slow motion, his last blink seems to take an age, the skin slowly closing over his piercing red eyeballs. Then his eyes are open again, pierced, fixed, its beak wide, angry, ready to catch. The pollack head reaching its zenith beginning to drop. As crunch! The beak snaps shut on its prize, just at the very same moment as the baseball bat crunches into the base of Tim's skull.

The crunch of human bone sends a vibration through the deck that Adrian would swear he could feel in his teeth. A crunch he could feel at 30 feet, over the roar of the engine, the vicious cacophony of the gulls and the crash of the sea. A crunch that sends Tim's body head first over the transom down into the churning white froth pouring from Kitty's propeller.

Matty hardly even looks as Tim's body hits the water and spins away like a ragdoll in the wake. Matty simply tosses the baseball bat into the sea over the stern and slowly turns to walk back up the deck to the wheelhouse.

Adrian can't move. This moment is a freeze-frame. A live pause. An out-of-body experience. As Matty now leans into the wheelhouse past Adrian's frozen stare, to reach the GPS plotter controls, where he calmly presses the prominent red button, with the bold capital letters 'MOB' embossed across it.

Man Over Board. Pressing this button creates an emergency waypoint registered on the GPS.

"Man overboard," Matty says quietly, smiling as he picks up his Zippo and lights the dog-end of the joint still hanging from his lips.

Adrian swings the Kitty K around 180 degrees and points her back through the tail of her own wake. Scanning the water on either side of the fading froth, searching to catch sight of Tim. There is no sign. Adrian not daring to take his eyes off the water in case he misses the boy. In case, God forbid, he accidentally runs over him with the prop. He doesn't take his eyes off the surface of the sea, but he can feel Matty, standing beside him, huffing out a cloud of bitter-sweet dope smoke that billows into Adrian's face.

"Don't go too fast," says Matty. "Last thing we want is to fish him out alive."

Adrian sees a flash of white. The skin on one of Tim's wrists, exposed, where his fleece bunched up when he hit the water, pushing his sleeves up to his elbows. Tim face down in the water. His arms outstretched, neck bent forward. Not moving. The water round the back of his neck, at the base of his skull, is coloured. Something is seeping out of Tim, making the green blue sea turn brown.

Man Overboard exercises are part of every licensed skipper's training. The protocol dictates when such an accident occurs; any deck hand should immediately shout 'Man Overboard' and point exaggeratedly in the direction of his fallen crew member. Crew are taught to continue pointing at the man in the water, without lowering their arm or taking their eyes off him, all through the ensuing manoeuvres. This is for the skipper's benefit, because the first thing a skipper has to do is look at his GPS to hit the MOB button. The quicker the exact location of the fall is electronically recorded, the better.

Then, should the fallen man not be found immediately after the boat swings round, there'll always be a reference point; a firm record of precisely where it was that he fell overboard. This also provides useful information for the skipper of the lifeboat that may get sent out to conduct a wider sea search. The lifeboat's coxswain calculating, using tide tables and electronic data, the exact rate and direction in which the fallen crew member should have drifted. So, if they don't get to him while he's still alive, at least they have a good idea where to go to intercept his corpse.

Matty isn't following protocol. He isn't pointing at the boy in the water, or shouting distance and direction to help guide his skipper's steering. Matty is standing in the wheelhouse finishing the joint. While Adrian flings the gearbox into neutral and runs out on deck, leaning right over the gunwale as soon as the Kitty is close enough for him to make a lunge with the boat hook at Tim's downward-facing body.

Leaning as far as he can over the starboard side, Adrian tries to jab the bend of the boat hook into the neck of Tim's fleece. The bright steel curve of the boat hook in the water showing clearly that the stuff seeping out of Tim's head is red.

"Fuck's sake, help," Adrian says, as he tries to pull Tim's head and shoulders out the water with the hook. Tim's soaking back pressed against the hull. Even straining with both his hands, with the hook twisted deep into Tim's sopping fleece, Adrian still can't shift the boy any higher out the water. The weight of Tim's sodden clothes and the angle making him impossible for one man to lift.

Adrian turns at the sound of the winch jib roller rattling, to see Matty, calmly stretching a length of pot rope through the jib and round the winch wheel. He ties a running bowline in the rope and tosses the loop-end at Adrian. Matty getting ready to winch Tim's body out like a crab pot.

With no choice and no time to lose, Adrian slips the wide loop of the knot down the handle of the boat hook and manages to pass it under one of Tim's heavy, floppy arms. Before he has a chance to get the other arm into the loop the winch begins to whine, as Matty presses the rubber control button.

With the boat hook still tangled in his clothing and the rope biting into his neck and shoulder, Tim's body is hoisted out the water until it hangs over the gunwale, swinging from the jib. Watery blood dripping from his fleece.

Matty stares at the white face and the rivulet of blood that cascades down over the collar. Matty's own face blank of emotion. He looks like he's daydreaming. Adrian manhandles Tim's corpse to the deck and loosens the rope now biting into his flesh. Then he releases the boat hook from the twisted clothing. Adrian falling to his knees, thrusting Tim's head back, clearing an airway. Just like they taught on his Marine Service compulsory Day Skipper course module. The one called 'First Aid At Sea'.

Adrian had practised and demonstrated on a hard rubber dummy that was only a torso with no legs, which Owen, the big fat ex-miner instructor, called Legless Lucy, even though it was clearly a man's torso. Owen had gone through the steps, clearing an airway, listening to the chest, compressing the chest, pinching the nose, blowing in through the mouth to inflate the chest. But it's all pointless. Tim is as dead as fuck, although blood is still leaking from the back of his head.

Adrian's hands and legs covered in Tim's blood. Matty looking down at his brother.

"You killed him," says Adrian, knowing he's stating the obvious. But can find no other words.

"I just saved you, and me, 16-and-a-half grand a piece," says Matty.

"What?"

"Made everything fuck of a lot simpler."

"You *killed* him!"

"Accident. You told me yourself. Time and time again. One in four commercial fishermen die at work."

"Fourteen!"

"OK, one in *fourteen* fishermen die at work. And, this is the one."

"I don't believe ... You ... just–"

"He would've run his little mouth off to any fucker would've listened," says Matty. "From the moment he stepped foot on the quay."

"But…"

"Old Bill would've known all about us, in a blink. Someone would've got wind and then someone grassed us up to make a quid," says Matty. "Or else to cut a plea deal."

"You…"

"Done us a favour. Done *you* a favour."

"You're fucking crazy."

"Call the coastguard," says Matty. "Now. Report it. We got the MOB mark logged. Tell them what happened. He was lashing pots on the roof of the wheelhouse when he slipped, or missed his footing, or something. You don't really know, 'cos you were at the wheel. Next thing you heard a sickening crash and then me, I called 'Man Overboard'."

"I …"

Matty looking down at Tim's white face. "Must've hit his head on the hauling jib as he fell. Say that. Cos when we got to him, he was face down, in the water, bleeding out."

"We can't just–"

"Ring 'em. Do it now," says Matty. "That way it looks right with the times and all. Enough time for you to try CPR and shit, and not get a response. Then… soon as you could, you called it in. So…"

"What?"

"Call it in!" says Matty. "*You're* the skipper."

God, she looks cute in her stab vest. Was something about a woman in a stab vest that really works for Tug Williams. Has to be a fit woman, with a proper figure. Not like one of them great lardy, lumpy ones worked back in the nick at Weymouth. Like Jackie, who just ate doughnuts all day from the Krispy Kreme counter in Asda. Doughnuts for breakfast. Doughnuts for lunch. Doughnuts and a Cornish pastie for dinner. Sitting at the desk in the Custody Suite, signing in perps, sometimes she'd have a pastie, a doughnut and *two* meat samosas.

You'd think it'd spook her they were just called 'meat'. Not any specific kind of meat. Like lamb or pork or beef. Just 'meat'. She'd warm them up in the break room microwave, and stink up the whole suite.

He likes Jackie though. She's a great Custody Suite Sergeant. Knows when to be tough and throw on the cuffs. But never resorts to force as a first port of call, like so many of her colleagues do. Jackie was smart. Could talk the birds out the trees. Tug had seen her make violent drunken repeat offenders cry with shame at finding themselves banged up in a cell, once again, due to be sent up in front of the Magistrate first thing.

"What's your mum think?" she'd asked a 21-year-old gang-banger with one blood-crusty closed eye and vomit down the front of his Southampton football shirt. "What's she think, when you keep getting in trouble, Mikey? It doesn't make her sad?"

Sure enough, Tug had seen Michael Keane, one of the most mental little thugs in Weymouth, cry big snot-bubbly tears at the questions Jackie probed him with, in her quiet, warm, motherly tone. Questions she asked between bites of a pink-iced doughnut.

She was a good cop was Jackie. Fat. But good. Tug wouldn't want be stuck in a car with her for a day doing surveillance. Wouldn't want to see *her* in a stab vest. But he was always glad to see her big grinning caster sugar-dusted face behind the Custody Desk when he brought in a 'client'.

Sara Chin was a different kettle of cop altogether. Half Chinese or Japanese or Taiwanese or some kind of 'ese'. She'd transferred, from the Met, three weeks ago. Detective Constable. With full firearms ticket and a whole list of tech surveillance qualifications. Way more than Tug had, if he was honest.

Which he wasn't.

Because, in this new partnership situation, even though they are both of equal rank, he is more than happy to assume the upper hand. He does after all have the local knowledge. He was Weymouth born and bred. Knows everyone. Knows more bad guys than good ones. And more than anything he loves nicking people. Absolutely *loves* it. Always has. Ever since the early days when he was only giving out speeding tickets and out-of-date road tax violations. Sometimes Tug actually looks back on his uniformed career with a real sense of fondness and even regret.

Of course every young cop in uniform wants to grow up one day and wear his own clothes to work. Tug used to think that part, the no-uniform part, was great. Just like school. You have to wear uniform through all the first five years of school. Then, a select few go on to sixth form where, suddenly, you can turn up in your jeans and trainers wearing your best Stussy top. All dressed up like you was on a Saturday night down Wetherspoons.

His main regret about moving up to plain clothes into a detective rank was he lost the opportunity to just go out and nick people committing crimes. The chance to nick people, who he could hold down on the floor, kneel on the back of their neck, and write up that very night as another statistic on his arrest record, was sadly missing. As a detective, nicking people happened way too infrequently. It took too long. Was too complicated. It involved far too much paperwork. And time and time again, it just ended up in a courtroom with two smart lawyers, being smart with each other, while a perp walks free, on account of some 'legal technicality', at the fag-end of some painfully long court case.

And more often than not, the 'technicality' was to do with the arrest, or the evidence, or the surveillance, or the *lack* of surveillance. So then, it was yours truly who'd get a bollocking. While the guy – who without a shadow of doubt, had done *exactly* what he was accused of doing, and which everyone from the judge to the prosecuting barrister, to the bleeding court usher, *knew* he'd done – flipped you the finger as he walked down the courtroom steps. Sometimes being a detective isn't all it's cracked up to be. Today though, just now, this very minute, the job appears to have its perks. Not least, watching Sara Chin slip into her extra small, female-cut, regulation-issue West Dorset Constabulary stab vest.

God, she looks cute in a stab vest.

They are stood on the small forecourt of a classic car showroom, down a side street in the middle of Sandbanks, on Poole Harbour. Real estate on Sandbanks, a long chunky spit of land that was once an island but is now joined to the smart end of Bournemouth by a narrow causeway – the English Channel on one side and Poole Harbour on the other – is the second most expensive real estate anywhere in the world. Houses and apartments on the half-mile long, 400 yard wide, spit of sand and concrete, are more expensive per square foot than anywhere else, except Hong Kong.

Maybe Detective Chin is from Hong Kong? Tug thinks. Chin certainly sounds Chinese and Hong Kong is in China. *Isn't* it? He'd have to ask her. Not now. Not in passing. Not just chitty-chat. No, he'd save that for when they had a beer and a bite some evening after a shift. Which they were bound to do, one day. Weren't they? Because that's what partners do, right?

He could ask her about where she was from originally, and put his chin on his hand and act all interested at the things she says. Because women love all that shit. He might even try to find out if Hong Kong is in China *before* then, so he doesn't make himself look like a dumb Dorset country cop. Yeah. He'd Google it.

Tug looks around, he's never seen a second-hand car lot as small as this one. He supposes it's to do with the Sandbanks property prices. If land is so expensive, you can't really expect a local Sandbanks car dealer to have a lot the size of a football pitch, not like the dealers on the edge of Weymouth. Mind you, the cars in this tiny little lot – just a glass-fronted showroom with an apron of concrete outside – aren't exactly ordinary cars. No Nissans or Fords or Vauxhalls in this guy's inventory.

In total there's only a handful of cars parked skinny-bitch close to each other and none of them has everyday car names. These all called things like Lamborghini, Maserati, Bristol, Alvis, Bugatti. Tug has driven some motors in his time. Pool cars, rental cars. He'd owned a whole selection of his own over the years too, especially in his early twenties, when he swapped cars like most guys swap boxer shorts. But he'd never driven a single one of the makes on show on this forecourt, or parked behind the showroom glass window of this posh little classic car dealership.

The dealership is called just Sandbanks Classic Cars. Tug isn't impressed. You'd think if you were selling such fancy-name cars, you'd want to have a fancy-name business too. It's because of the showroom's glass door that Tug and Detective Chin find themselves standing on the forecourt this morning.

A neighbour had called the police on 999 to report that the glass-panelled door to the showroom was smashed. "From the outside," he'd said to the Emergency Operator, like it was significant. Everyone these days thinking they're in an episode of *CSI*. The neighbour saw the inward-broken glass when he was walking his dog at precisely "11.19 am".

Sometimes Tug wonders why the county even bothers to employ police detectives at all. Because just about every crime ever committed these days is discovered by a dog walker. It's like everyone who owns a dog is now some kind of wannabe Sherlock, or Kojak or Hercule fucking Poirot.

The dog walker in question now stands on the forecourt too, with the dog in question – some sort of long haired lap-dog thing, with a ribbon in its head hair. Doesn't look much like a man's dog to Tug. Like it must be this guy's wife's dog maybe. Unless he is gay. Which is certainly possible around here. Fact quite likely. Unlikely in Weymouth though. Don't get a lot of gays in Weymouth. Probably 'cause they all moved to Poole.

"You didn't hear any alarm?" asks Chin as she shuts the Velcro straps along the sides of her stab vest. "No," says the man with the little poofy dog.

"Or hear any crash in the night," he adds. "And I *would*. I'm only two doors away."

Chin points with her stun-stick to a burglar alarm fitted to the outside wall of the flat above the little showroom. Just in case Tug hadn't clocked it. The burglar alarm with a blue glass light attached to it. The blue light designed to flash when the alarm is triggered. The alarm then sending an electronic relay to the local police, or some private security service. The blue light supposed to warn the owners that there's possibly intruders inside and, Tug supposed, to also warn intruders that the long arm of the law is about to feel their collar. But this blue light isn't flashing.

"You know the owner?" asks Chin.

"Not very well," says the dog walker, shuffling from foot to foot in his blue yachtie deck shoes. Like he needs the toilet. Chin now checking data on her iPhone. "We got him down as one Robert Rock?"

"I know him as Robbie. Not well," says the dog walker. "Just to say hello."

"Robbie's not here, I take it?" asks Tug.

The man shrugs. Not wanting to commit. Although in fairness, was a pretty dumb question. If he was here, he'd be down here. Standing out on the forecourt asking these fine police officers why they didn't go catch the low-life scum that broke into his classic car showroom.

Unless, of course, Tug thought, unless Robbie Rock is *inside* the showroom, lying on the floor in a pool of blood with his throat cut. Sliced through by some low-life burglar scum. Now, that *would* be a crack. A real honest-to-God murder to investigate.

With a big case like that to solve, he'd be sipping fancy cold beers and eating nachos with Detective Chin before the week was out. But statistically speaking, the chance of a juicy murder case cropping up this Thursday morning, in the over-priced chi-chi neighbourhood of Sandbanks, is pretty fucking slim.

Detective Chin finishes Velcro-ing up her vest, holsters her Taser and unleashes her stun-stick from the boot of the detective pool car, because there is, theoretically, still a possibility that whoever smashed the glass door is still inside the premises, crouching, hiding, cornered and dangerous.

Wouldn't that be sweet, Tug thinks. A proper fight, and proper messy, kneel-on-the-neck style arrest. Show Sara Chin just what her new partner was made of. He may be just a Dorset county cop, but bet he could show her some moves. Little Tae Kwan Do. Little hand-to-hand combat stuff he learnt on a special course he did up in Bristol, back in the day when the county still had some funds to spend on police training.

"You got a mobile number for Mr Rock?" Chin asks the guy with the deck shoes. He shakes his head. Guy doesn't waste his words, thinks Tug, as he slips on his own stab vest. His own vest looking worn and old and well-used – just how he likes it. Gives him an air of history, he thinks. Truth is, he put it in his Nan's tumble dryer with a handful of pebbles from Chesil beach one Saturday afternoon, when she was out at bingo. It had made the most ungodly rattling noise but 20 minutes' abuse gave it exactly the 'distressed' look he wanted.

Chin has edged to the broken glass door and slipped a gloved hand in through the shards, before Tug has even properly tooled up. He wants to tell her to hold up. *He* wants to be the first inside the premises – you know, as lead partner of this partnership and all. But before he's got a chance to even Velcro up his vest, she's swung the broken door open, having turned the latch from the inside.

Tug has to do a little run-skip thing to catch up with her as she steps across the threshold. Picking her way through the broken glass, he is right behind her, carrying his big-arsed Maglite torch and his stun-stick. He'd moved so fast from the still-open boot of the pool car, he'd forgotten to put on any gloves. Chin spots his schoolboy error in a heartbeat, and takes a spare pair of latex gloves from her pocket. She holds them out to him. Doesn't say a word. Just looks at him with one fleeting expressionless glance. Tug feels about the size of a prawn, as he slips on the gloves hurriedly, holding the Maglite uncomfortably between his knees.

"Why'd the alarm not go off?" asks Chin, almost to herself, as she walks across the narrow showroom floor, checking in between each of the cars. Back seats too.

"Not set properly?" says Tug.

"Why have an expensive alarm and not set it?"

"Maybe," says Tug, thinking about his throat-slit on the office floor theory, "Maybe cause the owner didn't leave the premises."

"Hello!" shouts Chin, her voice controlled, hand flexing around the Taser. "Hello. We're police officers. Investigating a break-in."

A piece of glass crunches under Tug's foot, but otherwise everything is quiet. There's four cars parked along one wall. All beautiful. All built before 1975, each one with a square of white muslin laid beneath their engines, pristine muslin on a pristine polished oak floor. White muslin to show that not one single drop of oil had dripped from the sump or the gearbox of these perfectly preserved specimens of automobile history.

On the other wall are only three cars, in similar perfect condition, although they're for sale, none of them displaying price tags or figures written up on the window. Nothing so crass. The space for a fourth car is taken up by a tiny office with frosted glass windows and a door covered in sparkling chrome decal badges from every make of fancy classic car you could care to mention, and a few more besides.

The door of the office is open just a crack. On the floor, just outside the door is one solitary drop of blood.

Chin points at it. She eases towards it slowly, stun-stick in one hand, Taser in the other. "Hello," she announces. "Police officers".

It was at times like this that Tug would like a gun. No shit, that's a lie. He'd like to carry a gun *all* the time. Like on TV. On *The Wire*, or *The Shield* or *Southland*. In one of those holsters that goes under your armpit, with the strap that goes up your back.

Chin doesn't even hesitate a beat. She pushes the office door open with her foot and walks straight in. She has some big 'nads, thinks Tug as he moves to follow her. *His* heart thumping. When he gets inside the office, he finds Chin standing, hands on hips staring down at a big green leather-topped antique desk, with a brass lamp angled across it. Huge great desk. Takes up most of the room in the tiny office. The brass lamp is switched on, getting hot, illuminating a pretty cream-coloured Persian cat that is lying across the centre of the desk.

The cat has no head. Just a large gooey pool of blood that spread half way across the desk and is dripping down over the side where a large leather swivel chair is parked. Chin stares at the fur and the blood.

"Jesus," says Tug. Can't help himself. It just comes out.

"Not a cat person, huh?" says Chin.

Tug can't work out if she's referring to him, to whoever broke the door and decapitated the cat, or to Robbie Rock… He's about to ask her when his mobile rings. The work one.

As Tug takes the call, from his commanding officer at Weymouth nick, Chin takes photos of the cat corpse, the blood, the desk, the chair.

"Where's the head?" asks Tug, cupping his hand over the phone, as he half-listens to what Detective Superintendent Firth has to say.

A moment later, Tug's walking back out the office into the showroom, listening intently now. He nods and makes 'uh huh' noises a few times. He even says "Yes, Sir" twice, then hangs up. Looking chuffed with himself. He walks back into the office now, where Chin is opening and closing drawers in the filing cabinet.

"No head," she says.

"We got a body," says Tug, barely able to conceal his excitement.

Chin looks at him blankly. Tug looking like he's about to deliver some killer punchline. When he realises she thinks he's talking about the cat with no head.

"No," he says. "I mean, we got a body. A <u>real</u> one. *Human* one. On a crab boat."

He knew the fish in the pond were Koi carp. Wasn't really a pond though, more like a sunken bath. Made him think of Romans. Sort of thing the Romans might have in their villas. With those big amphora vases at each end. He could imagine someone in a toga, bathing their feet in the carp-filled sunken bath. Made him wonder if carp would suck your toes or nibble off your foot-skin, like those little fish in tanks in beauty parlours that do pedicures. Garafolo fish or something.

One of them opened in the little mall of shops on Salter's Quay next to the boat dealership, beside the hair salon. Was called Dr Fish. Run by a little Korean couple. Man and wife. He'd stopped to read the price list once. Eighteen quid for a half-hour treatment. Must've been a dozen, more, maybe 15 tanks inside. Women sat flicking through glossy magazines, feet in the tanks.

He wonders could they be making any wedge. Shit, the hiked-up rent at Salter's Quay must sting like a bitch. Business rates'd be crippling, even for a tiny unit like that. Could they really be earning good scratch? They was Koreans after all. Koreans don't chuck their money at loser-ventures. Too proud. Too scared of looking like failures to all the other Koreans.

No, if Koreans thought the little fish-nibbling-your-feet business was good business, then it probably was. Maybe he should look into it? Check out the figures. Couldn't be that bad. Just a few tanks, few comfy benches to sit on. Big water bill though. Yeah, that'd be the choker. Still, you wouldn't be shelling out a lot of wedge for fish food, *would* you? Not when the little bastards are snacking on all that dead foot-skin all day long. Not exactly going to get hungry.

God, that is *so* what he could do with right now. A nice little business with minimal overhead, and a steady cash flow. Somewhere where punters came in and fed your livestock and then paid you for the privilege. *Nice.*

Anything would be better than classic cars. That business has just got way too volatile. Sure, when the economy was all rosy and all those hedge fund mangers were creaming off their fat bonuses, shiny chrome classics was the place to be. These guys'd buy a classic Corvette Stingray, or a TR3, just as a little 'high-five' present for their best tennis bud.

They'd buy a bright orange 1976 Ferrari Dino V8 with a crossflow head, because they've already *got* a sky blue one. At home. In the garage. They'd start to tell him how much they just *love* their sky blue one. And so that's why they want to buy the bright orange one too. Like somehow it made perfect sense.

Like he could give a toss what mental contortions they went through to justify spending 30 grand on something they already had. Albeit in a different colour. He was just happy to be the man they came to.

But the hedge fund guys, the derivative traders and the mergers and acquisitions guys, weren't buying bright orange Ferrari Dinos this month. If they came in his showroom – which most of the time they didn't – it was to see if he'd buy *back* the powder blue one. He has a showroom stuffed with cars he can't sell, and yet they'd get all pissy with him, cause he wouldn't give them back their money, three years after they spent it with him.

These guys, they love swinging their dicks when their pockets are full. Love playing the big man. But when times get tight they turn into spoilt little foot-stamping toddlers. Who get all infuriated that he isn't prepared to clean up their little potty-mess. Jesus Christ, not like he didn't have enough of his own mess to wade through, without getting dragged into theirs.

*This* place for a start. Three-and-a-half grand a week? Three-and-a-half grand, and she says she doesn't even get her own room! How the fuck can that be right? You could stay at the Ritz for that money; probably get a suite at the Savoy. OK, maybe not for the whole week. But you sure as hell wouldn't be sharing your breathing air with a couple of drying out alcoholics and some clucking crack-whore.

Koi carp were meant to be soothing. Probably that's why they were here, in the 'atrium'. He looked up at the ceiling; it was way up above three flights of dark wooden banisters. Right at the top was a glass roof, shaped in a sort of cone shape like the inside of a circus tent. So this is an atrium? He thinks. Receptionist had said, "Would you like to wait in the atrium, please", all smiling and soft-spoken, a small green badge with her name on it – 'Lottie'.

Carp are meant to be soothing because of the way they swim. Holding their body stock-still in the water and just fanning with their big graceful tails. Or else paddling slowly, only using their pectoral fins, like little chubby angel wings. He knew all about Koi carp because of the Discovery Channel. Saw a special documentary all about Koi carp breeders in Japan. He loves Discovery Channel. Never watches any of the other channels any more. Except Sky Sports for the Formula One.

Some of the top fish can cost upwards of 300,000 dollars. All bought and sold among Japanese collectors. The really big bucks was all to do with the fish's markings. The white splodges on an orange background, or else white splodges on a black-bodied fish. Collectors only really caring about these markings. Was all to do with achieving the perfect symmetry. Or was it asymmetry? One or the other. It was to do with exactly how and where the splodge of white was positioned upon the orange or black background. And if the base colour showed through the white splodge. Or if the colours bled around the edge of the splodge. Serious Japanese carpists liking the splodge to be pure white. With no bleeding at the edges.

The fish in this sunken bath atrium pond don't look like they cost 300 grand a chuck. Although the money they must be making in this place, renting out shared rooms at the price he was paying, would've bought a whole shed-load of Koi carp.

He'd bet no one was still paying 300k for a Koi fish anymore. Certainly not in Japan. Those would have been the good old days. These days, Koi carp, even in Japan, were probably the same as his Maseratis, just big fat arse-ache on the inventory.

"Mr Rock?" The voice making him jump.

"Hi, I'm Josephine." She held out a slim brown hand for him to shake. "Elsa's counsellor."

"Getting clean isn't the problem," says Josephine. "It's *staying* clean, that's the really hard part." They'd moved to a corner of the atrium, to a small stone bench. So he can't see the Koi any more. Robbie sitting square on the bench, his generous buttocks squashed right up to the arm on one side, he can feel it, cool and clammy through his D&G jeans. Josephine perched like a bird on her end. Only one of her tiny buttocks only just half-perched on the edge of the stone bench. Her legs angled underneath her, toes pointing down, in a pair of heeled sandals, with long string straps that criss-crossed her calves twice before they were knotted in a bow, below her knee.

Robbie was torn; he didn't know whether to stare at her little brown ballerina legs in the criss-crossy Roman sandal type things – thinking what *is* it with the Romans and this place? Or, to stare at her rings. She had a rock on her tiny left hand that was fucking unmissable. A proper rock. Chinking and blinking in the shafts of weak sunlight that fought their way through the atrium roof.

Robbie knowing a thing or two about jewellery. His first wife had her own antique jewellery pitch in an indoor market complex in Brighton. In The Lanes. It turned out to be a sweet little earner, which took him by surprise at the time. Made him wish he'd paid more attention. She wasn't no expert, but she made some nice cash out of it, from time to time. And it was real cash too. Most of the time. Folding money. Proper stuff. Stuff the tax man didn't have to get all involved with.

"For an addict or an alcoholic to stay clean in a treatment centre, is an achievement," says Josephine. "But not anywhere near as hard as it is on the outside. Back in their normal environment."

Robbie wondering now about *Josephine's* home environment, with a rock like that, somebody somewhere sure as hell loved her badly. No wedding band though. Just the big old sparkler. Engagement ring? He wonders. Nuptials pending? She is certainly very well preserved, but the tiny crow's feet at her eyes and the thin smile lines etched about either side of her mouth – which she did a good job of hiding with an expensive foundation – suggested she was nudging 40. Maybe even 45. Kinda late in the day to be getting engaged, he thinks.

Robbie was doing a lot of thinking today. Subjects rattling around his head like ball bearings on a pinball table, clacking off the flippers, clang-clanging against the bumpers. Thinking way too much, he thinks. Sure sign of stress.

"Elsa has shared a bit about her current domestic situation," says Josephine, her brown eyes searching his face for a response. Robbie could now feel this is where it was all about to get difficult. Meeting her eyes before he opens his mouth.

"What'd she say?" he asks.

"Obviously, I don't want to break any client confidence," says Josephine tactfully. "And we'll have a session later, together. All three of us. But I thought you and I might want to explore *your* perspective on the circumstances, that have led Elsa to where she is today."

Robbie swallows hard. This isn't exactly how he expected this visit to pan out. Didn't think he was going to have to answer any questions about anything to do with him. Shit, Elsa was the one booked into rehab. He is just the poor guy paying for it! Three-and-a-half grand a week for a shared-room and a sunken bath full of Koi carp, which right at this moment aren't doing nothing to calm his nerves.

He could feel a trickle of sweat meander down his lower back and run between his butt cheeks. He shifts his weight, uncomfortable on the stone slab. He might have some meat on his rump, but he can still feel bone on stone, and can really see how these benches could do with a little padding.

"She said you've not been together very long?" says Josephine, her voice all gentle and her perfectly shaped eyebrows lifting together into a tiny concerned frown. Oh shit where is this all going? thinks Robbie. And all he can find to say back, in answer, was "No."

That just created a pause. A pause where Josephine smiles at him. Saying nothing. Like she's waiting for him to fill the silence. Which he isn't about to do. What was she thinking? That Robbie's about to tell her and her big sparkly ring all about how he first met Elsa in a lap-dancing club in Westbourne, just a couple of blocks back from Bournemouth Pier?

How he'd bought her ridiculously over-priced drinks and paid for 'private dances' in a little curtained-off booth, where she'd let him feel the sensation of her tight little arse rubbing against his crotch and even let him suck her little sultana-like nipples, but "no touching" she'd say, every time he tried to cup her butt with his hands. Wagging her finger with a playful smile, "Is management rules."

He'd paid for private dances, and paid for the stupid cocktails that never had any booze in them, three, maybe four times, over a couple of weeks. She was very cute and very easy to talk to, even though her English had that Polish accent to it, with some crazy-weird sentence constructions.

"You not work like the hours of the office?" she'd asked once when he came to see her in the middle of a Wednesday afternoon. He guessed she was asking if he had a proper job and he just pointed at his own chest proudly and said, "I the boss of my business." Like the bad grammar was catching. "I boss," he said again, a bit louder this time, fighting against the strains of George Michael's *I Want Your Sex* pumping out from the dance floor's crackling speakers. Elsa nodded and smiled, seeming to understand the complex hierarchy of his tiny empire.

Next time he saw her she wasn't smiling. Her face was contorted into a tight angry grimace. And she said something fast in Polish to the club bouncer-type guy, which sounded like swearing.

"Problems?" he'd asked cheerily, trying to turn the moment around. He had enough crap going on in the rest of his life outside, without paying good money in here to experience someone else's crap.

"I hate fucking this place," she said setting her jaw and half closing her eyes. Robbie not sure just then if she meant the club, or Bournemouth, or England.

"D'you want to dance?" he asked, already feeling like it was about the stupidest thing he could possibly ask.

"No," she said. "Give me your phone." He handed her his mobile without even thinking. She punched in a number and saved it into his contacts and put 'Elsa' on the address book list.

"I do escort service now," she said, as she walked away towards the Staff Only door at the back of the dimly-lit stage. "You want to see me, call me."

It took him a week. He looked at the number in his phone address book a few times before he got round to calling her. The first time, a little nervous, but she sounded nice on the phone again. Friendly. Like she was genuinely pleased he'd called. And so he started seeing her. As a paying client, at first. By the hour. Sometimes 90 minutes. Then, later things evolved. And then they lived together in his flat above the car showroom in Sandbanks.

Except, now... Now she was staying here, in Cloud's House, a drug rehab treatment centre, in Wiltshire. Had been for the last ten days, detoxing from her coke and pills habit. And booze too, he guessed. She could get pretty crazy around booze as well, especially when the coke and pills weren't readily available. And Robbie was footing the bill. Like he footed the bill for some of the coke. Not *all* of it. But towards the end, *most* of it. Mainly because he'd rather pay for it than her go and earn the money to pay for it. Because he felt weird about her seeing other men – clients – even though she always had, and was when they first started 'seeing each other', or whatever it was you called it when two people did what they did with each other.

Sure, he was twice her age. She was Polish. He was from Harpenden originally. She was an escort – a hooker – part-time, and she was coke and pills addict pretty much full-time. But that didn't make her a bad person. And certainly didn't stop him loving her. Because he did. He couldn't find any other way of saying it. Deluded or not. Reciprocated or not, he fucking loves her.

And does skinny Josephine, with the Roman sandals and the big juicy rock of a ring, really expect him to rip open that big old can of worms? Here? Right now. In front of the carp? Because if she does, then it's *her* who needs some fucking therapy.

For the first ten days of rehab treatment, clients aren't allowed to make contact with the outside world. They could send letters or postcards, but no phone calls, or visitors. None of the clients, no matter how long they'd been in treatment, are allowed to have a mobile phone. And any phone calls, made after the first ten days of the stay, had to be made from the one and only coin-operated box, mounted on the wall in the middle of the corridor that led from the atrium to the client dining room.

Today was to be the first day Robbie has seen or spoken to Elsa since the morning he drove her to Clouds. That morning she bumped half a gram of coke and a bottle of sparkling Rosé in the passenger seat of his Range Rover as he drove along the M27. She cried a lot too, mascara running into little black deltas beneath her eyes. She looked about as bad as she'd ever looked in all the months he'd known her.

So, seeing her today, walking into the atrium, in the pink velour Juicy Couture lounge suit he'd bought her in Poole Quay when they went shopping after lunch in a shellfish restaurant one Saturday a few weeks back, made his heart jump.

Her hair was swept back, her eyes were clean and sparkly, her face, without any trace of make-up, was as beautiful as any face he'd seen in all his 53 years of life. She looked like an angel.

She put her hand on his shoulder, touched his cheek. But there was no kiss. He stood up, awkwardly, thinking he might try for one, make it look natural, but Elsa sat down in the space that Josephine vacated as she moved off the bench. "I'll leave you two to catch up for a few minutes," she says. "Then, we'll go on through to the Kreitman room, for a 'family' session. The three of us."

And Josephine then left, pausing to put her hand on Elsa's shoulder as she went. The two of them exchanging a smile. A smile that feels to Robbie, like a 'knowing' smile. Like these two are suddenly all tight. Close. Like they've shared something between them, that he isn't party to. In a heartbeat he feels excluded from

Elsa. Was like Josephine already knows more about her, could claim more of Elsa than he could.

Robbie takes Elsa's hand in his when she sits down. He's looking at her fingernails. All wiped clean of nail vanish. Just sweet and pure, clean, unpolished nails. He's never seen them like this before. Her hand somehow now looks like the hand of a little girl. It looks tiny and alien, inside his chubby brown, wrinkled, liver-spotted hand.

"So tell me, how is she?" asks Elsa, smiling, eyes wide, excited.

"What?" Robbie, waking from a day-dream, is confused.

"Suki? Does she miss me? And you feeding her the tuna, like I said?" Robbie smiling now, glad to have something to share with this beautiful girl who he can already feel is slipping out of his life.

"She's fine," he says. But, yeah… Missing her mummy."

What is it about some women and convicted felons? Adrian never understood the phenomenon. There's a breed of women, usually mothers; single mothers of a certain age, who seem sexually predisposed to prisoners. In terms of the evolution of the human race, it makes no sense at all. Being attracted to *successful* crooks – ones that are canny, career criminals, men who make good money, provide for their progeny and evade the law – that makes sense. But falling for guys who've already been caught and banged up several times on the trot, is just lemming-like in its self-destructiveness.

Tim's mother, Carole, now lives with Rich Tovey, a man whose ragged and ink-smudged collection of prison tattoos first started when he was 15, serving a 'custodial' at an old fashioned boys' reform school in Kent. Rich's array of DIY ink, started simple, with the one word 'Rich' worked deep into the flesh of his forearm. It was inked upside down, using a compass needle and a bottle of Quink. And still looks like the early learning scrawl of a remedial six-year-old.

Carole fell for Rich when he worked on a day-release programme from Portland Prison. He and six other, long-serving, soon-to-be-released, inmates were tasked with painting over bad graffiti at Preston Skate and BMX park, in preparation for new graffiti-style murals, to be created by a 'street art workshop' from Portsmouth.

Carole met Rich, while she was searching for her then ten-year-old, errant and delinquent son, Tim. She hadn't seen him for 48 hours, which wasn't that unusual. Rich and the day-release team helped her search. Later they got talking, over a roll-up and a Cup-a-Soup. And the rest is history.

Rich has been back inside three times since they first got together. Rich pretty much hates Tim, who *definitely* hates the brief, bitter periods when Rich is out of nick and sharing his mum's bed. And yet, Rich now stands beside Carole, on the quayside, looking and sounding like a very angry, very bereaved father. While Carole just stands silent, shoulders slumped, eyes dry, as she watches her only son being zipped into a black rubberised body bag, and loaded onto a waiting ambulance.

Carole is in shock. Rich is stoned. Prison has given him a proper taste for crack and speed, both pharmaceutical and home-made, and as a result, his attention span is no longer than a gnat's, while his temper is badly-balanced on a knife edge. Carole might eventually cry, Rich is definitely going to kick off.

Adrian thought he must be suffering from shock himself. He couldn't think of any other reason why now, at this precise moment in time, and for the last 40 minutes or more, there has seemed to be two Adrians in his head. One of them was doing normal practical stuff. Stuff, like hosing down the deck with the deck wash, and scrubbing it with the long-handled scrubbing brush, just like any skipper at the end of any normal day.

Except, what was pouring out the scuppers wasn't normal day stuff. It wasn't just bait-jizz and pot slime. It was Tim's cranial blood. While one Adrian sprayed the big oval patch of blood in the centre of the deck, skooshing the red liquid with the hose, until eventually it ran clear, the other Adrian was watching the first Adrian perform these mechanical tasks, wondering how the fuck he could do it and still look so normal. Because inside he was fucking screaming.

He saw himself, only 20 minutes ago, pull the tarpaulin off Tim's body to let the paramedics crouch down beside Tim, to perform their medical checks. To tell everyone standing around what they already knew. That this 15-year-old was dead.

And he could see himself talking to Kitty's owner Paulie, who was already sweating bullets about Tim's illegal, untrained, uncertified presence on a commercial fishing vessel. Adrian even watched himself standing, squeezed into the wheelhouse with the two police detectives. The one he knew from Preston Park Comprehensive, who was just starting in Year Seven back when Adrian was about to finally leave the school after his A Levels.

And now, the prawny little Year Seven's grown up to become a detective, who, looking at the size of his shoulders, obviously works out in the gym. And wears a lot of hair gel. To make it sit up all spiky along the middle and fan outwards at the front. Adrian could smell the smell of the schoolboy-turned-detective even over the smell of the pot bait. He didn't smell like any other man Adrian knew. He smelled of perfumed fruits and herbs and spices.

As Adrian was showing the fruit-smelling detective the MOB waypoint that Matty'd recorded on the electronic chart plotter, a couple of miles or so inshore of the Kidney Bank, Adrian notices how the policewoman is looking in every corner of the wheelhouse. She's even peering into the boxed-off gap between the sink drainer and the bulkhead where Adrian stores various bits of paperwork and licenses relating to the Kitty K. He is watching out the corner of his eye as the cop with the hair gel and the name like a nickname asks him to display the MOB waypoint not on the chart, but as lat-long numbers. So he can write them down in his notebook. All the while Adrian watching as the Chinese cop slides her tiny hand into the mess on the shelf and pulls out a packet of king-size Rizlas with the cardboard fold-over cover all ripped off.

By the looks of it, the packet has been in there for months. It's wrinkled and the top cigarette paper is stuck to the cardboard from weeks of overnight condensation. Adrian didn't even know it was there all this time. Anyway, she only looks at it for a beat and then pops it back on the shelf, never once making eye contact with Adrian.

And Adrian can see himself watching as Matty climbs up the metal ladder at the side of the harbour wall and approaches the ambulance. Just as the doors are being shut. Carole standing looking vacantly at the closed doors, Matty reaching out to put his arm around Carole, as Rich pushes Matty away. The forearm with 'Rich' tattooed across it, thrust hard in Matty's chest, heel of his palm coming up against Matty's cheek. Not quite a punch. But enough to

**108**

make Matty stagger back a step, as Rich jumps at him now, hollering face to face. Rich shouting, swearing, spittle flying from his mouth. Shouting, showing his yellow nicotine-stained teeth and his crack-pipe-shrunken receding gums.

Adrian now watching as the tiny Chinese-looking cop lady scales the harbour ladder in a blink. The hair gel cop behind her, thinking he's fast – what with all that gym-training and stuff – but in fact, he's clumsy, compared to her. She stops when she reaches the two fighting men, assessing the situation, working out her choices, when hair gel puts an arm up in front of her, as though to stop her getting too close. Like to protect her, although she looks in no need of any protecting. So she pushes his arm aside but then can only watch while hair gel dives between the two men. He's acting the tough guy hero. But actually just making the whole scene kick off a lot worse.

Because it's Rich on the front foot, jabbing and shouting at Matty, Tug addresses him first. Telling Rich to calm down. Rich too fried to even know what calm looks like. Tug grabbing Rich's 'Rich' arm and bending it up behind his back, to pacify him and neutralise the situation. Which doesn't work, because it's the one thing that wakes Carole out of her shocked day-dream phase. And now she flies at Tug. Matty trying to calm her. Grabbing her gently as he can, around her waist, to hold her back from attacking the cop. While Rich's swinging back with his one free bony elbow, hard aiming it at Tug but, because Carole's lunging in his direction, the spider web tattooed elbow accidentally connects with Carole's forehead, just above the eye.

So while Matty's holding her, from behind, around her waist, she crumples. Going down, like a stone. Tug using the moment of confusion to finally fell Rich with a Hendon-trained move, designed to 'demobilise and disincentivise' a suspect. Rich going down hard, right on top of Carole's spread-eagled legs, and cracking her kneecap into the Portland stone cobbles. Causing Carole to scream like a stuck pig.

Adrian, at the top of the harbour ladder now too, still feeling like there's two of him. One whose life has suddenly spiralled out of all sense of control, and the other, who is out there watching this car crash unfold in slow motion and is kind of buzzed and excited by the whole gruesome and bloody spectacle.

At Weymouth nick, Tug explains to Jackie that although Rich is currently wearing cuffs, he still might not actually be charged with anything. And even though Carole is sitting on the Custody Suite bench, he might need her driven up to Dorchester Hospital A&E department in one of the squad cars.

Tug wanting to use one of the Custody Suite interview rooms, now Jackie telling him that if he has three detainees present in the interview room, he will need to be monitored by a Custody Suite officer.

"But she's not being detained," says Tug, pointing at Carole, who is sobbing and trying to light a Silk Cut at the same time.

"Can't smoke in here, Carole," says Jackie.

"Fuck off," says Carole.

"I can certainly do that. But *you* still can't smoke in here, love."

"My fucking Tim's *dead*," Carole shouts in explanation. Jackie crinkling her brow, looking at Tug.

"Is he?"

Tug nods back.

"Accident on the Kitty K," says Tug.

"Oh, bless. Smoke away, Carole love. I'm sorry," says Jackie, reaching for a vending pack of Bourbons. Jackie beckons to Tug to come closer. And says in a low voice, explaining, "I thought Rich'd just been caught giving her a kicking again."

"Tried to give me a kicking, instead."

"Got ya," says Jackie. Everything now crystal clear. She passes the dongle, which will unlock one of the interview rooms across the counter, to Tug.

"Take Number Two," she says. "Number One *still* smells of puke. And let me know if you want a cell for Rich." Jackie looking over to where Rich is cuffed to the bench, making a big show of nursing his police-inflicted bruises. "Was beginning to think you'd *forgotten* us, Richie," says Jackie to him. "Matty," she says, nodding in his direction now, smiling. "Always lovely to see our regulars".

Tug ushers Matty towards Interview Room 2, using the dongle to open the door. "Where's your new partner?" asks Jackie, as Tug leads his group away.

"Trying to find out what happened, before this lot started fighting."

The inspector from the Maritime and Coastguard Agency had a clipboard in his hand. He seemed to be writing down the things that Paulie was saying. Paulie looking sweaty and angry and nervous all at the same time. He shoots a wary look at Adrian, standing now inside the wheelhouse, with the oriental cop. The Coastguard Inspector wanting Paulie to walk him through all the vessel's safety equipment. As registered owner of the motor fishing vessel, Paulie has a responsibility to maintain all fire extinguishers, life jackets, rescue flares and correct signage. Truth is Paulie doesn't even know where most of it's located and is getting seriously fucked off at being put on the spot and made to look like a cunt.

Paulie owns the vessel. He doesn't run it. This is what he keeps on trying to point out to the clipboard guy with the uniform. Who in turn keeps on pointing out that Paulie, as registered owner, has 'legal obligations'.

Adrian, seeing the look on Paulie's face, wants to step out the wheelhouse and help Paulie with his bureaucratic nightmare, except Adrian now had problems of his own to deal with.

"Just talk to me like I'm a child," the Chinese detective is saying. "Like a child who's never even seen a crab boat. Let alone one who has *any* idea how they work."

"Right. Well… We bait crab pots. We leave them out in the sea for a couple of days," says Adrian. "Then, we come back. Pull them up again and take out any crabs."

"OK…"

"Or lobsters. Or whelks."

"Right."

"Only we're not whelking just now."

"So," she says. "Why's he climbing on the roof?"

"Stowing pots. Strapping them down. Making room on the deck."

"While you were boating?"

"Boating?" he asks, confused.

"Driving? Moving the boat through the–"

"Steaming."

"Right. Steaming," she says. "Why's he strapping them down while you're steaming?"

"Saves time. We get home quicker."

"And he just fell?"

Adrian could feel his throat tighten.

"Yes."

"And you saw him fall?"

"I was steering."

"So you saw him or you didn't see him?"

"Didn't."

"You hear him fall?"

Adrian hesitated… "No… Not really. I think I heard a bang. *Maybe*. But if I did, I was still trying to work out what it was, when Matty shouted."

"You think that bang was him falling?"

"Don't really know," says Adrian. "It all happened so fast. Lots of things bang on a boat. Engine's really noisy. Old boat like–"

"What'd he shout?"

"What?" Adrian's mouth dry. "Matty?"

"Yes."

"What did *Matty* shout?"

She nods. Once.

"Ahm… Ah.. 'Man Overboard'. He shouted. 'Man Overboard' And, then, I turned the–"

"Man overboard?" she asks.

"Yes"

"Not 'Tim' or 'Him' or 'He's gone over!'"

**114**

"It's the training." Adrian nodding towards the man in uniform with the clipboard. "We get trained in Man Overboard procedure at MCA courses. And the drill is, you shout 'Man overboard'." Adrian feeling glad the bloke with the clipboard is out on deck now. Seems to make his answer sound more credible.

She wrote something down in her book. "Where was he standing when he shouted?"

"Matty?"

"No one else shouted, did they?"

Adrian hearing a note in her voice now. Little grain of sarcasm. Picking up on him keeping asking her if she meant Matty. Like she thought he was a bit simple. Or maybe she thought he was stalling. Buying himself a little breathing time before answering so he could get his answer straight in his head. Now Adrian worrying this could probably make her suspicious, so maybe he should be more spontaneous with his answers. All the while though, Adrian feeling his heart beating in his chest. Little bubbles of nervousness fizzing in his blood. "On the deck," says Adrian.

"*Where* on the deck?"

"Near where Paulie is now."

"What was he doing, just before Tim fell?"

"I don't know exactly," says Adrian. "I was steering."

"What *should* he've been doing?"

"What d'you mean?" Adrian now feeling like he's losing his footing with her questions.

"Tim is doing his job. Stacking crab pots on the roof. What should your brother have been doing?" she asks.

"Clearing up. Sorting the deck out."

"Passing stuff up to Tim?"

Adrian can feel like she's sliding a little trap into place, for him to trip over, so now he's watching his step. Trying to work out if she's suspicious, or this is just the way she asks questions. Either way, he can see he's got to tread carefully.

"I guess if he was so far back he couldn't be passing stuff up," says Adrian, looking at where Paulie's standing. Thinking about what he said about where Matty was on the boat when he first shouted. "But maybe he'd *been* passing stuff up to Tim. A pot maybe. And so he was walking back up the stern to collect something else."

"When he shouted?"

"Yeah." Adrian's tongue sticking to his mouth now. Maybe all this is just in his head, but it doesn't feel like he's coming over too good. But what did he expect? After all, he is lying. Lying to a police officer, about the death of a 15-year-old boy, murdered by his little brother. Murdered for the sake of a third-share of a load of someone else's black dope. So, with every word coming out Adrian's mouth he is digging himself a deeper hole. Is digging himself into the centre of a very cold grave, where he is choosing to lie down beside his fuckwit brother. No wonder he's nervous. He's acting as an accessory. Perverting the course of justice. Putting himself in the frame for a prison sentence. All because of Matty.

Adrian could feel bitter rough acidic bile seeping into the back of his throat. He could feel his head sweat. He felt a wave of sick rise up inside him as he jammed the flat of his palm across his mouth and ducked around the Chinese cop, and ran onto the deck. Adrian vomiting before he reached the gunwale; all brown creamy stuff with greenish froth.

He spat and spat to get the taste out his mouth. His eyes now resting on the cuff of his tattered hoodie, where Tim's blood, thick and gloopy was congealing in the corrugations of the sleeve. He felt his gut heave again, but nothing came now out except a 'yack' sound.

"You alright?" says the Chinese cop.

"Just the shock," he says, wiping his mouth with the other sleeve. Feeling his hot face turn cold as he looks up at her. She doesn't smile. Or look sympathetic. Or even look bored. She just looks straight at him. Deep into his eyes. Unblinking. Adrian holding her gaze for an uncomfortably long moment, then turning away to spit.

Jackie didn't like to come out from behind the Custody Suite reception desk if she could possibly avoid it. For the 12 hours of her shift, this is her domain. The throne from which she rules her empire. On the receiving side, the counter stands chest high, to even the biggest 'clients'. On Jackie's side, the floor is raised, like on a stage. So clients are always at a disadvantage. And the stainless steel reinforced rings mounted at four points along the receiving side are designed to accommodate handcuffs. With their cuffs looped through the rings, even the lairiest of late night street-fighters are forced to stand upright and pay attention to Queen Jackie.

Jackie sits on an hydraulic cushioned executive typing chair with four roller-ball feet. She can steer her throne anywhere within her semi-circle of power, just with the toes of one foot. In front of her are two CCTV monitors, both split into six boxes, which show her 12 different camera points of view at any one time. From the car park to the plastic-covered mattress in Cell 4, she can see it all. She is like the Queen and Big Brother all rolled in to one.

Jackie has a two-way radio console with which to reach any of the six constables who share her shift, and a PA system through which she can talk and, of course, listen to any cell or interview room. She'd described it to her little sister once, said it was like being Captain Kirk on the bridge of the *Starship Enterprise*...

"Only better," she'd said. "'Cos I can keep a pair of fleecy slippers in my drawer."

Some days the only time she'll come out from behind the reception counter is to have a wee. She'll even take her breaks behind the counter. Much more comfortable than the Break Room – and staying put saved her having to slip her shoes back on and retie the laces. Some days she'll even refuse the odd mug of tea when it's being made by Cliffy, her most senior Custody Constable, simply because she knows her tea intake is proportionally related to the number of times she'll have to slip off her slippers, slip on her shoes, slide her well-supported bum out of her well-cushioned executive typing chair, bend over – which isn't easy – retie her laces, and come out from behind the counter.

Jackie doesn't like to come out from behind her counter. Unless it is really, unavoidably necessary. But Jackie knows if she wants to get Rich Tovey, Matty Collins and Carole Shorter out of her Custody Suite without a whole lot of screaming, swearing and paperwork, she is going to have to get up and get out from behind her counter, and go and stop Tug Williams from fucking things up.

"You know what my only concern is now?" she asks Rich. He wasn't going to humour her with an answer. She knew this, but still gave a little pause to let him make a sucking noise with his horrible teeth. "*Carole,* Rich. Carole is all I'm concerned about. Right? She's lost her boy today, Richie. And now she's going to have to go on up Accident and Emergency. Get that knee X-rayed. You with me?" she asks Rich. "You think it's right she should have to go there alone?"

Jackie moves an inch closer to Rich on the bed bench. He is still handcuffed, but she wouldn't be frightened of him even if he wasn't. Jackie isn't frightened of anyone. Certainly not any man. She'd seen some of the baddest of the bad, burst into tears, piss themselves, crap themselves, puke on themselves. All just like little toddlers.

"She shouldn't have to sit in any hospital waiting room alone. Not today, of all days, Richie. Should she?"

Jackie can now see that whatever buzz was vibrating through Rich's brain cells when he came in the Custody Suite today is well and truly wearing off. This is too easy.

"What d'you say I get Detective Williams to forget about what happened on the Quay, earlier," she says. "And in turn, you forget any upset you might have with Matty. God knows neither of you need to be up in front of a beak tomorrow, eh? Then, you'll be free to accompany your lady up to A&E?"

Rich shrugs. Saying like he could give a fuck. Jackie smiling at him now, acting like he just made some big effort, and she was going to let him step up out the 'Naughty Corner'. "She needs you, Richie. Needs you to be a man. Be there for her." Rich juts his chin out, in what could pass as half a nod. Jackie leans closer to Rich and speaks in a confidential whispery tone.

"You behave," she says. "And I'll make sure Supercop keeps Matty in here, *least* another hour." Rich liking this idea, showing her a little receding gum. "Yeah?" she says. "*That's* what we'll do. You get out first. Matty has to wait. That sound good?"

The Chinese woman cop had explained how the Coroner's office would need to send their people to the boat to take photographs and make measurements. The MCA inspector had then explained to Adrian and to Paulie – but mostly addressing his words at Paulie – how the boat would be required for detailed safety inspection within the next three days and how nothing significant should be altered or moved before the inspection.

Paulie immediately asking how his crew were supposed to haul pots if nothing was to be moved. His tone nasty. Paulie's tone *always* nasty. The Inspector explaining that in order to continue to enjoy commercial certification – as required for the landing and trading of fish and crustaceans – they would be required to comply with his agency's wishes, to the letter. Telling Paulie in a polite, official way, that if Kitty K was to go pot-hauling tomorrow or the next day or the one after, she'd be stripped of her MCA license, and so could not legally sell so much as a whelk.

Paulie in turn explaining that accidents happen every day and that people still had to make a living. The Inspector agreeing with him and ensuring him that once the inspection had been completed, the vessel would be free to continue in her line of work. So long as all basic health and safety requirements had been met. Adrian now seeing Paulie struggling to keep his temper. Three days with Kitty K tied against the harbour wall, while all the other Weymouth crabbers were out at sea making money, this eating away at Paulie like a fucking cancer.

"Sweet," said Matty, when he heard the news. "Couldn't be better. Gives me time set up Stage Two." The brothers sitting in the front seat of Adrian's Nissan Navara pick-up. The truck smelling as bad as the Kitty K's deck. Worse even. Least the Kitty got flushed through with fresh sea air most days. The truck, full of ropes, broken pots, tarps and rusty tools, just got the occasional warm-up by the windscreen-demister, making the stink inside it bloom with the heat.

"I got some people up in Bristol, need to pay a visit," says Matty. "Talk around the potential, see who might be interested in what. Maybe even see if I can get a little cash up-front." He smiles at Adrian. "That'd be very cool. If I can pull it off, right?"

In the gap between throwing up in front of the Chinese cop and seeing Paulie have a hernia over the MCA Inspector's imposed three-day tie-up, Adrian had been trying to work out what to say to Matty when they next spoke. He'd tried to work out how to put into words the bubbling cauldron of anger, fear, hatred, disbelief and just naked fucking shock that he now felt. It was impossible. So Adrian didn't put it into words. Just as Matty was telling Adrian how he might be able to rustle up a little 'seed capital' from one of the 'high end money-men' he'd be able to 'access' in Bristol, through a Sikh guy named Max, Adrian lost it.

He threw himself sideways across the centre console and the gear stick and landed on top of Matty, punching, gouging, shouting, biting. He grabbed Matty's face in both hands, his stubby fingernails digging into his flesh while he mashed the back of Matty's head against the door pillar and the passenger's window. He hoofed his knee up trying to drill it into Matty's chest. He roared himself hoarse as he tried to crush Matty's stupid head between his hands. No actual words came out of Adrian's mouth, just the animal sounds of rage and frustration.

Matty brought his elbows up high to shield his face. He managed to raise a knee to fend off Adrian's blows, but otherwise Matty didn't fight back. He did his best to protect his head until the fit of blind big brother rage eventually died away and Adrian was left hanging over him, panting, sweating, spent.

Adrian slumping back across the console into the driver's seat and looking blindly at the now steamed up windscreen. His hands shaking violently in his lap. He opens the electric window to let the damp cold night air suck away the fog of his fury.

Matty says nothing. Just folds down the sun visor and checks his face in the vanity mirror. A ragged flap of skin hangs open and bleeding, below his left eye. He wipes the blood away with the cuff of his sleeve. And he says, "We do this right, everything changes. I get the fuck out of here, for good. You get a new boat, new business, whatever."

*"Right?"* asks Adrian, incredulous.

"Do it right," explains Matty. "Make us some cash. Invest it. Move on up."

"When you smashed Tim's skull, you didn't think – about me? Or Helen? Or my boys?"

"Exactly."

"You make *me* part of this. And you make them part of it too. If I go along with this, I–"

"Stand a reasonable chance of giving them a life."

Adrian balling his fists. *"Jesus,* you really think I want my boys to have–"

"Something?" asks Matty. "Yes. Otherwise they going to have nothing. Because that's all you'll ever have to give them. Because you got shit," he says. "Until today."

"I wasn't an accessory in a murder."

"Well now you are. Nothing you can say'll change that. And what you going to do? Walk away from 50 grand? Shop me to the law?"

Adrian stares out into the Quay car park, all lit up by the orange fizz of street lights. The clanging of cables against aluminium yacht masts beating a rhythm all across the marina. A hundred thoughts clanging, in his brain, turning it to mush.

Matty saying, "Face it, bro. I took an executive decision. Bought you *and* your boys a future."

The pick-up is parked in the shadow of the huge Victorian house where Matty rents a bedsit. Half a dozen wheelie bins clustered outside, all daubed with the number 17 in white, drooling gloss paint. One lay on its side, around it a scattering of bin bags ripped open by dogs or cats or foxes or seagulls. A tin take-away tray glinting in the headlights, picked clean of its scraps.

A small fridge with its door open is propped against the rotten wood gate leading through to the back garden. Not one of the lit windows appears to have proper curtains. Blankets, clothes on hangers and even an upside down American stars-and-stripes flag are in use to protect the residents' privacy. Adrian has no idea which window is Matty's, if any. And didn't want to know. He only knew this is where Matty lives because he'd given him a lift to the same shadowy spot with a second-hand fridge stuffed in the flat-bed of the truck. A fridge that Matty had been given or sold by someone he met in The Sailors. It might even be the same fridge that blocked the back gate. Adrian couldn't care less.

"We can't touch the boat for three days. Police and MCA," he says.

"Good. Gives me time to go and see Max the Sikh."

"We should do nothing."

"*You* do nothing," says Matty. "You always bitching about how you doing everything. So you do nothing for a change. *I'll* go do some business."

"No," says Adrian. "We both do nothing. Let things settle down."

"Strike while the iron is hot."

125

"*No.*" Adrian feeling his anger fermenting again.

"Longer that gear's around, more chance us getting in trouble. Am I right?"

"Not when it's under the sea."

"In one of *our* pots?" says Matty, like its incriminating.

Adrian shrugs. "It's the safest option. Let it lie."

"I'm going to Bristol. Tickle up some interest."

"Why? Just wait a few days."

"You wait. I'm moving on up."

"Think about it. What you going to do? *Talk* about the dope?" says Adrian. "*Tell* them what it's like. Ask them to take your *word.* Come on. Even I know they're going to need a sample."

"Fuck yeah," says Matty.

"And all the dope is in the pot," says Adrian, spelling it out. "Out on the Kidney Bank. And we can't go anywhere near the Kitty for three days."

"Don't need to."

Adrian looks confused. Matty winks at him, now with his swelling left eye. Matty enjoying the moment.

"You really think I'd put all that dope back in the sea?" he says.

Matty slides his hand down the waistband of his trousers, into his pants, down into his crotch. When his hand reappears, it's holding a lump of black dope half the size of a matchbox between his fingers.

"Come on, big bruv. You know me better than that," he says, as he slams the truck door and walks away past the wheelie bins.

Robbie opens the lid of the small Neff chest-freezer that stands in the larder off his kitchenette. "Was my girlfriend's, really," he says. The two plain clothes police officers squeezing into the tight space beside him. A light going on as he lifts the lid, illuminating the pitifully empty wire baskets that hang inside the top-of-the-range little freezer. Domestication has never come naturally to Robbie. He was always more of a restaurant/bistro type diner than a cook.

That didn't stop him *yearning* for a little home cooking. Didn't stop him having mini fantasies about preparing dinners to be consumed at the kitchen table, or even out on the patio furniture, with or without the warm red glow of the patio heater. The one that he'd bought on the same love-flushed shopping trip with Elsa, at the John Lewis Home store on the outskirts of Poole old town.

Together they had burned another big hole in one of his many maxed-out credit cards in a Cava-and-coke fuelled spree, intended to turn his flat above the car showroom into a home.

"You put it in the freezer?" asks the cop with the hair gel.

"Didn't really know what else…" Robbie trailed off. His voice sounding weird in his own head. "Just thought it'd give me some thinking time."

"Thinking time?" says the cop.

"To think what to do with it."

Sara Chin picks up one corner of the pristine-looking Ziploc bag and holds it up. The freezer light shining through the plastic, profiling the frozen outline of a stiff Persian cat, with something brown and papery where the head should be. She looks at Robbie, with a question.

"Filter paper from the coffee maker," he says, as if reading her mind. "To soak up the blood." He shrugs. "Didn't know what you're supposed to do."

"Most people *bury* dead pets," says Tug.

"Not much of a garden," Robbie says in explanation.

"But, freezing it?" Chin asks.

"I don't know. I thought she might want to see it. Say goodbye."

"Without its *head*!?" says Tug. Put like that it sounded stupid. What was he thinking? Freezing it? Fuck. He could've put it in a bin bag. Chucked it into the harbour, maybe. Left it out for the urban foxes to chew on. But instead, he put it in a Ziploc and put it in the freezer! Now Robbie *knows* he's losing the plot.

The really stupid thing is he'd actually felt quite pleased with himself when he'd first thought of freezing the dead cat. At least he'd be using the freezer for *something*. So many times he'd heard it humming away at night, knowing all that was inside it was half a tub of Chunky Monkey and a freezer gel pack that he likes to use on his lower back when he got one of his sciatica attacks. With the shooting pains down one leg. At least, for once, all that humming and electricity was being used for freezing *something*.

Even though the freezer lid is open and freezing cold air is tumbling out, and even though Robbie's only dressed in his bathrobe and slippers, he can feel two trickles of sweat leach their way down his sides, from both arm pits. As he shifts his weight from one foot to another, he catches a whiff of his body odour billowing up from under the robe. He stinks. He stinks like he's never stinked before. A new kind of body smell. Not like his own. Like some other man. Another *species* even.

Robbie hadn't been able to sleep all night, his legs all twitchy, kicking, aching. His armpits leaking. Now he could feel the sweat glands all up and pumping again, as he stood in the kitchenette, discussing Elsa's headless Suki, and the broken glass door downstairs.

"No one?"

"No."

"You can't think of anyone who might have done this?"

"No," says Robbie "Local teenagers?" he suggests, just to make it look like he's trying.

When he says this, the police officers take their eyes away from the cat in the bag and look at each other. They say nothing. They don't move either. God, Robbie just wants them to go. To leave the kitchen. To close the downstairs door with the 24 hour emergency boarding repair tacked across it and leave him to think. To think about what the fuck he should do next. Like he'd been doing all night long, staring up at the shade on the central ceiling lamp. The one with the squiggly design that Elsa said reminded her of a lampshade her mother had bought when she was a little girl in Warsaw. That too coming from John Lewis. The Lighting Department. Stick it on the Mastercard.

Oh, Jesus he so just wants the cops to leave. Give him space. Let him try to get his brain back to work.

"Thing is," says Tug. "It doesn't seem very random. Seems like very specific."

"Targeted," says Chin.

"Like you were targeted by someone, to be the victim of a very specific criminal act."

"Cat mutilation."

"Committed on your desk."

"Inside your office."

"Like," Tug says, his face very close now, the mixed aromas of after shave and hair gel hanging around his head like a thick cloud. "Like someone is sending you a message."

"Someone you know maybe?" says Chin.

"No. No one I know. Least no one I can think of," says Robbie. Making a 'serious' face like he's just wracking his brains to come up with a likely candidate. But failing. "No. Uh-unh. No one."

"Because if someone *is* trying to send you a message. Trying to make you aware of something," says Tug. "Doesn't seem like it's a very kind sort of message."

"More of a threat," said Chin.

"That what this is, Mr Rock?" asks Tug, "A threat?"

There's something about pushing a buggy and watching Josh skip along beside it that makes him feel worse. When he offered to take Josh to nursery and push Jack along for the ride, he thought it would help. Help him flush away some of the clinging sickness he felt about what had happened on the Kitty. To be with his two boys, full of innocence and fun, should rub off a little. Make *him* feel more innocent and fun. Of course, it didn't. It made it worse. He felt dirty and wrong and like a fucking fraud of a father; pretending to listen to Josh's prattle about why he loved hot school lunches, but one day wanted to have a packed lunch, so he could sit in the playground on the bench with Aaron and Liam, who always had packed lunches, in boxes. Liam's was a *Transformers* box and Aaron's was *Spiderman*. And if Josh got one, for his one day of packed lunch, he wanted a *Cars 2* one, that looks like a mechanic's tool box.

Adrian's Helen sometimes joked about how small and banal her life has become; working part-time, two days a week, as a teaching assistant, for no money. Just a way of clocking up her 'classroom-time credits'. Spending every single day of her week deeply embedded in the lives of the under-sevens. She said she found it hard sometimes being in adult company after so much time with the children. She was scared she had nothing to say, because all her points of reference had been boiled down to words of no more than two syllables.

Just now, Adrian felt jealous of Helen. He'd love nothing more than to lose himself in a world of sticky-fingered innocence. But he couldn't. Even with Josh, skipping and chatting, Adrian could still feel the crunch of bat against bone and taste the diesel and the bile in the back of his throat. Adrian dreaded his phone ringing. It would either be Paulie, the police or Matty. Was hard to say which he dreaded most.

"Sunseeker 52-footer," says Tug, pointing to a large white motor yacht, moored up against a pontoon. "That's about one-point-eight million. The one with the teak deck on the back and the dining table, that's a Moody. More old school. Still set you back just over a mil-and-a-half."

They're sitting in the Windjammer Brasserie at Blue Haven, the next bay west along Poole Harbour shore, after Salter's Quay. The view looks back across the harbour towards Sandbanks, except they can't really see Sandbanks, because of all the big yachts moored alongside the decking in front of their table.

They're waiting for coffees to be delivered. Chin had asked for a cappuccino and Tug ordered an Americano, waving her hand away when she tried to give him some pound coins for her drink.

"Nah. My shout," he said, trying to sound all 'hey-we're-partners, aren't we?' While, also trying to remember which one an Americano was. Did it have the frothy milk or the flat milk? Normally, he would have just ordered a Diet Coke and a bacon sandwich. That's if they'd gone to Wimpy, like he would've done normally, if he was on this job with any of the boys from the squad.

Way he saw it, he was doing her a professional favour. Chin didn't know the area. Didn't know the lie of the land. Didn't have the full picture of the socio-economic rollercoaster ride that occurs in the 30 as-the-crow-flies miles, from the stinking whelk pots of Weymouth quay, to the blinding-white multi-million pound gin palaces of Poole Harbour.

Should he actually call her 'Chin'? Tug runs the idea through his brain. Sounds kinda cool. But then it might be insulting. Or sexist. Or racist. Maybe Chinese don't like using just surnames, like it's an insult to their family name, or something.

Anyway, so Tug thinks, this is like providing part of her professional education about her new manor. Helping her to grasp a geographical and social awareness of her new surroundings. He certainly wasn't just showing off. Or trying to impress her, by bringing her somewhere that had real teaspoons instead of plastic stirrers, and where they served your coffee with a little shard of hand-made chocolate on the saucer.

He didn't even realise what it was at first and left it by the cup too long, so it got all melty and then stuck to his finger when he picked it up, which meant he ended up sucking his finger, like a child. He tried to wipe it on the napkin but then the napkin looked sort of disgusting, and he had to ball it up, wanting to hide it somewhere, when Chin says, "So, what do we do, then? Just wait until it's *his* head that gets chopped off?"

Tug shrugs. "What can we do? He don't want to tell us who's scaring the living shit out of him, we can't make him."

"He turns up, floating face down in the harbour," says Chin. "You not going to feel like you should've done a bit more?"

"He's a grown up. We gave him plenty of chances."

"You see the sweat running off him?"

"Fuck yeah," says Tug. "But if he don't want our help, can't force it on him."

"So we do nothing?"

"We were sitting in the squad room now, phone'd be ringing off the hook, with people *begging* us to help *them*," says Tug. "We asked him. He said 'No thank you' even when we was offering."

"What about the girlfriend?" says Chin.

Tug looked at the dried froth around the inside rim of Chin's cup. If it was his cup he'd run his pinky round the inside and suck at that froth. He could even see some chocolate dust around the edge from the sprinkle stuff the waitress put on the top of Chin's coffee. Next time, he must remember not to have the Americano, because he really liked the froth. The flat stuff he had was just like regular white coffee. Only in here you pay best part of three quid a cup. Jesus that must be some mark-up they got going.

"Didn't make a lot of sense," says Tug. "What he says about the girlfriend. He really didn't want to tell us where she's at, did he?"

"That's if he even knows," she says.

"What d'you mean?" asks Tug. "Like, you think maybe she's run out on him. Walked out and he don't know where she's gone?"

"No," says Chin, her voice flat as she looks out at a grey-haired man in shorts, tying a big plastic owl to the mast of a yacht with cable ties. "Like maybe she's been kidnapped. And he's sweating it, in case someone cuts *her* head off next."

Helen had a pig. A small pig. Oxford Sandy and Black. Runt of the litter. Stunted. Bullied. Always hungry. Every time it sucked on a teat of its fat supine mother, a brother butted it out of the way. As the brothers' bellies grew tight and chubby, the little pig shrunk. As it shrunk, its squeals swelled to a knife-slash shriek of hunger. Piercing the air with pity. Pity that none of its brothers felt. Pity that its pink mouth-drained mother easily zoned out, as she lay eyes closed, head flat in the crusty mud, letting her fat-filled juice flow into her strongest babies. Not her hungriest. Suck to survive. Squeal and you die. A mouth full of nipple lives. Mouth full of scream doesn't.

When she was nine years old Helen wasn't scared of pigs. Big boars could be mean to each other and to their young. Snapping. Butting. Stealing food by menace and brute strength. But they seldom snapped at Helen. She was an ally in the supply chain of food. And she never had her face in the trough ahead of theirs.

Plus she had a kick. And a stick. And she knew how to use them.

Piglets were no problem to Helen. Even as a wiry streak-of-piss little girl she could toss them around the sty like scatter cushions. She'd pull a swollen wet-mouthed fat boy, its whiskers creamy with clotting milk, off a teat to let the squealing piglet runt get a turn at the dripping nipple tap. Doing this, shuffling pig boys off the breast to let a sickly runt get a suck, was the only time a pig ever scared Helen.

Wasn't the tusk-snouted old boars. Or the hyperactive, ear-piercing piglet boys. But a mother. A sow. A huge fat-bellied vessel of birth and cream. When she got fucked off with Helen disrupting the natural order of mouths on her teats. Moving off the strong to make way for the weak. When Helen interfered with her spawn. Swapping a winner for a loser, one too many times, she'd raised her head out the mud, broke off her flow of creaminess, and stared at the spindle-thin-legged girl who was fucking with her babies. Pig eyes glowering hot hate.

Helen might be some sort of misguided wannabe surrogate mum to a milk-starved runty piglet, but this 100 kilo sow was the real mother to nine fat butter-ball piglets. Survivors. Suckers. Not squealers. Helen understood that look. Read it in the sow's eyes. Felt it in the marrow of her bones. No mistaking the message: *I am hot. My tits hurt. I am having life drained from me by my selfish starving progeny, so fuck off now, or in a heartbeat I will hurt you. I don't care how many buckets of growers' pellets you've poured into my trough. Come between me and my babies and I will tear chunks off your bones.*

So, Helen backed out of the sty. Closed the gate. And bolted it. Folding the bolt key flat to lock it in place. As the sow's head returned to the mud, nine-year-old Helen walked towards the back door of her house, a little skip in her step, a plan forming on her lips.

"Never give a pig a name," said her granny. "Not if you're going to eat it." To attach a moniker to an animal that is destined for the abattoir or the freezer, or the sausage pusher, is not a good idea. So goes the accepted wisdom. To assign a name to a meat-bearing animal is only going to make the killing, cutting and rendering to flesh all the more difficult.

With a name comes feelings. With feelings comes attachment. With attachment comes the desire to protect and preserve. You won't want to eat what you once loved. You can't kill what you called by name.

Only the breeding stock had names on Helen's dad's little farm. The big sows, and the occasional boar. The babies, the piglets, the animals due to be fattened and slaughtered remained anonymous and nameless. Distinguished only by their 'kill weight' at the abattoir.

Helen's plan was to raise the runt piglet in the lambing pen in the corner of the tractor shed. Wean it on cow's milk and mashed growers' pellets, mixed with a tub of out-of-date molasses stacked in the garage between rusting tins of red zinc primer and dock leaf spray.

Looking down at the skinny, squealing, starving piglet, her father hesitantly agreed. It wouldn't survive without a teat to suck on. And once dead, its mother and the biggest of its brothers would only eat its wizened little corpse anyway.

She could wean it. She could raise it. But if it survives, it goes to the slaughterhouse just like all the others. It's a pig. Not a pet. It's meat. It's money. Its days are numbered. And you're not its mummy.

Little Helen agreed, as she filled a washing-up liquid bottle with soured warm milk.

"I'm not its mummy," she said.

As she decided to call it 'Bugsy'.

Bugsy grew fat on kitchen scraps. Garden waste. Crab apples and acorns. Fatter than her brothers. Helen siphoned off extra portions. Prime chunks and hunks that caught up Bugsy with her bullying brothers, and then took her beyond. Plumping her. Stuffing mini pillows of fat under her brown mottled hairy flesh. So that when Bugsy moved out of the tractor shed back into the pigsty, she was bigger than the bully boys. Her shoulders and her rump, swollen from love. Food love. Fat love. Love that gave her the edge in the battles over the feed trough.

A hard snout and a big arse are the winning weapons of a trough battle. Head down. Snout in. Hind feet anchored in the mud with bulging leg muscles is the way to keep your mouth full. Even with their hard heads and baby budding tusks, the boars couldn't dislodge their once runty sister from pole position in the trough. Law of the sty: the fat get fatter as the weaker get less.

And it's not just quantity. It's variety. Greed. The ability to be rabidly omnivorous. Adapt. Eat anything. First.

Helen's father would shoot rabbits with his Anschutz .22 rimfire. And once skinned, he'd keep the saddles and back legs for stew. Front legs, shoulders, skins, feet and heads – all surplus to requirements – would be tossed into the pigsty. As an experiment at first. To save arse-ache sweat digging a hole to bury the bits – only to have some fuckwit badger dig them up again.

Not all pigs will turn to carrion-eating quickly. Some never do. The hungry usually will. The greedy always. A rabbit head, ears erect, eyes fixed open in death, would hardly hit the mud floor before Bugsy's teeth would crunch into its skull, hoovering brains, bone and fur into her acid-bubbling stomach juices, long before her hesitant brothers had time to make up their minds what sort of a pig they were.

Bugsy loved to eat. Loved to chew. To crunch and swallow. The smell of blood and gas-filled rabbit guts filling her with pig joy. Bugsy loved to eat. Anything. One rain-pouring Sunday afternoon, Helen's mum took a washing-up bowl full of potato peelings and mouldy corn cobs to the sty. So thick and deep was the mud seeping up around the pigs' elbows, that she hadn't the heart to toss the peelings on the filth and watch the soaking wretched animals suck lumps of peel coated in mud and shit into their mouths. And unable to reach the trough, she laid the plastic bowl on top of the mud. Give them a fighting chance of a clean mouthful. She could always hose off the bowl in the morning.

In the morning, the washing-up bowl was gone. Casting an angry eye around the sty, Helen's mum caught a guilty glance from Bugsy. There was no doubt in her mind that pig had eaten her washing-up bowl. No peeling-thin sliver of a doubt. Bugsy had munched her way through a third of a kilo of industrial plastic. Just because she could.

Bugsy loved to eat. Her favourite being anything that bled. Helen knew this about her. Knew she loved the dead things most, because of her tail. Bugsy's tail was like all other pigs' tails, a tight spiral corkscrew of muscle and cartilage, most of the time. Except for moments of deep pig joy. When Helen scratched her fingernails behind and between Bugsy's ears, or raked at the hairy dimpled valley at the base of Bugsy's spine. Or gave her a pair of rabbit skulls to munch. Then Bugsy's tail was transformed. It was the barometer of her happiness. When Bugsy sucked on rabbit guts, or bit down on splintering bone, her tail uncoiled. Her tail stuck out straight behind her, semi-erect. Almost wagging.

At 65 kilos Bugsy was big enough to die. And by this time she would willingly follow Helen anywhere. All Helen had to do was shake a bucket of pignuts in Bugsy's earshot and she'd come trotting. Snout high. Ears flip-flapping. Happy as a pig in shit.

Although she'd never been in a trailer in her entire life. Bugsy would follow Helen's rattling bucket up and down a tailgate boarding ramp all day long, with just the rattle and a sniff of nuts.

Her brothers were suspicious. They smelled more than nuts. They smelled a far off whiff of treachery. A trailer-box, sprinkled with straw and stray feed pellets has a certain allure, but the boys didn't trust it. Too weird. They would need much more tempting, coaxing, pushing, nudging and pulling, to get them in that box.

Not Bugsy.

If Helen, the girl who saved her from starvation and hand-raised her to fuck-off fatness, wanted her to trot across broken glass and barbecue briquettes, Bugsy would give it a stab, in exchange for a few pig nuts and a scratch behind the ears.

That Bugsy should trust Helen, even when all she was going to do was abuse that trust and lure her up the ramp into the trailer of her doom, unsettled young Helen. She'd given Bugsy love. Bugsy trusted her implicitly. And now that trust was her easy undoing. That love-fed trust made the biggest and most brutal of all this year's pigs turn into the simplest to load in the trailer. And the first to die at the slaughter man's bolt.

Love would be Bugsy's undoing.

And so, Helen pleaded with her father. The pig she should never have named was the one she begged her father not to take to the abattoir.

Of every litter raised each year all but one would go to the slaughter man's bolt. To be killed. Hung. Bled dry. And finally sliced in half. Snout to arsehole. Sold onwards wholesale, in two identical bookend halves, into the butchery business.

One pig each year didn't go to the slaughterhouse. One pig stayed at the farm. To be shot in the forehead by her father's .22 rimfire. Hoisted up on the tractor shed beam. Throat-slit and blood drained. Before being sliced and sawn and boned and bagged. Packed away in trays in the garage freezer for the family to eat through the coming year.

Helen's dad naturally assumed what he was about to witness was the ploy of a broken-hearted girl. A ploy to prolong the life of her favourite pig. A ruse to dodge the trailer. To buy some days. To beg for the pig's life.

But no. Helen knew Bugsy had to die. She just felt that as Bugsy had to die, she should die the best possible death. At home. Without the terrifying trailer ride and a bolt from another man's gun. She should die at the farm. Amongst those who loved her most.

If Bugsy was going to die – which very soon she was – Helen just wanted to be there when she did.

So yes, she begged. Pleaded and begged. But not for her dad to spare Bugsy's life.

Helen begged for him to let her pull the trigger.

Dressing up to meet a drug dealer is an irony lost on Matty, as he scrapes his chin with a blunt disposable BIC razor and some hot water, poured from the kettle into his grubby bedsit sink. Thing he uses the sink for most is taking a piss in the middle of the night – siphoning off a couple of pints of cider in the wee small hours.

There is a shared bathroom across the hall, which probably has hot water. But, there's something about today's ritualistic preparation for his step up into the big league of drug retailing that Matty wants to experience in private, without the poisonous bitch across the hall banging on the shared bathroom door.

Matty didn't want to look, or smell, like a whelk potter from Weymouth today. OK, he wasn't quite at the point of kidding himself he could look like a 'player'. But, didn't have to look like a complete waster-loser neither. Somewhere in the middle was where he was aiming, as he splashes ten-year -old Kouros on his raw, smarting face and eyes the grey jacket on his bed.

He last wore it to his dad's funeral and the wake, where he got trashed and asked his Uncle Derek to give him a business start-up loan. Uncle Derek and Matty's dad, although brothers, had not been friends. Matty's dad thought Derek was a 'sanctimonious prick' and so, when Derek turned Matty's drunken request down flat, Matty told Uncle Derek what his dad called him. Not that it was news exactly. Still, it rounded the ceremony off with a suitably familiar sour family note.

Maybe the jacket would even bring him luck, he thinks, as he slips it on over the River Island shirt he'd bought from the boot of Black Dave's car, one night outside The Sailors. With this ensemble he wears the only pair of jeans he possesses that haven't been splattered with pot bait.

If he actually gets to meet Max the Sikh, he wants Max the Sikh to feel he's talking to a man who really does have access to a lot of very high quality black hash – at the right price. Didn't want him thinking from the outset that he was talking to just another fucking pikey tyre-kicker. This, today: this is business. And Matty needs to look like he means business.

The funeral shoes didn't look right with the faded jeans though. Like they were from two different outfits; two different men, and shouldn't really ever be put together. Only option was his trainers, but he'd worn them one day last week on the Kitty, after an all-nighter. And they reeked of pouting guts. If he's going to be in a confined space with Max the Sikh, like in his office or his car, the trainer smell would definitely become an issue.

The funeral shoes would have to do.

Matty looked at himself in the reflective window of the Clinton Cards shop in the High Street, on his way to the station. He just glanced at his reflection in Clinton's window, which freaked him out a little bit. So now he stops and has a proper good look when he gets to Greggs the Bakers. His reflection superimposed on a backdrop of pasties and jam doughnuts isn't any better. He looks like a fucking Jehovah, or a guy selling replacement PVC windows. Or, a plain-clothes cop, he thought.

Was that a good thing? Or a bad thing? Does dressing like a plain-clothes cop make you seem less likely to be one? Yes, definitely, he decided. If he was a real plain-clothes cop, he certainly wouldn't dress like one, especially if he was about to go and set up a massive drug sale. No way. So, in a strange sort of round about way, looking a bit like one was the perfect disguise.

As he passes the Spar shop, Matty checks the money in his pockets, again. It is still 18 pounds and 47p. A return to Bristol was 16 quid. He knows that. He's taken the train up enough times to buy skunk and sell it again back in Weymouth. All watered down with some shitty home-grown and some old stalks and seeds to give it extra bulk.

He'd punt out the watered-down skunk in 'wraps' rather than by weight, in order to make his money. Selling late at night round the back of the pub, or in Monty's Nite Club. Selling to people already so fucked they didn't really know what they were buying. To be honest, he thought, they probably *expect* to be ripped off. It comes with the territory of buying drugs in toilets and car parks. Drugs bought in toilets and car parks are meant to be over-priced and underpowered.

And Matty's 'primo Bristol Skunk' was certainly that.

Matty did get the irony of the fact that during this visit he was completely turning around the normal tide of drug flow. He was going to *sell* puff to the place where he usually *bought* puff. And it'd be truly primo puff, at that. Was something to be proud of, he told himself. Putting right the wrongs of so many other crappy deals he's done. Stepping up in the world.

Matty needs to save back at least a quid, minimum. In case he needs to buy a cup of tea in a café somewhere, up in St Paul's or Fishponds, while he's out scoping for Kelvin. He needs to find Kelvin and persuade him to intro Matty to Max. Which in itself isn't going to be easy. Kelvin being very wary of upsetting Max the Sikh. Keeping back a quid would leave him enough to buy one can of Scrumpy Jack or White Lightning. Matty so wishes he could afford vodka, even if it was only one of the little cans of Vodka and Tonic Mixed Doubles. That way he won't turn up at Max's smelling of cheap cider. Which isn't cool. Not when you're doing business.

Matty looks across the road at Kenny's Tackle shop. He could see Fat Kenny in there, standing behind the till, weighing out lugworms into a newspaper parcel. Matty thinking to himself how Kenny's just like a big old drug dealer himself too. Weighing up his skanky wraps of lugworm. Matty thinking how Kenny's shop till would have more than enough cash inside it to buy a bottle of vodka, a bottle of tonic and a packet of breath mints to chew afterwards. With a few quid out of Kenny's till, Matty could have a proper drink on the train. Arrive all mellow and buzzed up. Ready for anything.

But Kenny would no sooner lend cash-money to Matty than he would stir his big old mug of tea with his dick.

Matty had burned that particular bridge many moons ago. Kenny fucking hated Matty.

So, just one can of Scrumpy Jack it was then. And Matty thinking that he'd be real classy and save the cider for the train. Drinking from a can in the street is not the behaviour of an aspiring businessman.

Hunting for Kelvin was never going to be easy. Kelvin's mobile going straight to voicemail, which means Kelvin has no credit. Which is normal. When Matty checks his own available credit on his EE Pay-As-You-Go, he sees he's got less than four quid's worth of credit himself. He really hopes tracking down Max the Sikh isn't going to involve a lot of phone calls, because between them they got a total of about 12 minutes' airtime.

Maybe Kelvin's got cash, Matty thinks. Then realises, as he walks in and straight out of his third pub in St. Paul's – wearing his best just-looking-for-someone-face – that if Kelvin had cash, then he'd probably have phone credit. No credit. No cash.

Exiting the side door of The Palm Tree, Matty decides to go back and kick at the metal bars outside Kelvin's squat once again, just in case Kelvin's returned inbetween now and the last time he kicked the bars and shouted through the letter box.

This time, when he's hammering at the door, he's thinking how it's not like Kelvin to be up and out before 4pm. Unless just maybe he's already gone to score. Though there's not that many crack dealers, even in Bristol, who open up shop this early.

As he straightens up from hammering at the door through the steel bars, Matty takes a pace back and just catches a movement out the corner of his eye. Something bobbed behind the loose bricks along the top of the wall of the house next door but one. Could've been a cat.

Curious, Matty walks through next door's garden, which is just a ratty pile of rubble and mouldy green plastic outdoor toys, to peep down over the crumbling wall. As he leans over the top, he sees a man, crouching head bowed on the other side of the wall. Hiding. The man looks up to see Matty leering over the wall and he jumps backwards, in shock. Like he's just been shot. Or seen a ghost. The man wearing four rings in one eyebrow and two huge circle-ring hoop things in the middle of his ear lobes. Looks like a cross between a circus freak and a fashion experiment. And now, he's gasping for air and he paws at his chest, like he's having a heart attack.

"Fucking hell. Fuck! Oh fuck! Don't *do* that!" he says.

"Kelvin mate," says Matty, trying to put some kind of nonchalant cheer in his voice. Like the two of them just bumped into each other at the supermarket or snooker club or something. Like normal people.

"You got an *evil* fucking knock, man," says Kelvin. His face now ripe with indignation. "Could fucking hear you all the way up the next street! *Not* cool!"

"Trying to roust you up, is all," says Matty, indicating the locked metal grill on the squat.

"Wasn't in. *Was* I?" says Kelvin, pissy now. "Signing on day, innit? I come round the corner. Hear this knocking: Bang-Bang-Bang. Jesus! And see this guy... Fucking guy like an undercover cop, hammering on my door... Nearly crapped myself."

"Sorry," says Matty. "Was looking for you..."

"You got cash?" asks Kelvin, already mentally calculating how this day might now pan out. Matty only ever coming to town to score. An event which normally would have positive implications on Kelvin's day.

"Not exactly," says Matty. Kelvin staring at him, very chilly now. Not the answer Kelvin wanted.

"Better," says Matty.

"Better than cash?"

"Yup."

"Crack?" asks Kelvin.

"No," says Matty. "But something we can turn *into* crack." Kelvin's face not expressing any joy at this news as he wearily walks past the mouldy toys, to his metal-barred squat. Kelvin takes some keys out his pocket and shakily unlocks the grille, as now he looks Matty up and down, from his sticky-looking hair to his black shiny funeral shoes.

Matty now asking, "You *really* think I look like a cop?"

"We go in. Don't say anything. Let me do the talking."

"He works in a shop?" Matty's voice now sounding a little pissy.

"He *owns* the show. It's *his* shop," says Kelvin. "Not like he's a shop *assistant*. He's boss of the shop."

Matty can see the guy, behind the counter. In his thirties. Smart, slim, Asian-skinned, with a neat but complicated beard on his chin. And, on his head, a turban. The guy leaning on the counter top, all relaxed, typing text into a shiny new smartphone. Big sign above the shop says '*Cash Converters – We convert your goods into cash.*' A list down the side of the window saying – '*We buy: Gold, Silver, Jewellery, Electronics, Computers, Games etc etc*'.

Going into a shop to do a drug deal – marching up to a counter, all packed with watches and Xboxes, to do your stuff – doesn't seem right. In Matty's little fantasy, the one that he enjoyed, sitting on the train, the deal was going to take place in an office, or back of a private club, or front seat of some top-of-the-range Range Rover. Maybe they'd be overlooking the Clifton Suspension Bridge. Or, maybe in a hotel. A suite, sort of thing. Not just a bedroom. Drinks from the mini bar. Maybe a couple of cute girls, doing lines off a glass-topped table. Whatever, in his mind it was something a little more Quentin Tarantino.

As they walk in the door and step on the mat, a tiny speaker somewhere goes '*Bing-bong. Bing-bong*' twice. Max the Sikh, the turban-wearing guy, looking up just with his eyes, just once. Not moving his head. Not changing his expression. Not a flicker, before he goes back to his texting. Was like he's clocked them, catalogued them, and gone back to more important matters.

Matty pleased there doesn't appear to be anyone else in the shop, either on his side of the counter, or the other. Sure, there could be someone behind the mirrored door that must lead to some sort of back office place, but wasn't any one else buying or selling just now. Which is good. Otherwise he'd have to have done something, like hang around looking in cabinets, or flicking through display boxes of used DVDs, while he's waiting for the right empty-shop moment. Would've been sweaty and nervy-making, even more than it is already.

Whole thing would be so much easier if he'd had a proper drink first. Little buzz, to give him the necessary swagger and a bit more flow with the words. Instead of one measly Scrumpy Jack, drunk so long ago the buzz already seeped out his cells, leaving an even bigger hole in his confidence. Making him feel, right now, like there's a piece of him missing. Like he's not all there. Not firing on all cylinders. Like the engine on Kitty K.

And the shoes don't help.

Kelvin is standing at the counter now. Max still not looking up from his iPhone. Still typing with one finger. Kelvin saying, "Alright, Max?" Trying to sound relaxed. Max saying nothing. Just holding up one finger of his other hand. One finger. Index finger. In between him and Kelvin. The finger saying 'Hold on.' Or 'One moment.' Or 'Not just yet.' Or some such finger-words. Whatever, it stops Kelvin in his stride. His hand half-buried into a deep pocket of his big woollen old man's, charity shop overcoat.

Kelvin now fiddling with something in the pocket, not quite bringing it out, but wanting to. Matty having to look in the cabinet at the watches and the second-hand mobile phones, like he is interested, not just nervous. His eyes moving to Max's iPhone, parked in the centre of the counter. His finger tip-tapping letters out on the screen's keyboard.

Matty entranced by the sight of Max's hand. So clean. So soft-looking. The nails all white and an even length on all the fingers. A gold watch, hanging loose from the wrist, with a metal strap and a huge chunky face. The gold metal of the strap articulating silently as he types. Looking makes Matty suddenly aware of his own hands on the edge of the counter. All cracked and rough, with rope burns and months of ingrained, poorly washed silicon grease from the pot-hauler bearings.

Matty takes his own hands off the counter, puts them out of sight. When suddenly he realises he's staring directly at Max's text-typing finger. Looking like he's trying the read what he's typing, upside down. Which he isn't. But it makes him think that's what Max might be thinking, and doesn't want to get off on any wrong foot. So instead he makes a big gesture of looking elsewhere. On the shelves again, in the cabinets. Anywhere. All of which makes his heart beat a little bit faster and his alcohol-starved tongue just that little bit drier.

Kelvin empties his pocket and puts a four-inch screen TomTom sat-nav on the glass counter top. Again Max's eyes flick for just an instant, to assess the black electronic gadget proffered by Kelvin. And then back to his perfect finger, typing on his perfect iPhone. Max keeps on typing, but now asks a question while he types.

"Got the box?"

"No," says Kelvin.

"Got the leads?"

"No."

"Proof of purchase?"

"No."

"Tenner," says Max

"It's third generation with the Europe-wide map card," says Kelvin, an expert on in-car satellite navigation systems, even though he's never, ever used one. And doesn't have a car. Or even know how to drive.

"Tenner," says Max again. "And I need to see ID".

"How about 20, Max?" says Kelvin, pulling what looks like a laminated library card from his trouser pocket and laying it on the glass.

"What about nothing?" says Max, like it's a genuine enquiry. "And you go away and take it somewhere else?"

"OK. Tenner," says Kelvin, pushing the TomTom across the counter.

"And you need to sign a receipt of sale," says Max, picking up the library card and reading it. "Mr Patel."

Kelvin eyes Matty, as Max takes a ten pound note out the till and lays a receipt on the glass for Kelvin to sign.

"This's my mate," says Kelvin, nodding towards Matty. "I vouch for him and all that. Got something you might be interested in. To sell, like."

Matty caught on the hop. Not quite sure what to do. Does he just bring out the lump of hash, in the shop now? Or set up a meet elsewhere? Or what? This bit not rehearsed. None of it rehearsed really. Except in his head. On the train. Taking a piss in the train toilet. Seeing himself in the toilet mirror. Acting out a little drug deal scenario in his head and in the mirror. Pulling the facial expression he thinks he should use when he's with Max. Seeing his reflection. Holding his head in the way he thought made him look cool. All at ease. Bit nonchalant. Like he's done this stuff before. *Loads* of times. Like Max the Sikh would know he was dealing with a professional.

None of it ever looked in his head like it looks now, in the real world. In a Cash Converter in Fish Ponds, next door to a funeral director and a Marie Curie Cancer Shop.

Max's expression not making things any easier. Max not showing any interest or expectation. No attempt at engaging. Or even looking the least bit curious, just those flat brown eyes staring out at him under a green turban, the colour of kelp.

Matty puts the lump of black hash on the counter beside the iPhone. It was exactly half of what he's snuck off the Kitty in his pants. He'd felt it tucked under his scrotum all the time he was in the Weymouth Police Custody Suite. Pretty sure then that no one was going to frisk him properly, because he'd committed no offence as such, and even though he had plenty of previous, the scuffle on the quayside not being a drug-related incident. All the same, it'd been pretty sweaty, knowing he was sitting right inside the nick with that stash in his pants.

And when he was released, feeling chuffed that he'd sat it out, ice-cool, no one any the wiser. Thinking he really did have the balls to be a bit of a player. Even imagining himself walking through Customs at some airport with a load of coke in his luggage, showing no sign of nerves, nothing. Like maybe he really was cut out for a life of high-end crime, after all.

"What is that?" says Max. His black eyebrows meeting. His jaw set firm.

"Afghan black," says Kelvin, butting in, and saying "He's got *lots* of it." Like he's worried the one lump looks a bit small.

"Why have you brought that in my shop?" Max's voice sounding all serious and official, like a headmaster, or a judge, or something.

Matty caught on the wrong foot "I thought, you might–"

"That is a Class B controlled substance. Get it out of my shop now. Or I will be forced to call the police."

Matty frozen now. Fuck! This is so not the way his train toilet fantasy went. His mouth open now. Jaw working up and down, slowly. No words coming out, feeling like he's a codling, lying on the deck, gulping air.

"Take it. Now. Go!" Max's voice raising up louder, as his perfect smooth fingers swipe at the lump, like it's a cockroach or a bee, sending it clattering off the glass counter onto the floor.

Matty's eyes torn between Max's ferocious glare and trying to follow the trajectory of his precious chunk of black. "S'alright, Max," says Kelvin. "He's alright. Like I said, I can vouch. He's cool."

Matty not feeling too cool as he scrambles on his hands and knees, trying to follow the hash, which has rolled under a metal wire basket stand, full of used DVDs, two for five pounds.

"Out!" shouts Max. Matty, chin almost down on the brown thin carpet squares, stretching under the stand trying to wrap his fingers around the lump. Kelvin stepping back from the counter, his hands raised, palms out, like Max is pointing a gun at him. Which he isn't.

"It's cool. It's cool," says Kelvin, backing away.

But nothing about what's happening in this shop, at this moment in time, seems cool to Matty, who gets up off his knees, slipping the dope in his jacket pocket, and '*Bing-Bongs*' back across the mat and out the door, just a few paces ahead of Kelvin's '*Bing-Bong*' as he follows Matty out the shop.

Next door to the funeral director is a car park. Walled in on three sides. Signs painted on the brickwork mark the designated parking slots for the undertakers. There's a hearse parked in one slot. Other slots are empty. Some are closed off with chains. In one corner of the car park is a skip and a pile of carpet remnants.

Matty is panting now, furious. Freaked. Kelvin is clutching his ten pound note like his life depended on it. Matty starts marching back and forth in front of Kelvin, his shoes hurting, repeating over and over: "What the fuck. What the fuck? What the fuck was…? He searches for words "You… Fuck. The *Fuck*?"

"He's a cool guy," says Kelvin "I done a *ton* of business with Max. I don't get it."

Matty now marching away four paces. Then marching back. Fierce. Looking like he might punch Kelvin. Thinking he *definitely* might punch Kelvin.

"It's the jacket," says Kelvin, looking to shift the blame. "And the shoes. I said, didn't I? You… fucking you look like a Fed."

Matty squaring up to Kelvin now. His weight evenly spread between his feet. His stance wide. Shoulders up. Ready to swing.

"That… in there. That was about my fucking *shoes*?" he asks. "That what you saying?" Matty all set to let a fist fly. Ready to swing one up from his hip, and crack his rope-hardened whelk potter fist into the side of fucking Kelvin's fucking head. Release all his tension and embarrassment and nerves in one knuckle-bruising, bone-crunching, right hook. Then he'd take Kelvin's fucking tenner too. And go get himself a proper drink. Get his head back in gear. Work out what the fuck he was going to do next. When suddenly Max the Sikh walks into the car park. Kelvin's back is towards Max, not seeing him walk up behind him, cool as a cucumber. Matty's fist now dropping a little, wrong-footed again, confused. Shit, where is this going?

For the first time Matty is seeing the bottom half of Max the Sikh. Seeing the guy's legs and shoes now. Designer jeans. Brown leather shoes with little gold chain things hooped across the front. Like little identity bracelets.

Matty finding something very weird about this guy now being out from behind his counter. Really disconcerting. Like he wasn't supposed to be exposed to the outdoors and sunlight. Like he's exclusively an indoor-guy with smooth hands, clean white nails and shoes with jewellery on them.

"Show me that," Max says, walking up to Matty, never once breaking stride. Pointing at Matty's jacket pocket where he'd slipped the dope after he'd scooped it up off the shop floor. Matty's fists still balled up. Matty still half-ready to swing. Looking wired and dangerous, but the Sikh guy, with the tight trimmed beard, doesn't even look fazed. Holding his soft hand out, palm up, his fingers curling and uncurling slightly, like he's beckoning for Matty to hurry up.

Matty, wary now, puts the dope in Max's outstretched hand. Max puts the dope to his nose, smelling it. Studying it. Now bending it, like he's trying to break off a chunk. Matty watching. Aware of shoppers walking past the entrance to the car park. Matty's eyes searching for police. Or for more Sikhs. Or anything sinister. Feeling like some sort of shit is about to kick off. At least, Matty thinking, that if someone wants a fight, he'd know exactly what to do then. It's just all the rest of this confusing drug transaction thing he didn't understand. A fist fight in a car park. Now, *that* he could manage.

"Where'd he get this?" Max now asking Kelvin, as he takes a slim gold cigarette lighter out his jeans pocket. Kelvin shrugs. Max holds the naked flame to the corner of the black lump and sniffs the smoke that curls off it.

"How much you got to sell?" He addresses Matty now.

Matty silent. Still staring directly at Max. Matty showing a little beef at last. Like he wasn't just going to be pushed around.

Max crumbles the corner of the block between his thumb and forefinger. The dope turning soft and creamy, with the heat of the flame, like window putty. Max smearing it between his fingers, smoothing it out, letting the oils leak out their aromas. He holds his thumb and forefinger to his nostrils, sniffing, rubbing, sniffing again.

Finally, Max looks at Matty. His eyes roaming down now, from Matty's face, down his jacket, across his jeans to his uncomfortable shoes. And then back up again. Until he's eye to eye with Matty, asking him once more. "Where d'you get this?"

Matty still doesn't have an answer. And has no idea how to counter the question. Definitely he knows he doesn't want to get into explanations about crab pots and baseball bats. So instead he just stares back. Saying nothing. Desperately trying to find the right words.

"He came to *me*, see…" says Kelvin. "'Cause he knows I'd know the right man to go and–"

"Go away," Max says to Kelvin, quietly. Kelvin doesn't move. "He wanted to find just the right…"

"Am I talking to you?" Max asks Kelvin.

"No," says Kelvin.

"Then go away. And don't say another word."

Kelvin pauses, but not for long. Then he walks to the edge of the pavement, beside the undertakers and watches Matty and Max from a safe distance. Kelvin crossing his arms and leaning against the wall like he's in a huff.

Max now leaning close towards Matty, and saying, "I don't know you. I don't know where you're from. You come into my shop. You pull out a piece of hashish in front of my CCTV camera and you talk about *me* buying your gear. What kind of crap is that?"

"CCTV?" says Matty. Unable to keep the wobble out of his voice.

"Camera behind the counter. Not exactly hidden," says Max the Sikh. "Round thing with a little red light on top."

"We were… on CCTV?"

"I'm a registered pawn broker. Says so on the window in big gold letters. Is a legal requirement that I have constant surveillance of all transactions."

"Shit," says Matty. Couldn't help himself.

"Where you from?"

"Weymouth," says Matty, the word out of his mouth before his brain even knew it was coming. Just like that. One question. One word. Already he's shooting himself in the foot.

"You don't have CCTV in Weymouth yet?" says Max.

"Yeah, 'course. All over the…" Matty's ragged brain realising too late this wasn't a question that needed an answer.

"You don't walk into a shop… A man's place of business. _Licensed_ place of business. And start talking about this stuff. It's basic common sense."

"I just thought… you know, Kelvin said you…"

"That Kelvin," Max points over his shoulder to where Kelvin is leaning against the undertaker's wall, "Is a crack-head. I don't do business with anyone smokes the pipe. I'll buy stuff off them, if there's profit in it. But I don't do business." He looked at Matty, with piercing eye. "You smoke the pipe?"

Matty shakes his head. Which of course is a lie. Matty'd smoked a fair few rocks in his time, but, to be fair, it wasn't his drug of choice. Plenty of other highs he'd choose instead.

"Good," says Max. "Because if you've got some more of this, and we can agree on some prices, we just might be able to do some business." Max takes a set of car keys out of his pocket and presses the button in the centre of the black fob. A black BMW Seven Series parked three spaces away from the hearse beeps, as its four indicator lights flash simultaneously.

"We can talk in my car," says Max, walking towards the Bimmer. Matty follows, already feeling much better just at the sight of the sleek black leather upholstery.

It wasn't until much later, when he's sitting on the train heading back to Weymouth, looking out at dusk to green fields dotted with black and white cows, that it dawned on him. The thought creeping up. Chilling. Unsettling. Crawling like a damp slug down his spine. The thought messing up his deep warm vodka buzz.

The thought that he'd just arranged the biggest drug deal of his entire life – in a car park.

If you want to catch a crab in a pot, you have a choice between two basic types of trap: inkwell or parlour. Inkwell pots, also known as 'creels' are an old fashioned, traditional style of pot. And not surprisingly, they look like an inkwell: a stubby cylinder with a hole in the top. Couple of generations back, potters would make all their own pots. Constructing them and repairing them, when weather was too harsh to go to sea and work their gear. Back then, they'd use bent willow to make the staves, and tar-greased rope to hold them together. After the war, when steel was cheap again, creels were made with steel ribs and staves, usually fashioned from concrete reinforcing rods bent, hammered and welded into shape.

When rubber got cheap and every breaker's yard in the land was filled with piles of part-worn tyres, crab fishermen would use the tyres, by slicing them apart with short-bladed gutting knives. They'd slice the tyres into inch-wide strips, to weave around the bottom edge of creels, to bind the arc-welded structure together and create a thick rubber foot for them to sit on. The tyre rubber also reducing the rate the steel would rust away, and making the whole thing about as bio-degradable and eco-friendly as a Russian nuclear sub.

Fishermen, like farmers, used to be multi-skilled. They could weld and cut, do basic carpentry and boat building. They were competent motor mechanics, could sew sails, rig ropes, splice cables, even mend and make nets. Not anymore. Like the farmer is now reduced to sitting in his multifunction tractor, or programming his computerised milking parlour, so most big scale commercial fishermen are reduced to sitting in a fully-automated wheelhouse checking satellite and computer-generated data, pressing the odd button to activate some motorised winch.

When Matty's dad started fishing, most men worked off wooden boats, with little single cylinder diesel engines and a sheet of square-rigged sail to help the old boats lie broadsides to the tide when hauling pots. The boats were wooden. So they would rot. So they needed to be maintained, or else they would sink.

And these vessels were fragile; just a careful selection of cut, shaped wooden planks held together with glue and nails. They needed to be treated with respect. They had limitations. You couldn't take them out and pound them day-long against violent rib-cracking storm-induced seas, or they would quickly fall apart, and send their careless owners spiralling down to their watery graves.

Because the boats were basic and the engines were so slow, no one could go fishing when the weather was shitty. Consequently the fishing days were fewer, so fishing pressure on the fish stocks was much lower, catch rates were smaller and therefore the amount of fish and crabs left in the sea was far greater.

Fibreglass fucked up the fish. Fibreglass and cheap diesel.

The 1960s witnessed an orgy of fibreglass manufacture. Everything that could once only be made in wood or steel could now be made in fibreglass. All around the coast, small entrepreneurial boat builders would make a detailed mould of their most popular and successful clinker-built wooden fishing boat, and set about layering sheets of fabulous new age fibreglass into their mould. Few layers later and out would pop a shiny new fibreglass hull. It was like shucking warm mince pies from a greased baking tin.

Wood became the boat-building equivalent of vinyl records, exclusively the territory of fanatics and freaks.

An unbreakable, nigh-on unsinkable fibreglass hull, shackled to a huge many-cylindered fuck-off motor, satiated with an endless supply of government-subsidised cheap red diesel, seriously shrunk the size of the seas. Boats and fishermen who had never previously strayed outside a six-mile radius of their home port, were unleashed upon the seas, churning twin prop wakes behind them as they harnessed the full force of post-war technology to help them empty the oceans of fish.

Nobody makes their own inkwell pots anymore. Not out of steel rods and sliced up tyres, and definitely not out of willow and tarred string. In fact, no one really uses inkwells anymore. Not seriously. A few old boys might have a shed full of inkwells that they've kept going for the last 20-odd years and are determined to work with until they die or until they sell their valuable crabbing-licence and catch quota to a broker – whichever comes first.

Mostly inkwells are a thing of the past. Parlour pots are what most serious crabbers use. Flat-bottomed dome-roofed cylinders with an entrance lobby leading to a 'parlour'. A place of no return. A room with no escape route where bait-engorged crabs and lobsters go to await their fate at the calloused hands of the pot-hauling crabber.

Inshore commercial potters used to make their own parlour pots too; constructing frames out of scrap steel, plumbing pipes and some lashings made of sliced-up tyres and inner tubes, all joined together with panels of nylon netting. Not anymore. No fisherman has time to make pots now, because every day he's a runner in the race to grab the lion's share of what little life is left scuttling nervously across the seabed.

Nobody makes pots anymore, parlours or inkwells, because the Chinese do. The Chinese make pots. Not great pots. Not lifetime-of-loyal-service pots. Actually not even very good pots. But they do make cheap pots. Cheap enough to spray liberally across the seabed in the hope that they'll earn their keep, before they quickly rust and rot away.

From Dover to Devonport, all along the floor of the English Channel, thousands of little rusty-staved boxes of Chinese low-grade steel are crumbling and corroding to a pile of wet dust. The nasty cheap steel is melting away to leave behind screeds of nylon and rubber fixings that will tangle and roll around the seabed for the next thousand years or more.

Apart from inkwells and parlours, there is one more pot in

common use amongst crabbers. The keeper pot. It isn't a hunting pot. It's not a pot shot out on rough ground to trap wild creatures of the deep. It is a prison pot. A pot of emasculating incarceration, designed to hold the already captured crabs in a state of rendition, awaiting the next phase of their certain death.

The keeper pot is a necessary evil. A tool of imprisonment that ensures the inmates can be kept alive until just the right time for them to die.

Keeper pots are a busy crabber's saving grace. His thinking space. His buffer to cushion the spine-jarring price hikes and jolts of the rollercoaster commercial crab market. Keeper pots are a sanctuary, a time-out from the daily grind of the catch and sell, where a clever crabber can park his haul, in a strategic bid to second guess the vagaries of consumer demand versus weather patterns, versus the good or bad fortunes of other crab men.

The scheming two-faced bitch that is the Lady Luck of crab men can be very cruel, very often. You might have had the best day's hauling of your adult life, pulling up big beautiful cock crabs, with virgin white flesh and claws the size of a baby's arm, since the tide first swung to the ebb and the sun first poked its baldy head above the flat horizon. You might have emptied hundreds of pots filled with crabs as big as badgers. Stashing them below deck, in your seawater-fed live well. Indeed, your on board vivarium may be rammed to the rim with top grade crustaceans. And yet, if every other fucker with a crab pot and a hauling jib has had a Blue Ribbon bonanza day too, then today's unit price of your hard-earned edible brown crab is going to be shite.

So, what are you going to do? Sell your prime load for peanuts, just because today the crab market's swamped? You can't hold it in your live well for more than a night, because you've got to be out hauling more gear again before dawn, and of course you'll need the space for more crabs.

You can't stash your haul of crabs on land, because they'll die without fresh seawater, and then they'll be worth less than the blood sucking fish merchant's offering you today. If they're dead, they're worth nothing. Therefore, you are basically bum-fucked over a fish barrel.

Unless... unless you are one of those well-organised crab potters who has already bought, built, borrowed or stolen himself a little armoury of keeper pots.

A keeper pot is a cage. Anything from the size of a dog kennel to a small caravan, depending on the grunt of your hauling winch. A cage into which you load your catch and then drop back down to the seabed, where it can sit, in naturally-oxygenated water with the crabs safely locked inside. Waiting until the hopefully not-too-distant day when the market is once again crying out for good quality crab, and yet none of the rest of the crab fleet is landing diddly.

No one else is landing, either because the weather's turned so bad no boat is able to get out of the bay. Or else because the fishing's just switched right off and the crab aren't feeding. If that happens, the crabs won't give a monkey's nut what sort of bait you've loaded your pots with, because they're just not interested. They're not climbing into any lobby, any entrance, any parlour, inkwell or creel, they're simply not playing. When these days do occur, a crab fishermen with a keeper pot, already rammed full of big brown edibles, is a wise and happy man.

By and large crabs are pretty basic, hungry, sex-obsessed mechanical creatures, who go from day to day, and season to season, and year to year, fucking, fighting and eating. Not too much interrupts the flow of their primal needs and wants, but when it does, they can go weird for weeks.

Sex and shell-moulting can throw them off the hunger for food for long periods at a stretch, which makes them impossible to catch in baited pots.

Storms don't bother crabs. If the seabed gets too rough in shallow waters, they'll go deeper. They'll just walk to where it's calm. Apart from sex and the business of changing their shell at least once a year, the thing that really does jam a spanner in their mandible, is algae.

An algal bloom is a period when the algae that naturally floats around within seawater is triggered to massively and outrageously reproduce. It can happen in the summer when sea temperatures are high, and it also happens nearly every spring, when the 'May water' arrives. May water is a milky-green opaque colouring to the normally clear or blue sea, which is caused by the exponential and dramatic reproduction of algae in inshore waters. This is caused by a sudden increase of sunshine, day length and the arrival of warm currents flowing in from the Atlantic.

An algal bloom is like a gas cloud. It robs the sea of oxygen. It affects visibility and so makes hunting harder. But most of all it creates a miasma of gloomy oxygen-starved suffocation, which puts most sea life off their food, sometimes for a month or more.

When the fish and crabs are off the feed and boats steam home with near-empty live well tanks, that is the perfect time to have a battery of keeper pots, ready to unleash your carefully stored crabs on a crustacean-starved fish market.

Keeper pots are cruel, sad places, where inmate crabs need to be neutralised in order that they can be safely kept incarcerated together, imprisoned in one big communal cell. And so, to minimise fatalities, big crabs will have a tendon in their crushing claws cut through with a gutting knife, rendering the once-fearsome crushing mechanism useless. Their vice-like death grip now reduced to a spastic hug. They can't rip or tear or crush or crunch, so they can't really feed themselves. They can't even do battle with their natural crab enemies, other than by hugging each other with embarrassing impotent embraces.

Keeper pots are a great idea if you're a canny crabber, but they're a rare type of godless purgatory if you're a crab.

For all their market-playing savvy, keeper pots do have one big weakness, and one real nemesis: the recreational weekend diver.

Commercial crabbers hate divers. And most of all they hate dive clubs. Those cluster-like organisations of hobby divers come from far off landlocked towns, like Coventry and Stroud, Birmingham and Stoke. Towns where men and women who have invested heavily in neoprene wet suits and nitrox tanks, all club together to organise diving trips to famous dive sites around the coast.

The best of these sites are found amongst the wrecks and reefs and sandbanks of Weymouth Bay.

Commercial crabbers hate hobby divers and their well-organised beer-drinking, high-fiving, YouTube-posting, car bumper sticker club mentality. But most of all, commercial crabbers hate the local dive boats and their treacherous back-stabbing skippers.

Dive boats are local boats, licensed to a harbour, and run specifically for the purpose of taking groups of divers, normally bound together in individual clubs, out to dive on specific local sites of varying degrees of difficulty and interest.

These boats were once commercial fishing boats. These skippers were once commercial fishing skippers, or else the sons of commercial skippers; men who once made their honourable and traditional livelihood, hunting for fish and crabs and lobsters, to catch and sell.

And yet these men betrayed their heritage, gave up the work of hunting and killing fish, sold their commercial fish-catching licences and used the money to buy big fast new diving boats. So now these men no longer sully their once-noble calloused hands with the real work of fishing; catching and killing. Instead, they take groups of portly office workers lined with sporty neoprene out to sea, to play beneath the waves.

They have given up the real job of fishing to toy with out-of-towners and their air-filled tanks.

And, of course, now it transpires all these local dive skippers have much bigger and better and faster boats than the commercial fishing boys. They have bigger and better trucks. More holidays. More friends. More money. More free time. More freedom from the castrating grip of fish merchants. More confidence. More people skills. They have websites and chat rooms. They have Facebook pages and Twitter feeds. They have online videos of their bright yellow dive boats christened with such fucking annoying names as Skin Deep or Pressure Seeker.

And so, for very good reason, commercial crabbers now hate dive boats and dive skippers. They hate them because they feel a mixture of jealousy and betrayal, but above and beyond these reasons, commercial crabbers hate the divers that these boats and skippers ferry around with them. They hate the divers, because it is these divers that have been known to commit the most heinous of all sea-based crimes: they fuck with keeper pots.

Recreational divers, who have no understanding of the real work of commercial fishermen, regard keeper pots as cruel inhuman inventions. And, if they happen upon one during their nature-loving recreational dive, they'll often open and pin back the door of the offensive keeper pot, to let what might be a ton or more of incarcerated crab run free.

So, commercial crabbers hate hobby divers. And hobby divers in turn hate all commercial fishermen. Divers want to come and play in the very same places where commercial fishermen go to work. The reefs and rocks and wrecks and sandbanks that are the fish-holding places where netsmen and crabbers ply their gear are exactly the same underwater features where hobby divers want to pursue their hobby.

And these hobby divers also nurture a powerful sense of

self-righteousness. They see themselves as a benign and nature-loving force. Peaceful crusaders who seek to visit these wondrous underwater locations, not to rape and pillage and kill and remove, but only to observe and marvel, and make videos to post on websites and YouTube.

They are not hunters. They are simply spectators. They want only to photograph aquatic wildlife, not remove it and sell it to the Spanish and French. They are even prepared to part with substantial amounts of their hard office-earned cash for the privilege of being able to sink beneath the waves and record the mating displays of a tub gurnard or a spawn-heavy ballan wrasse.

In their eyes, the act of diving is all about observing, documenting and conserving what is a beautiful natural asset, in which we all deserve an equal share. The crabbers and commercial fishermen, on the other hand, believe that as their families have earned a living by removing fish from these locations for generations, long before neoprene was even invented, it is they that have a God-given right to continue to bugger and molest fish stocks.

And those playtime chubby rubber-wrapped dive buddies can just go and fuck themselves.

The mutual animosity means that some divers believe they're doing a right and just and noble thing when they tamper with the awful keeper pots, by releasing those horribly and unfairly imprisoned crustaceans from the evil crabbers' clutches.

Sadly, what they don't do is think through the logic of the act they're committing. If a crab's had his claw tendons clipped in order that he can be safely incarcerated and not eat or crush his fellow inmates, it means he'll be unable to defend himself, hunt or even just survive, in the wild. More likely he'll just starve in a horrible, slow death, when he's released back to the wide open sea, where good food has to be fought for.

Walking back across town, from the station, cutting through Asda car park and over the Town Bridge, Matty hangs a left towards The Sailors, and that's when he first sees them, parked in The Loop car park. Two big bright orange RIBs – rigid inflatable boats – towed behind two almost identical four-wheel drive VW people-carriers. Both sporting the same self-adhesive decals and bumper stickers, announcing that these vehicles have travelled from Kidderminster, and reminding anyone, who might have possibly forgotten, that *'Divers do it Deeper'.*

The cartoon character of a neoprene-clad comedy diver grinning from the arse-end of a VW Caravelle eight-seater, catches Matty's eye as he makes a beeline for The Sailors. Matty feeling confident that he can find someone in the pub to bankroll him a couple of drinks and maybe even a quarter Charlie, or at the very least a couple of Es.

The presence of the two dive RIBs in the car park tell Matty that the recreational dive fraternity clubs are here tonight in force. Probably means there is some big club outing or competition or something equally pointless going on. The roar of laughter from the Wetherspoons telling Matty that the massed body of divers were in the middle of some jolly drinking game and that the RIBs, and probably all the local dive boats too, would be out on the early morning ebb, aiming to catch the slack between the tides. The slack being the time the divers would most want to shoot their shot-lines and descend to the wrecks, reefs or maybe even drift-dive on the sandbanks.

Matty feeling a stiff breeze whip down the harbour making the tethered boats swing and jostle with each other and causing the wires on the yachts to clack and clang against their masts. He is almost at the door of The Sailors, well past the parked dive club RIBs, when it hits him, like a fucking toe-punt to the testicles.

There must be upward of 50 divers hoping to dive tomorrow morning, the rash of RIBs and people carriers and 4x4s in The Loop car park could hold that many, at least. And, what with a southerly wind whistling up the harbour mouth, this means the sea will have a big old ugly chop on it in the morning.

The chop wouldn't affect the divers' pursuit of pleasure when they were beneath the waves, but the chop would make their journey out across the bay very bumpy and very painful. Out-of-shape townie hungover hobby divers might well enjoy a feeling of weightlessness when they're deep under the waves supported by salty seawater, but they do *not* like the sensation of pounding across short, sharp, spine-jarring white horses as they make their way to their chosen dive site, sat astride the narrow hard saddle of a RIB.

Tomorrow's bad weather would seriously compromise the divers' travelling range. They won't be able to reach the far wrecks or the bigger reefs without pounding their tender kidneys to a painful mush. And so, they will reduce their expectations. Each of the dive masters and the local dive boat skippers will no doubt at this very moment be making executive decisions to change plans and dive some much nearer marks instead, rather than punishing their hangovers in an attempt to reach far off wrecks.

Matty realising that what they'll most likely choose to do instead is to drift-dive over some of the nearer sandbanks, looking for blonde rays, undulate rays, turbot, brill, plaice, spider crabs and big red gurnard. Maybe even dropping off the rough rocky southern edge to collect a few scallops.

Meanwhile the cheekier divers amongst them will definitely make it their business to fuck with any keeper pots they might happen upon. And maybe even steal or release any lobsters they find incarcerated in any parlour pot that might, by some fluke chance have been shot along the edge of the sandbank.

Drift-diving a flat sandbank can get very boring even by the standards of your average office-working weekend-diving gas monkey. By it's very nature a sandbank is an underwater desert. Not too many fish earn a living on sand. Sure, rays and plaice, turbot and brill are all equipped with the right kind of camouflage to make the sand a safe place for them to hang, but no one grows fat living on sand.

Kidney Bank is one of the favourite bad weather drift-diving sites and, although there's rarely much potting gear on the bank, with that many keen-as-mustard divers descending at slack water, you can be pretty fucking sure *someone's* going to have a close look at any pots they do find, on that sandy barren seabed. Probably stick a gloved hand in there too.

Adrian couldn't eat. It felt like a knot had been tied in his stomach. Making his gullet feel raw and stingy. Helen was worried. She'd put meals in front of him and the boys; Jack and Josh attacking their platefuls like terriers with tapeworm, while Adrian sat staring at his baked potato like it was a galaxy of stars in a far off universe. Never even lifting his fork. His eyes wet and glazed.

He blamed the shock and the grief. She blamed the shock and the grief. But he *felt* nothing. No grief. No shock. Nothing. Like his insides had been hollowed out and repacked with polystyrene balls.

To make her feel better, he told her he felt hungry now and was going downstairs to eat his dinner, which she'd covered with a plate and left in the fridge. They're in bed and she's asking him questions, and telling him he should talk about it. Suggesting that if he just talked a bit about what happened and how he felt then, and feels now, it'll soon begin to shift things. It'll feel a bit better, less huge. Will lighten his load, if he shares his pain.

All he can see now, lying in bed, in the semi-darkness with his eyes shut, and his neck propped up on the mountain of decorative pillows – which seemed to be breeding and multiplying every week – was the back of Tim's head. Didn't make any difference if he shut his eyes or opened them a crack. All he could see was the dirty lank hair, the ring of spots around his grimy neck and the meat of the baseball bat crunching into the thick curved bone at the base of his skull. He could see it all again. A perfect replay, the noise, the vibrations, the shudder through the bat, as it made contact. Only now he could hear it louder and more sickening than ever before.

He lied and told Helen he was feeling hungry, but all he can taste is bile. She wants to warm his dinner for him, watch him eat. He manages to persuade her to stay in bed, knowing the long-term fatigue of running around after two toddlers all day will have her snoring in her mountain of pillows in a matter of minutes.

Even though he can't eat, Adrian still puts his plate of dinner in the microwave for two minutes and lets the timer ping. Their house is so tiny. Sounds, especially at night, can travel half way down the street. She'll be dozing. She'll be listening for the timer to ping. Listening, trying to catch him out about not eating. Once the two minutes is up, Adrian takes the plate out of the microwave and sits and watches his dinner cool and congeal for the next half an hour, until finally he can hear the rhythm of her gentle snore from the bedroom above.

He opens a Tesco carrier bag and scrapes the cold thick food from the plate, feeling the knot in his stomach tighten and heave. He ties the handles of the bag together and opens the back door onto their tiny back garden. Adrian sneaks out the back gate to hide the evidence in next door's dustbin, just in case tomorrow Helen decides to snoop for proof that he still isn't eating.

In the lane, just outside the dim glow of the one weak street light, Matty is waiting.

Matty talks too fast and way too loud, Adrian pushing him further down the lane away from his house, in case the sound of Matty's rant wakes Helen. There is no love lost. Helen is the kindest, purest-hearted woman Adrian has ever known: she finds the good in anyone and never, ever bitches about other people – even the ones who totally deserve it – and yet even Helen will bristle at the sight or sound of his little brother.

Matty ranting about divers. Boat-loads of them. The stench of vodka and cider and Golden Virginia making Adrian's eyes water as Matty swears now about the weather forecast. The Met Office giving it fives increasing to sixes by midday. He swears about the size of the swell, the incline of the waves, the seas that will stop the hoard of divers making it out to the bigger wrecks and force them to execute their dives inside the shelter of Weymouth Bay instead. So they'll dive on the sandbanks instead of further out amongst the sunken twisted ships.

"They'll be trying to spear plaice on the fucking banks," he said. "They'll be scalloping on the ledges. No way they won't dive the Kidney."

Adrian could feel the hairs prickle on his neck. Matty's rant reaching the point where it finally makes some sense. Weekend divers simply cannot leave crab pots alone. Any gear they come across during their 'down time' – whether it's trammel nets, tangle nets, gill nets, cuttle traps or crab pots – bet your baby's eyesight, they'll fuck with it. Especially on a sandbank, which by its very nature is a desolate, desert-like feature, without much to entertain a hyperactive gas monkey, except the pursuit of the rather too well-camouflaged flatties. If they happen upon pots on the bank they will investigate, at the very least, to see what lurks inside. And if they find a pot rammed full of plastic wrapped black hash, what then?

"No fucking way can we leave it out there," Matty says.

Adrian staring into his face, like it's another plate of congealing chilli con carne and baked potato. Adrian lost in doubt and shame and fear. Then, snapping out of it, as his coping mechanism kicks in.

"We can't use the Kitty," he says. "She's impounded. For forensics."

"Fuck that," says Matty. "She's still tied to the harbour wall. We can be out and back before anyone knows."

Adrian found himself looking at his watch, calculating, mentally factoring in the big ebb tide that was about to start flowing east to west which would give them a boost if they got out the harbour within the hour.

Adrian now thinking about Helen waking up. Shifting over to find his side of the bed cold. Padding through the house in her slipper socks, looking for him. Seeing his boots and overalls gone from the back door. She knows the Kitty is impounded. So her subsequent interrogation of him, about where he disappeared to in the dead of night, will be razor-sharp. His answers would need to be watertight. Or else, she'll smell rat all over him.

Bugsy didn't die that winter after all. Not because Helen begged for her life. Or cried or pleaded with her father to save her favourite pig. Bugsy didn't die that winter because Helen's dad decided she should live. Boy pigs are ten-a-penny, and useless for anything other than meat. Girl pigs can be tupped. Served. Impregnated. They can carry piglets. Spill them in the straw. Suckle them. Grow them into little weaned butterballs of sausage filler.

His big sow was 12 years old. She would need to be replaced. Sooner rather than later. Of course Bugsy was no pedigree. She wasn't going to win any mantelpiece of ribbons at the Melplash Show, but she had heft. Her pelvis was wide. He could always buy a new boar for less than 50 quid this time of year. No one wanted to feed animals through the winter only for them to have lost weight by February, and cost good money in the process.

He could buy in a new boar. Probably even swap something with one of his mates over in the Marshwood Vale. Not even have to put his hand in his pocket. Which he never really liked to do. He's got a pair of new trailer tyres that don't fit on his current pig box. Someone'll trade. Give him a boar. Bring in new blood. He can't cover Bugsy with her father or a brother. But he could cover her with a new boar.

The Ridouts over in Toller Fratrum keep a strain of wild boar crossed with saddleback. Long snouted things with scrawny rear ends. Still, wild boar-cross meat makes good money. Pubs loving to put 'wild boar sausages' on their blackboard menu, a few places up above the sticky toffee pudding and six local cheeses.

Cover Bugsy with one of the Ridout wild boar-cross boars. Why not? Those hairy boys can eat for England. He definitely wouldn't need to be digging more holes to bury any rabbit guts and heads. Not with those boys in his sty.

He knew about the tape. Adrian had seen the crime scene officers stretch the blue-and-white 'Police – Do Not Cross' tape all around the deck rails of the Kitty K before he left the harbour on the day of Tim's death. He'd seen the forensic guys tie her up to the inside harbour wall; the Harbour Master, directing proceedings, wearing his peaked hat and carrying a walkie-talkie, which everyone in the harbour knew didn't work. He was trying to look officious and efficient for the benefit of all the official guys in uniforms.

Adrian had seen them wrap an adhesive sticky version of the 'Police – Do Not Cross' tape around the mooring ropes and wrapping it over the cast iron bollard on the quay. But what he hadn't seen was what they'd done to his wheelhouse door.

Matty and Adrian now staring down at the police-issue tamper-proof seal, that'd been drilled and threaded through the door and door pillar. They'd drilled holes in his door for fuck's sake! To insert a thick cable wire connected to the police tamper-proof seal. Adrian supposing they did it because the wheelhouse door was the only part of the whole boat they could actually secure. Only part of the whole vessel that made any sense to them.

Couldn't do fuck all with the 36 foot open steel deck. But show them a door, that's different. They can secure a door. No problem. Just drill it. Wire it. Clamp on a tamper-proof seal. Job done.

Adrian now looking at the seal in the glimmer of the dull sodium yellow street lights, with a sense of hopeless dread. They're fucked. No way can they open the door without breaching the seal. No way can they steer the boat, even start the engine, without opening the wheelhouse door. Could ask to borrow someone else's boat maybe, if he rings around a few numbers Adrian could find one of the skippers who'd be prepared to drive down the harbour and hand over their keys. Maybe. For a price. Which wouldn't be the real problem. Real problem would be the questions. Why do they need to borrow a crab boat in the dead of night? Did it have something to do with Tim's death? What are they going to do while they're out at sea? And why can't it wait until daylight?

The more Adrian stares at the police issue tamper-proof seal, the more his heart sinks and the higher up his throat the level of bitter juice rises. He's distracted by a noise behind him, sound of the toolbox lid closing and Matty moving up beside him. A claw hammer swings across his field of vision and smashes into the tamper-proof seal. One big meaty strike, ripping it from its steel wires.

All the way to the Kidney Bank, the amber engine warning light of the Kitty K flashes on and off intermittently. She is sick. This is her cry for help. Her amber light. Her warning. Her way of telling Adrian she is about to cough up her lungs and die, with his hands still warm on her wheel. The blinking amber light could not be a clearer signal of impending mechanical doom. And yet, it barely registers with Adrian. Mainly because he already feels that all is lost.

All the way out to the Kidney Bank, as the amber warning light blinks, Adrian is scouring his brain. Searching every corner and crevice to try and find any excuse that would help him explain, to whoever asks; the police, the Harbour Master, his wife... but most of all the police, why he had defied their warnings and consciously contaminated a potential crime scene.

He had been expressly told not to use or touch his boat until the crime scene officers had finished investigating. What he was doing now constituted the crime of tampering with and attempting to conceal evidence.

Matty stands beside him, both of them staring out into the pitch black, the distant flash of Portland Bill lighthouse on the portside and the eerie orange glow in the sky over to the east was cast by the street lights of Bournemouth, 25 miles around the Jurassic coast, hidden by Old Harry's Rock. Kitty's navigation lights are all switched off. They don't want anyone on shore, or at sea, to notice them, or have any chance of tracking where they've been.

All the regular instrument panel lights are switched off too, as is the GPS plotter screen and the echo sounder. The instruments all off, in order to reduce any glare, and give their eyes a better chance to adapt to the dark. The fact that every other light is switched off makes the blinking amber engine warning light ever harder to ignore. But they do. Neither brother even mentions it. They just stare out at the sea ahead, searching for a pot buoy.

Carole's neighbour had a bottle of Valium. In her bathroom cabinet, left over from when her husband died, six years ago from cancer. The doctor prescribing them for depression and grief. She'd taken a few back then, but they made her feel woolly. If anyone needs them now, it's Carole. Her eye black and her cheek swollen. The A&E department's bandaged up her knee and put it in a temporary nylon splint with Velcro straps to keep it in place.

Carole took two of her neighbour's Valium and soon started to nod off in her chair, her leg stretched out on the coffee table. Rich took four Valium, had a can of Special Brew and snorted two chubby lines of speed.

As he feels the bitter rivers of industrial strength chemicals run down the back of his throat and feels the end of his nose turn cold and wet, he thinks to himself what a perfect cocktail Special Brew, speed and Benzos is. The Valium giving a smooth, heavy, mellow base-coat on which to pour the belly-fire of booze, then tuning it to pitch perfection by the corrugating, pulsating ripples of the speed. High notes, melody and a thumping bass, running along underneath. A chemical symphony.

The only thing that could possibly improve the combination would be a rock of crack, smoked in a glass pipe or sucked down a biro tube stuck in the arse end of a Red Bull can. A rock of crack would be the perfect addition, if he was just going to stay home and mong out. Perfect if he was intending just to watch the telly and maybe drink a few more Brews.

But the job that Rich is determined to do tonight will not be improved by crack. Careful negotiations with a cunning snake-like negotiator is not something that crack would enhance. If all goes well and he achieves the desired result from these negotiations, then that will definitely be the time to celebrate with a rock or two. Before the negotiation begins, he needs to stay sharp and focused. Speed is the way to achieve focus. A nose full of speed and two sticks of Orbit chewing gum to stop him grinding his teeth too loudly is the perfect pharmaceutical preparation for what he is about to do.

At The Sailors, Rich soon finds that losing a family member, even though Tim wasn't his flesh and blood exactly, is an excellent way to get bought free drinks. Men who'd normally blank him cold, are sending pints and shorts down the bar to where he sits on a tall stool, back resting against the wood and glass partition to the snug.

Those who make an effort to actually come over and talk to him – something that would never normally happen unless he owed them money, drugs or both – want to stand and talk about Tim. Not Tim while he was living, but more specifically, the circumstances of Tim's death. Very soon after expressing their monosyllabic words of condolence – "Fucking gutted to hear 'bout Tim, mate" – they rapidly move on to seeking details. They buy him a pint and roughly pat him between the shoulder blades a couple of times, before they start hunting for the graphic account of what Tim's skull actually looked like when he was fished out the sea. And how much blood was spilled on the deck.

As the night progresses, the questions get bolder and less inhibited by the conventions of grief and acceptable behaviour, and more like rubbernecking at a motorway pile-up. It wasn't long before Rich found himself describing the way that part of Tim's skull had been ripped clean off, clearly exposing a chunk of brain underneath. None of it was true. Rich had seen very little of the corpse from the harbour wall and by the time Tim reached the ambulance he was zipped up in the body bag. But with free booze flowing so unexpectedly thick and fast, Rich wasn't about to let fact get in the way of his good story.

Later, Rich would blame the booze for rounding the sharp clean edges off his speed buzz. Even though he snorted a finger-thick line off the lid of the cistern in the gents at The Sailors around 10.30 pm he still couldn't get the whizz to cut through the slurry booze fog that was muddying up his brain, and making him say some words like he has Alzheimer's, or some other brain-fucking disease. He is wobbling too. When he stands and tries to piss into the toilet, he can feel his knees knocking and almost buckling, sending his deep yellow piss stream all over the seat and floor, even splashing on his best white trainers. The ones he kept for prison.

On D Block, the whiteness and newness and overall pristineness of your trainers says everything about you. Status in prison is about a lot of different things, but you're a total non-starter nobody, if your trainers don't look like they were just plucked out the stock room at Foot Locker.

Rich blamed the spirits. Mostly he was a cider and super-strength lager man, especially if he was taking pills at the same time. Except when blokes kept asking him if he wanted a short, because at the time he'd already got at least one full pint in front of him. So of course he'd say yes. He'd say he was drinking "Jim Bean". Or even, occasionally he'd just say, "JB on the rocks" because it sounded very cool. Trouble is, no matter what it's called, it tastes like earwax and badly collides with all the Valium, to make Rich sound like a messy, fucked up drunk. Which is no way to start a tricky negotiation with a tricky negotiator.

So when the pub empties out a bit and Rich asks Paulie, who has been behind the bar most of the night, if they could "have a private word", he wasn't probably in the sharpest focus that he could be. Consequently, when he came to discuss with Paulie the real reason why he had come to The Sailors tonight, not just for himself "but on behalf of Carole too, see", he maybe didn't express himself as well as he might.

The words 'police', 'compensation' and 'insurance' were all part of Rich's badly-rehearsed and alcohol-muddled speech. The long and the short of it, he says is that Carole is "devastated" by her loss. Tim was her only son. No mother ever gets over losing her son. And when it's your only son, it's much worse.

Rich saying how he knows how terrible Paulie must feel because Tim had lost his young life so tragically on board the boat that Paulie owns. And of course everyone knows what a kind-hearted man Paulie is and how he'd want to do whatever he could to "square things" with Carole "in her hour of need".

And then Rich adding how complicated and ugly it could all get if police and legal proceedings were commenced on account of Tim's age, and him supposed to be at school, and him not having a Basic Crewman Training qualification, so the boat consequently is not insured for him to even be on board, let alone be working the pots.

When Paulie says nothing, absolutely and totally nothing, after Rich finishes his first five-minute-long speech about Tim's death and what Paulie should/might/could/ought to do, for Carole, in the aftermath of the tragedy, Rich decides to change tack.

Paulie's wordless silence throws him off his game. The booze doesn't help. They're sitting in Paulie's office, one flight of stairs up from the door at the back of the bar. The one with the bags of dry roasted nuts and pork scratchings hanging from it. Rich has never been in Paulie's office before. Doesn't know anyone who has, other than the barmaids and barman, who he assumes must come through it and up the stairs to the office, to bring Paulie the contents of the till and stuff.

Rich certainly doesn't know anyone who's been in Paulie's office to discuss business. Not like *he's* discussing business with Paulie now. Only the discussion still seems to be very one-sided, with Rich doing all the talking and Paulie just staring at him, mouth closed, an unlit fag between his fingers.

It strikes Rich as weird that Paulie could sit up here and smoke himself silly in this small box-lined office, and yet downstairs in the bar, no one was even allowed to light up. Instead, everyone standing out on the front doorsteps, freezing their tits off in a knife-cutting south-easterly wind, sucking on their snout like there's no tomorrow.

After Rich could bear Paulie's protracted silence no longer, he launches into his second speech, the one with the clever twist.

The one that made Rich not a bearer of bad news and the potential threat of legal proceedings (unless a suitable out-of-court financial settlement could be reached) but the clever man who can save Paulie from an unnecessary storm of shit.

It is Carole, he explains. In her grief and loss she feels bitterness and pain. She wants retribution. Revenge even. She wants to see someone made to pay for her loss. And that someone in her eyes is the owner of the boat on which her son died. She wants to see them suffer as she is suffering. In a way it's understandable. That's how grief hits some people, makes them mean and bitter. It makes them seek the advice of certain types of solicitors and legal advisors who will work on a 'No Win, No Fee' basis, because they specialise in compensation claims relating to industrial accidents and work-related injuries and deaths.

This special breed of legal professional knowing exactly how to wring the most compensation out of an institution or business, even if it means bankrupting that business in the process. Rich explaining that Carole's already researching into exactly this type of legal firm. Firms, which she's seen, advertised on Sky Living and ITV3, in between the *Jeremy Kyle Show* and re-runs of *Wife Swap*. Firms whose targeted advertising campaign is aimed directly at anyone who has suffered unjustly in any sort of work-related accident, where substantial compensation might be awarded, if the right legal buttons are pressed.

The way Rich spins his second speech is to try not to impose any kind of threat of his own to Paulie, quite the contrary; it's to offer himself up as the man most likely to be able to dissuade Carole from taking this particular course of action. He knows how her head works. He knows when she's vulnerable and when she can most easily be talked into or out of a specific mindset. He knows how to make her see sense when her head's full of nonsense. She listens to him. He is her man. She turns to him for advice and support on things that she doesn't understand.

So, if she needs to be steered away from a particular course of action, he, Rich, is the very best man to do exactly that. Left to her own devices, in her hour of gut-wrenching grief, she could become a lawyer-seeking missile, that might wreak financial havoc upon those she imagines are responsible for her son's death. But, with careful guidance from Rich, she could be pacified and neutralised. And would present no potential legal or financial threat.

That is, of course, if a mutually agreeable settlement can be reached between these two men of the world.

Rich is much happier with his second speech. He achieved much better control of his tongue this time around, and although the whole I-can-do-you-a-really-big-favour approach was totally improvised, after he'd experienced Paulie's first impenetrable silence, Rich is confident, second time around, he's nailed it perfectly.

So he is kind of surprised when this time around Paulie still says nothing, for a very long time after Rich has clearly reached the end of his very reasonable and very helpful offer.

Paulie finally lights his cigarette and finally gets around to speaking. Softly. "You finished?" he asks. Rich nods. Eager.

"Good. Well, get the fuck out of my pub now, and don't ever step foot in it, or even in its shadow, so long as you live. Do I make myself clear?"

His failure to achieve anything resembling the result he expected put Rich in a right skanky mood. Being barred from The Sailors for life had a very sobering effect. This just isn't right. Rich can smell that this is a golden opportunity. The woman he's been fucking for donkey's years has just lost her teenage son due to some very bad stuff occurring on a boat that belongs to the richest man Rich knows. And yet, here Rich is, stuck bang in the middle of it all, with his pockets hanging out and still no idea how to milk his share. He just knows there's a big pay day attached to this situation, and he's so fucking pissed off that he can't work out how to skin this fat cat.

It's because of being barred, and because of feeling suddenly sober, that Rich finds himself at the end of Weymouth Harbour pier standing on a bench pissing over the railing. It's just then, when he's shaking his dick dry, that he hears the low irregular thump of a diesel engine, no more than 50 or 60 yards out in the bay.

Rich can hear it's a four-cylinder single-stroke marine diesel. Rich knows a lot about single-stroke diesels, from all the workshop training certificates he's taken in various prisons. Rich can even tell from the sound that this four-cylinder marine diesel is a sick one. A cylinder is grinding, a dry growl coming from its main bearings, where the con-rods meet the crankshaft.

Rich can tell a lot about this engine just from the sound, but he still can't see the boat. Mostly because the spill of light from the pier lamps – the few that haven't been broken by glue-huffing teens hurling beach pebbles – is so piss-weak.

Rich stares into the blackness, searching for the source of the noise but doesn't even see any nav lights. Finally he just manages to make out the source of the sick growling thump, a light-coloured rusty crabber that seems to be steering a course tight-in close to the pier. Inside the wheelhouse he can just see the outlines of two faces, intermittently lit by one dim glowing amber warning light. The two faces look like... *brothers.*

What the fuck are they doing out on a crabber at night? And why are they doing whatever they're doing without any navigation lights? These are just two of the many questions rattling around Rich's tenderised brain. Then he hears the angry gearbox being slipped into neutral. The engine chugs with an unhappy rhythm as it ticks over and the boat coasts in close, almost touching the west side of the pier, moving deep into the dark shadow.

One of the faces disappears from the window. One, grim, tight-lipped face remains, illuminated by the flickering amber warning light. One brother's at the wheel, the other's left the wheelhouse, and is presumably walking out on deck.

Although it's rough and irregular, the tick-over of the ancient engine is still quiet enough for Rich to just hear a sucking, gurgling splash, as something heavy is slipped off the gunwale of the brothers' boat into the deep dark water up alongside the cast iron pier stanchions.

The same questions remain unanswered as Rich now hears the Kitty K being slipped back into gear and start chugging slowly up the harbour towards the quay. What the fuck are these brothers doing out at night? Why are they doing it without navigation lights? And now, he has a new question: What did they just dump in the sea alongside the pier?

Rich counts the upright railings from the far end of the pier to where he roughly judges the Kitty K was floating when he heard the heavy gurgling weight hit the water. Eleven upright railings along. Just to be sure, he stands an empty Thunderbird bottle he finds under a bench alongside the eleventh railing. Thunderbird marks the spot, he thinks as he walks towards the marina.

Far as Adrian is concerned, Matty is a liability. Everything Matty does is a danger to both of them. From the moment he swung that bat into Tim's head, he risked not just his own freedom, but Adrian's too and the future of Helen and the boys. By hiding the hunk of dope and by smashing the tamper-proof seal, Matty is drawing more and more attention. Adrian knows the police'll be all over them about the broken seal. Could see suspicion in that Chinese cop's eyes right from the start. If they can get away with returning the Kitty K to her mooring without anyone seeing, then at least they can blatantly deny any knowledge of how or why or who broke the seal.

And if Helen's still asleep when he gets home, he might at least have an alibi. If he can slip into bed before she wakes, then as far as she's concerned, he's been there all night. What they need to do now is get back to the berth, get tied up and get away without anyone seeing them any where near the Kitty K.

With all the navigation lights switched off they stand the best chance of avoiding being noticed. The cold south-easterly will dampen the urge of couples hoping for a grope or a shag on the pier benches. The tide's too small for any anglers to want to fish off the end of the breakwater, and the time of night should mean most normal people are tucked up in bed.

Of course Matty wanted to bring the dope back to the quay. He wanted to unload the pot and make a dash for Adrian's truck, which is parked half a mile away in The Loop car park. Which would have meant carrying a crab pot full of black hash right across the bridge and up along the harbour to the marina, under the full glare of the street lights and God-knows-how-many CCTV cameras.

**189**

For two men, who have already been brought to the police's attention, because of the violent death of a teenager at sea, to be filmed carrying a mysterious crab pot through the town centre at 2 am, would not be good.

"How's that going to look?" asks Adrian

"Fuck it," says Matty. "Be fine. Then we can stash it at mine. Bury it in the garden."

Matty is a liability. Adrian keeps telling himself. Everything Matty does is knee-jerk. Nothing thought through. Matty's going to get them both caught. Adrian can see it clearly now. Adrian at last waking up from his pathetic state of shock, and now he knows he's got to take control of this situation, or else Matty's going to get them buried.

"We don't land it," says Adrian.

"What?"

"We don't dock with it," he says, steering the Kitty around towards the dark side of the pier. "Anyone could be round there waiting for us now. Police, coastguard, harbour master... *Anyone* sees us and we're fucked."

The dim lights of the pier only a hundred yards away now as the Kitty K makes her way through the darkness towards the town.

"Cut the rope off the pot and drop it over the side, when we pass by the pier struts," says Adrian. "Drop it right close in. Half way along."

"No fucking way," says Matty.

"Think about it. We round the bend to the harbour and we see a reception committee, we got nowhere to go. We can't hide the pot," he says. "Too late to toss it over with everyone watching. But if we drop it in the deeps up against the pier now, we can come back on foot, drag it out later. Or tomorrow. When we know it's all clear."

Matty not happy. Matty didn't like the idea of tipping the pot into the water without any rope or buoy to mark it. But, he could see sense in what Adrian was saying; if they rounded the bend and saw a bunch of blue flashing lights parked up at Kitty K's empty berth, they'd be caught with their thumbs stuck well and truly up their arses.

Adrian wasn't prepared to argue. No debate. Wasn't taking the Kitty in the harbour with the pot on deck. They stash it beside the pier, or else he's turning the Kitty round and taking her back out to sea.

Matty hating to admit it, but Adrian's plan had merit. Even if they berthed the Kitty and there was no Old Bill waiting, they'd still have to get the pot off the boat. Whether they carried it to the truck or brought the truck to the berth, there'd still be way too much messing around with a pot-load of hash, in the centre of town, in the middle of the night

So, when the Kitty K glides in neutral into the thick inky shadow of the pier, Matty counts the railings along from the seaward end giving himself as clear a marker as he can, before slipping the pot off the gunwale into the dark water.

Matty counting exactly 11 stanchions from the end and then pushing the pot off, the plastic waterproof liner behind the mesh catching a last glint of weak light, before disappearing into the black.

Rich had stolen enough stuff from boats in the marina over the years to know exactly where the CCTV cameras are located and, more to the point, which ones are real. Didn't matter too much tonight, because he's still wearing his hoodie and he can just about hide his entire face inside it. Still, he doesn't want to tempt fate. Rich has been caught out by CCTV camera footage twice before.

Once, breaking into an old people's home just outside Bridport. He'd thought the drug cabinet would be a really piss-easy nut to crack. And old people do have some very nice prescriptions. Between the 40 or so inmates he'd reckoned there'd be a whole mess of pharmaceuticals to pop, swap and sell. "Bound to be some Rich pickings," he'd joked to Carole, this being one of his favourite word plays. Personally, he thought it was really clever, and was kind of bummed out that no one he ever said it to laughed more than a weak chuckle. Maybe was the way he said it.

Anyway two things he hadn't reckoned on in regard to the old folks' home, one was the state-of-the-art sophistication of their CCTV system, and the other was the vigilance of the night sister. He never even *found* the drug cabinet, let alone got a look inside to see the quality and variety of the old people's scripts.

The second CCTV disaster was a classic. Not only did it originally feature on *Crimewatch*, but it also crops up regularly on *Britain's Dumbest Criminals*. Which anyone might think would be an embarrassment amongst prison inmates, on account of it being televised proof of what a crap criminal Rich can be. But, in fact, the opposite was true. When his 20-second-long CCTV clip was broadcast as he was doing 18 months in Guy's Marsh, a huge cheer went up in the rec room. Was so cool. Inmates slapping him on the back telling him he's a 'star', for the next two weeks or so.

It *was* a classic CCTV gaff. Mainly because it was so dumb. Rich and two black guys he'd met when he was doing a short stretch in Dorchester, had driven to Sidmouth to rob a Spar store, that turned out to be closed, for a refit. So they decided on the spur of the moment to go and rob the Tesco Express in the centre of town, instead.

Rich went in, to buy a tube of Pringles and to case the set up, first off. Rich did the casing, on account of he was white. Sidmouth doesn't see a lot of brothers, so the two sitting in the knocked-off Nissan Micra parked outside are going to stick out like hammer-thumped thumbs.

Once he'd scoped the store and bought his Pringles, Rich gave the boys the thumbs-up, and the three of them slipped on their army surplus ski mask balaclavas, after a quick discussion about who was to do what when they went in, like which check-out cashier and which till each one of them was to intimidate and empty. The discussion taking place on the pavement two doors down, right outside the HSBC, a couple of yards from the ATM cash machine.

And to be fair, it wasn't the slickest game plan discussion. One of the black guys, Jai-Man, was as thick as a skip-load of thick shit. Rich had to keep repeating the same thing over and over again, about which cashier Jai-Man was to rob. He couldn't get his thick head around whether it was the second one from the entrance door or the second one from the far end. In the end Rich had said to him really slowly and really loudly: "Just rob *any* fucking cashier what's not being robbed by me or him. *Get* it? Don't rob any the ones we're robbing. Right?"

At the time Rich was as nervous as fuck and adrenalin was pumping through his veins which had the effect of making his voice sound really high and squeaky. They had the ski masks on their heads, but not pulled down over their faces while they had their little pre-raid confab. Then once he'd finished their squeaky pep talk, they all pulled down their masks, Rich checking what his looked like in the reflection from the HSBC window. Before leading the way into Tesco Express.

What none of them clocked at the time, because Rich was too wound up and the brothers were too dim, is that the HSBC cashpoint had a CCTV camera pointing straight out at the street recording everything that happened within a five-yard radius of the money dispensing machine 24 hours a day.

The whole thing, from Jai-Man and the other one stepping out of the boosted motor to the three of them striding into Tesco Express with their ski gear in place, was perfectly recorded in a wide-shot complete with sound. When the series producer of *Britain's Dumbest Criminals* first saw it, he nearly wet his pants.

So now, Rich has learned to be wary of CCTV, which is why he chose to cross the bridge and climb down onto the nearest pontoon of the marina on the far side, away from the centre of town. He knows when you're stealing from boats in the main marina, the far side near the fire station is the best place to start.

The boats on the side furthest from the town centre are the smaller ones, the cheaper ones with the least impressive moorings. If you got a big boat that cost a lot of money, you want it moored in a place where everyone can see your big boat and admire it and envy you. And of course, you want it to be in the place with the best security, the brightest lights, and CCTV cameras that are actually plugged in.

If on the other hand, your boat was small and cheap and not much to behold, you'd probably be happy over the far side in the gloomy shadow of the fire station, where the lights are dim, the CCTV non-existent and the mooring rents so much cheaper.

Rich didn't want to rob from a big boat on the east wall, not just because of the added security risk, which considering his current parole status was apt and pertinent, but because what he wanted to rob wasn't something a big fancy boat would have. What he needed was something he'd be most likely to find on a small, cheap crappy boat, tied up against the harbour wall. What Rich wanted was an anchor. Not a big fuck-off ten kilo Brent anchor attached to several metres of eight-mill chain. No, Rich wanted to find a thin wire grapple from a dinghy, or one of those folding anchors you get, like on rubber tenders, with a length of thin rope attached to it. Something light enough to carry, small enough to hide up his hoodie, and nimble enough to chuck off the pier, without causing too much of a splash.

In the front of a tatty fibreglass rowboat with an ancient Seagull outboard strapped to the transom, Rich saw a rusty grapple with a coil of sodden seagull shit-splattered rope, and his heart skipped a beat.

When the Kitty K cruised towards her berth, engine off, all lights out, creeping towards the harbour wall in the thick silent blackness with only the glow of street lights to guide her, Matty really wanted to have a go at Adrian. The whole dock was totally fucking deserted. Not a policeman, coastguard, harbour master or any other fucker in sight, whatsoever. Matty could seriously have kicked off and had a right good go at Adrian for being such an over-cautious pussy, who just took an even bigger risk, by dumping their precious cargo, unmarked, over the side, by the pier stanchions.

Matty could have rubbed Adrian's nose in it, but the truth is Matty was feeling a bit spooked now too. He looked at the smashed police tamper-proof seal lying on the deck and saw the tatters of blue 'Police – Do Not Cross' tape fluttering between the bollards on the top of the harbour steps, and he too now wanted to put as much distance between himself and the Kitty K as was humanly possible. If they were tying up and now carrying the pot off up onto the road that runs along the side of the harbour, in the glare of the street lights, they'd be feeling pretty fucking exposed. Truth is, he was glad not to be humping a heavy dripping pot full of someone else's hash across town at this very moment.

The Kitty's buffs had hardly touched the wall before Matty and Adrian were scrambling up the metal ladders, hooking the mooring ropes around the bollards still strewn with broken blue sticky 'Do Not Cross' tape, and legging it across the street into the shadows.

Adrian sprinting along the dark side of the lane leading towards The Loop car park and Matty trying to catch up with him. Matty wanting to beg a lift back to his flat. Adrian with no intention of taking Matty anywhere. Quicker he got home, quicker he got under the covers, and started pretending he'd been there all night, the more rock solid his alibi would be. If he didn't want to be jammed squarely in the frame for busting the seals on the Kitty K and ripping her mooring ropes out taped restraints, then he needed to be back in bed with his wife before she discovered he *wasn't* in bed with her.

The one thing he could not rely on Helen to do, for him or anyone else, was to tell a lie.

Robbie liked to do coke with Elsa, mostly because Elsa liked to do coke. Left to his own devices he'd probably never go and score a gram, just for his own consumption. And definitely he'd never go and score a whole eight-ball. An eight-ball of coke, on his Jack Jones, would last Robbie a whole year. But with Elsa around, they'd get through an eight-ball in a week, no problem. Elsa bumping twice as much as him. And then some.

When she was on one, she was crazy for it and wouldn't go to sleep for three nights in a row. She'd just do line after line, and then do mad shit, like dance or cook. She'd even do housework at three in the morning; cleaning the flat so it shone in every corner like a new pin. Then after three or maybe even four nights, she'd be begging Robbie to go and score some smack, or some pills; some downers to help her climb down off her eyeball-cracking high.

Robbie, now he was a totally different kind of coke user. Could take it or leave it. He'd reach a 36-hour limit, and have to sleep it off. A good night cap; couple of stiff whiskies, maybe even a sleeper, a Mogadon, Tramadol, Xanax, temazepam or two, from the old bathroom cabinet, and he was gone. Sparko. He'd sleep 14 hours straight. Get up. Piss for England. Drink a couple of pints of water. Go back to bed for another ten-stretch, and when he woke up second time around, he'd be golden.

Sure he'd need to eat a full English breakfast big enough to feed a rugby team; but once that grease and egg had soaked into his blood stream, he'd be 100 percent again and good to go. And afterwards, Robbie would not be inclined to touch the Charlie again for a couple of months, or more. Even if he still had a gram or two left kicking around the flat, he'd just wrap it up, stick it in the little drawer in the bedside cabinet thing and forget all about it, until the time felt right again, which could be ages.

Elsa wasn't like him. She could not have coke in the house without snorting it. She would have to finish every last crumb and lick every wrap paper clean, until her binge was finally over. Even then, she'd be debating scoring just one more gram, or maybe two, just to 'tail off' her buzz. Elsa did not have brakes. She had no natural ability to either stop or say no. If she was on one, she was full on. Pedal to the metal. Burning her candle at every end imaginable. Torching the fucker until it melted in a big pool of liquid wax.

So it came as a big surprise to Robbie to realise he was physically addicted to cocaine. And that the reason he couldn't sleep and was sweating so much his bed was wringing wet, like he'd pissed it, was because his body was reacting to the fact that its hitherto constant supply of cocaine had suddenly and emphatically stopped. Robbie had suddenly stopped using coke hundreds of times before, and felt nothing. Never missed a step, got on with life and work and everything – bish-bosh – like nothing was different. Which in his mind it wasn't. One day he was doing a few lines. Next day, he wasn't. That's the way he liked it to be. You use drugs. You never let the drugs use you.

Elsa was a whole different story. He knew pretty quickly she was an addict. She could not say no. And could not stop herself even if she wanted to. Which she didn't. In fairness, Elsa was addicted to just about *anything*: coke, money, sex, shopping, gambling, shopping, coke, eating, lying, shopping, coke.

Thing was, it didn't make her a bad person. Quite the opposite. It made her a fine person. Full of life. Full of passions. Crazy. Funny. Lively. Excitable. She made Robbie's life a mess. She spent all his money and made him neglect his business and got him smashed out of his can far too often than was good for his health. But she made him feel happier and more alive than any other person in his entire life made him feel.

He would do *anything* for Elsa. He didn't care what it would cost him. He really didn't. He would become a martyr to her cause and he'd die a happy man, just to have been able to spend the time with her that he'd spent already. Even if there was no more fun to be shared with Elsa, he wouldn't care, because in his eyes and in his heart, the times they'd shared together had been the best times of his life.

Beside the bed, on the bedside cabinet that they'd bought together in Southampton Ikea, was a framed photo of Robbie and Elsa in the basket of a hot air balloon. It wasn't a real hot air balloon. Not one of those ones that floats all over the countryside until it crash-lands in some farmer's field somewhere. This is just the hot air balloon at the Jubilee Gardens in the centre of Bournemouth, which is attached to the ground by wires. During the summer it's winched up to nearly a hundred feet every 20 minutes or so, and tourists and visitors and families pay to go up and look out over Bournemouth town one way, or out to sea and across to the Isle of Wight, the other.

Just after they were winched back down to the ground, Elsa had asked the lady who was selling tickets to take a photo of her and Robbie. She has her arm around his neck and she's pressing her cheek against his and grinning, a big open-mouthed grin for the camera. Her eyes wide, her face full of happiness.

Elsa got the picture printed and put it in a picture frame that she'd bought in Ikea without Robbie knowing. She'd bought it, with her own money. Then she'd put the frame by his side of the bed with a red rose Sellotaped to it, for Valentine's Day last year. They don't have Valentine's Day in Poland, she told Robbie, and she'd always wanted to celebrate it, back from when she was a little girl and first heard about it.

Robbie cried when she gave it to him. Big blubbing sobs and tears, and she cradled his head in her arms. She laughed at his tears, kindly, not cruel. And told him he was "the sweetest man" she had ever known. Said it was like his heart was made of "mash mallow". It was one moment of his life that he'll never forget.

And now as he lies in the bed, sweating, accepting that he's gone and got himself all messed up and strung out on coke, he starts to weep all over again, as he looks at the photo propped on his chest.

He now so wishes he'd saved the rose too. But when it wilted and went mouldy he'd thrown it away.

Robbie was just wiping away the tears from his cheeks with the cuff of his sweat-stinking bathrobe, when he heard the noise downstairs, in the showroom.

The unmistakable noise of a classic 1969 Chevrolet 350 engine with factory-fitted side exhaust ports and an all aluminium cylinder block, cranking over.

Adrian wakes Helen just after 4.30 am and tells her he's just got a call from Dougie, the skip on Nicola B. Dougie having some trouble getting her fired up, and needing a hand.

"All right, darling," Helen says brightly, but keeping her eyes firmly shut. Her bright voice a total contrast to the unmoving expression on her face. Now, Adrian has his alibi.

"Said he might be short of a deckhand, too," Adrian tells her. "If he is, I might crew for him. Be cash in hand."

"O-K," she said tunefully, her face still, like a burial mask. Adrian adding the bit about crewing, just in case things turn out to be complicated and he needs an excuse not to come home all day.

He'd agreed to pick up Matty on his way into Weymouth and they'd planned to then drive the long way around town, along the Esplanade and into the Theatre Pavilion car park, down by the pier. They could park the truck along the side of the theatre and walk across to the short pier, without having to pass any of the crab boats or netters, who'd be starting to steam out, around 5.30.

Even if it took them a while to hook out their stashed pot, no one would see them up there on the pier. The crab boats would be passing way below and most of their windscreens would still be misted, and most of the skippers and crew would be half asleep. They could dredge for the pot with a small anchor and if necessary, drag it out after the crab boats had all gone to sea.

Once they've hooked out the pot, then they'll run it back to Matty's, where he'll remove the kilo he's agreed to sell to the Sikh guy in Bristol. Matty insisting the kilo was only a 'test purchase'; the Sikh guy needing to check the 'quality and logistics' were smooth.

Matty already talking like he's some kind of big businessman. If they are smooth, then he said he'd go ahead and put in a 'proper' order. "Says maybe he'll buy the whole lot," says Matty. "His fucking watch alone must be worth five grand!" Matty totally impressed by the guy in the green turban.

What Matty didn't know yet is that Adrian is going to drive away with the other 21 kilos of hash in his truck, after they'd removed the kilo for the Bristol Sikh. And then he isn't even going to tell Matty where it's going to be stashed.

Adrian now realising he can't trust Matty not to fuck up. Not to tell someone where the stash is at. Or worse, lead them to it. No. Fuck-up amateur-hour is officially over. Adrian is taking charge until it's all sold. Matty can have it in bits and pieces as he sells it. And Adrian will produce the gear and wait until Matty produces Adrian's half of the cash from that sale, before they move on to the next buy. No way he's letting Matty have any control of the bulk. Time for Adrian to take control is now. The only good thing to come out of this will be if Adrian can get his share of the cash and get his independence from Matty and Paulie, and start his life with his family all over fresh, with his own boat or his own business. And that isn't going to happen if Matty has his hands on the reins and his head up his arse.

Two things Adrian is determined to do, is avoid getting ripped off, and avoid going to jail. In order to achieve these things he will have to keep Matty on a very short leash. Starting from today.

First though, they have to go get their crab pot of hash back from the base of the pier stanchion beneath the eleventh railing from the sea. And so, after he leaves the house, Adrian stops at his shed and digs under a pile of pot frames by his work bench to find the small grapple anchor their dad used to use on his tender dinghy, back in the days before he got a mooring against the harbour wall. Adrian grabs a short coil of polyprop rope and lays the two things quietly in the flat bed of his truck. Time to take control.

Rich was getting all wound up. He's on the pier, 11 railings from the southern end and now he's probably chucked the little grapple anchor more than a dozen times. Trouble is, the angle's all wrong for snagging anything. He's too high up and the rope's a little too short to give him much room to drag the anchor across the harbour bed. He needs to be lower, which is impossible, unless he was chucking from a boat down at the water level, or else got hold of another 15 or 20 feet of rope.

It's not that he hasn't hooked nothing. Second throw he snagged something big. Turned out to be a Morrisons shopping trolley, all covered in weed and slipper limpet shells. Must've been in the water for a year or more. The fucker was, once he'd hooked the trolley he couldn't *unhook* it. Again, he didn't have enough rope to give it enough slack, or else be able to walk down the pier ten yards and pull the hook out from another angle.

Instead, after tugging and shaking and tugging and shaking, trying to trip the grapple out of the stainless steel mesh of the trolley, and failing time and time again, he eventually had to pull the whole fucking thing up and out of the water. Weighed a fucking ton. Pulling it, hand over hand up and out of the sea, in the light of the breaking dawn, a big weedy shopping trolley.

Worst part was once he'd got it up as far as the pier railing, he had to flip it over the top rail, but it was so fucking heavy, and the wet rope was biting into his hands. In the end, he had to clinch the rope around the armrest of a bench, and just suspend the trolley on the seaward side of the railing. Then he had to lean right over and drag the stinky green weedy fucker up over the rail and on to the bench, where it stood now, smelling like a tub of over-ripe whelk bait.

He could've just unhooked it when it was the other side of the rail. Pulled the grapple anchor out of the stainless mesh and let it fall back into the sea. But then he'd probably just keep hooking it again and again, while he's trying to dredge and drag around the bottom of the stanchion. Rich also didn't want to make that much noise. Even though he didn't know what he was going to find, he knew he didn't want to share any discovery with anyone else.

By about 4.55am, after he's been fucking around with the anchor and the trolley for the best part of an hour, and now the sky was starting to lighten in the east, Rich began to wonder if he was just chasing some fat wild goose. He knew the brothers dumped *something* off the Kitty K. He knew it had to be something they didn't want anybody else to see, or to have, else they wouldn't have risked taking their police-impounded boat out, and they certainly wouldn't have done it all without navigation lights. But, just because it was something they didn't want anyone else to see, or to find, didn't necessarily mean it was something that was going to make Rich rich.

He thought about what it might be that was so dodgy they had to dump it at night. A body is what he kept thinking. But, whose body? And if they was going to dump a body, surely they'd dump it much further out to sea. Out to where the big west-east flood tide could catch it and drag it up to the Isle of Wight. They wouldn't just chuck a body by the pier where, it could be hooked by some kid with a crab line and become a lead story on BBC *Spotlight West* by the end of the week.

No, if it was a body they would've gone further out. And yet, thought Rich as his addled brain sifted through recent data, when he heard them pushing whatever it was that they pushed off the portside gunwale of their boat, the brothers were heading *into* port, not heading out.

Coming in. Like they'd already *been* out and now were heading home, carrying something. Something they'd just picked up maybe!

Out at sea. Something they didn't want to be seen bringing back to their berth, even though it was dead of night.

None of it made any sense. Still, Rich decides to give it another ten more chucks before he'll give up and jack it in. He could hear one of the crabbers start their engine, round the river bend, in the main town harbour. The crabbers and netters would be starting to head out soon and he could certainly do without any of them inbreds seeing him fishing Morrisons' trolleys out the harbour. Ten more chucks and he was gone.

On chuck number six, a chuck that he threw a little more down stream and much closer to the pier ironwork than he had before, he hooked up to something new. At first he thought he'd hooked the stolen anchor over one of the pier's cross braces, because when he pulled hard with both hands – the rope coiled like a snake up his forearm, to give extra grip – the thing didn't budge an inch.

He slackened his grip and repositioned himself on the other side of the bench, upwind of the stinking Morrisons' trolley and tried again. One more big pull before he'd try to unhook it by dropping it back down and jiggling the rope to rattle free the grapple blade. One more pull, only this time using the pier rail strut as a post to yank it around, and give it an extra angle of leverage.

So, with the rope wrapped around his forearm, over the top of his hoodie sleeve, Rich pulls so fucking hard his lips are stretched right back over his dying gums, as he sticks his once lily-white trainer against the seaweed-dripping, silt-covered bench and hauled like he was trying to bust himself a new hole. And yes, the fucking thing moved! Whatever it is moved nearly a foot. It isn't a cross-brace he's hooked, it's something big and heavy and his grapple anchor is dug right into it.

Next haul, he moves back downwind of the trolley again, so he's positioned directly above where the rope enters the water. Again, he uses a rail post like a capstan to haul around. Again, he pulls so hard he can feel his arsehole pop, but again the thing moves. This time it moves up off the seabed, up through the water by maybe a foot or more. Of course, as soon as he gives any slack to the rope, the thing sinks back down fast. Back to the seabed. Whatever it is, it's fucking heavy. So next pull he's prepared, and uses the bench armrest to loop the rope around, holding the thing up off the bottom. A few more big pulls and he'll be breaking the surface with whatever it was. The sky lightening up just enough now for him to probably see it, from the pier edge, if he hangs right over the rail.

Rich is like a ferret or a weasel or a stoat. Thin. Sinewy. Skin and bone and tight little stringy muscles. Naked he looks like a streak of badger piss. But Rich has learned how to use his wiry strength. Unlike the brawny muscle-bound guys who work out every day in the prison gym, and get the screws to smuggle in protein shake powder, rather than spliff, Rich can easily lift his own body weight. The drugs and the fags and the pipe are shredding his lungs, but his shoulders and biceps are still rigid balls of knobbly muscle.

By putting both feet on the rail and leaning right back into each haul, and whipping the slack around the armrest in between the pulls, he's making some ground. After one mammoth grunt of a pull, he can hear the noise of water splashing, way down below. Whatever he's hooked is now, at last, hanging above the surface dripping water back into the harbour.

Picking his way across the mud-splattered bench, Rich leans far over the rail and peers down into the greyness, to finally see what he's snagged on his stolen anchor.

Of all the different fish that swim in our sea, there are really only two basic types: fish that eat fish and fish that eat other stuff. The other stuff includes plankton, algae, weed, worms, sea lice, crabs, shrimps – although, to be fair, just about *anything* with a mouth big enough will eat shrimps. Shrimps are God's little gift.

The fish that eat other fish are predators. They have a well-developed appetite for other fish flesh, as well as their own. Cannibalism is not a taboo amongst sea life. Predator fish are generally as happy to eat their own babies, as they are to eat the babies of their foe.

There are even more subtle divisions amongst predators and non-predators. There are apex predators and there are lazy predators. There are predators who live to hunt, whose entire existence boils down to their ability to seek out, to chase and to devour other fish and their families. And then there are predators who are just way too idle to be bothered to do much predating.

The Atlantic sea bass is a warrior-like, gladiator-style predator, heavily armed and heavily defended with stiletto-sharp spines, a bony gill shield, razor-edged rakers, thick scales, and all the speed and agility of a snow leopard. But then, there's the lazy predators: pollack, whiting, coley, pouting, and the laziest of them all is the cod. Although cod are predators too, in that they will predate upon other fish and crustaceans in order to feed, they are idle opportunists with varying degrees of unfussiness and sloth. While a bass is not satisfied with hunting anything less than a live fish with a beating heart and a fear-blinking eye, a cod will eat just about anything, dead or alive. Fresh or putrid. Wriggling or rotten.

In fact, a cod is probably happier if its food is already dead, because that saves it the unwarranted effort of having to kill it first. If a cod can avoid work, it will, at any cost. A cod is the biggest, laziest, free-loadingest, scrounger, ponce and couch potato in the sea.

Researchers examining the stomach contents of large cod caught in the North Sea regularly discover polystyrene cups inside the bigger fish. Big cod see white shapes on the seabed, and assume they're dead cuttlefish. And, being very hungry and very lazy – as cod nearly always are – they suck them down, one after the other, in the vague hope that they might be food. In fact, they're just empty coffee cups.

Bass are very picky about what they'll hunt. Cod will hoover up any old shit, on the premise that it might just possibly be lunch.

And by far the easiest fish to catch are the greedy ones.

As Robbie pads across the kitchenette in his bare feet, heading towards the stairs, he stops at the spotless worktop, that's never seen much cooking action, and slides a knife out of a wooden block. The block is an angled lump of beechwood out of which bristles eight different knife-handles. Robbie can tell the big knives from the small knives just by the size of the handle. What Robbie can't tell is what each knife is intended for cutting. There's no label or guide. No map, like inside the lid of a box of chocolates, which tells you what fillings are inside what shapes. Robbie thinks they should have the same sort of shape-map on the knife block. Outlines of each knife, with a little description of what stuff you're meant to cut with it.

All Robbie knows now is he wants a *big* knife. He takes hold of the biggest handle and pulls a long knife out the block and walks down the stairs leading to the ground floor showroom and office. The meaty bass thump of the Corvette's eight polished aluminium pistons making the stairway windows rattle as he passes.

It wasn't until he opened the office door and stepped down onto the rubber Porsche mat that had once been on the luggage shelf of an ancient Carrera GT, that Robbie realises four separate things at once. The first is that he's not wearing any slippers. He can feel the rubber treads of the Porsche mat with his bare feet. Number two is that he is still clutching the photograph of him and Elsa in the basket of the Bournemouth wind-up-and-down balloon. Almost as soon as he realises this, he shifts it to his chest, glass front facing into his hot damp bathrobe, as though somehow he might be able to protect Elsa by clutching her to his breast. Third thing is the knife. The one he'd taken from the block with the big handle is outstretched in front of him now, the blade pointing into the office. Only now he realises the big knife he'd chosen was a bread knife with a serrated blade and a flat blunt square ended tip, instead of a point.

Fourth thing he learns in this avalanche of information is that he knows the man who is now opening the drawers of Robbie's small wooden filing cabinet and pulling out his folder of log books for the cars he currently has in stock.

He knows the man is Polish. He'd met him three times before, once with Elsa, when she introduced them, only later to tell Robbie, when they were cutting lines on the little mirror from the hallway, what exactly it was that the Polish man did for a living. Second time was when Robbie went to meet him for a drink, on his own, in the bar of the Sandbanks Hotel, after calling him up on the number he'd copied from Elsa's phone, while she was finally sleeping off a five-day binge.

Third time was when Robbie had taken his share of the cash to a Thai restaurant in Parkstone very close to the John Lewis Home shop, where he and Elsa splurged. They had sat across a small table from each other, a plate of mixed starters between them: spring rolls, sesame prawn toasts, carrots cut into the shape of small fish, and Robbie had given the man an envelope full of cash. And he in turn had given Robbie a sheet of A4 paper on which was typed a small set of numbers, which were the latitude and longitude references of a small green buoy, attached to a rope, attached to one single crab pot.

Although Robbie had owned a boat for nearly three years – owning a boat was practically *de rigueur* for anyone living in Sandbanks – he wasn't exactly a confident or adventurous boater. Mostly, if he took his boat out – which he didn't do nearly enough to justify the fees he paid to keep it at Blue Haven Quay – he'd just potter around Poole Harbour. He'd maybe cruise past Brownsea Island, see if he could catch a glimpse of one of the red squirrels that still enjoyed island-sanctuary there, unharrassed and unmolested by the scourge of the grey squirrel. He never did see one.

And Elsa wasn't a big fan of the boat. Probably because she sensed, fairly early on, that Robbie didn't really know what he was doing, and that made her nervous.

It was Robbie's lack of knowledge with boats that made him ignorant to the finer details of latitude and longitude. And, when he stared at the numbers, printed so tiny on what seemed like such a huge expanse of white A4 paper, they didn't raise in him any doubt or cause for concern. All he knew is that he could type them into the 'find waypoint' function of his very expensive split-screen NavMan chart plotter, and if he then pressed the right buttons, in the right sequence, the fabulous technology would give him a 'route plan', a 'total distance' and an 'expected time of arrival'. Thing was so smart it could even estimate the amount of fuel the whole journey would use.

As far as Robbie was concerned that's all he needed to know. So long as he could operate the onboard computer plotter then it would tell him not only where these mysterious lat-long numbers were located, but also exactly how to get there.

Of course, he would also have to know *when* the pot, the rope and the lime green buoy was going to be dropped at the location of the lat-long co-ordinates.

The Polish man had insisted on counting all the money in the envelope Robbie had given him. He had done it under the table, but not very discreetly. The waiter and the waitress, both in Thai traditional dress, had noticed the man in the very new-looking tweed checked blazer and pronounced widow's peak counting a stack of 50 pound notes out of an envelope and laying them one at a time on his thigh.

Robbie was a bit surprised at the man's lack of concern. He assumed someone in his line of business would be more discreet, take precautions and not want to be seen counting 25 grand in cash in public. Might at least go to the toilet to do it.

Robbie told himself to relax. The guy knew what he was doing. He did this all the time. Robbie is the new guy here. The guy bought and sold quantities of all sorts of things. He had connections to buy stuff. He had connections to sell stuff. What he lacked most specifically, in this instance, was a partner with half the capital and more importantly with access to a sea-going vessel and the wherewithal to reach a certain designated marine location, at a certain designated time, or at least, within a certain time window.

"Thursday," the Polish guy said, as he tapped the sheet of A4 with one finger that had an uncomfortably long pointed fingernail. "Wednesday night drop. Thursday pick up."

"Thursday it is," said Robbie confidently as he peered one last time at the meaningless numbers on the ocean of white paper, before folding it into three, lengthways, and slipping it into his inside right breast pocket.

Robbie had no burning ambition to be a drug smuggler, or importer or dealer. He did need to turn over some cash though. Elsa, God love her, was an expensive habit and he had no intention of making savings or efficiencies where she was concerned. He never wanted to say 'no' to Elsa. Only yes. Trying to do Elsa on the cheap would not be doing her justice. Whatever she wanted or desired, within reason, Robbie would provide. He wanted her to think of him as generous, big hearted, fun-loving and sweet.

In Robbie's varied lines of work, he'd met very many very wealthy men, and consequently seen some of the most appalling and unattractive vinegar-soaked meanness. Too much money made too many men into poisonous penny-pinching scrooges, who could see no further than investment-versus-return. Robbie didn't care how flash and how crass and stupid he looked – splashing his cash around like a Pools winner – he just didn't want to ever look mean.

Robbie never intended to become a drug smuggler or runner, but Elsa's Polish friend needed an equal share investment partner who could handle, and preferably who also owned, a boat. One fast enough and seaworthy enough to pick up drops made in the English Channel by a Dutch freighter. One that made regular runs from Zeebrugge to Milford Haven and Cork, carrying fishmeal on the outward bound and live mussels on the inbound.

Elsa's Polish friend, Lech, would set up the transaction, and pay the supplier – half with his money and half with Robbie's. The drop would be arranged, the collection then actioned by Robbie. Lech would take delivery of the dope as soon as it hit soil, and sell it on, in one single sale to his London connection.

After which, Robbie and the Pole would split the profit. They would, he was guaranteed, double their investment at least, on every transaction. The selling was to be kept simple: one sale, one customer, in order to minimise the length of time the dope was held. Bigger profits could be made by multiple sales, but Lech, was all about speed and simplicity. "Clean and quick," he said. "Clean and quick."

It wasn't until Robbie's maroon Arvor was lowered into the water by a huge fork-lift truck that zoomed backwards and forwards across the dock at Blue Haven marina, taking rich men's playthings from the enormous storage racks to the slip way, that Robbie fully realised the significance of the numbers.

As his two-litre VW marine inboard engine warmed up at 1000 rpm, Robbie switched on all the electronics and punched the lat-long numbers from the A4 sheet into the NavMan. And sure enough, when he stabbed the right buttons in the right sequence, it did give him a 'Distance to Waypoint' reading. At first Robbie assumed he'd made an error. Typed a wrong number. It told him there was a total of 39.6 miles between his current location and the selected destination. He read the lat-long figures again. Everything checked out. Fuck a duck. Robbie didn't think it was possible to travel 39 miles south out of Poole Harbour, without ending up practically in Paris. Dover to Calais is only 20 miles for fuck's sake!

So, he looked at the chart on the screen. Zoomed out so he could see where it was he was supposed to be heading. And sure enough, it was right out around the corner past Old Harry's Rock and way, way down south nearly to Jersey. Fuck.

Twice 39 is 78 miles, plus the two point sixes, that make 80 miles minimum. Plus add another ten percent for bad steering and searching around a bit when he got there. That's the best part of a hundred miles. Jesus. Did his boat even have a fuel tank big enough to travel over a hundred miles of sea? He looked at the handbook and as far as he could work out, the answer was no. So he'd have to fill the tank *and* go and buy some carry-on Jerry cans and fill them up too, and just hope to Christ he didn't run out of fuel half way out in the middle of the English Channel with a load of illegal drugs on board.

He'd thought, when the Polish guy said it'd be dropped in a crab pot, that the run to go get it would be a couple of miles, maybe five tops. What he hadn't thought was he'd be ploughing through a hundred miles of a rough and choppy sea.

When he looked at the electronic chart again and at the blinking point where the cursor indicated the precise location of the lat-long numbers, he now noticed two parallel lines running an inch apart all the way down through the centre of the Channel, and then turning a sharp left, when they got just past Dover. The selected destination was just south of the centre of these parallel lines.

Robbie stared at the lines a full 30 seconds before the penny dropped. Shipping lanes! The space between the two lines is the shipping lanes. On the electronic chart, a faint dashed line running down the middle of the lane marked the central reservation. The Shipping Traffic Separation Scheme. Like a motorway. The freighters and tankers and container ships heading west, were kept in the south lane while the ones heading east were up in the north lane.

The flashing destination dot was right in the middle of the south lane. Now, it made sense. A freighter from Holland heading west down the Channel, would have to travel in the south lane, and that's why the drop was where it was. Fucking Jesus wept, thought Robbie. He was expected to cross right through the centre of the busiest shipping lane in the world, dodging in between tankers that were hundreds of yards long in a little maroon play-boat that'd hardly been further than the harbour mouth.

This is a suicide mission. Right this minute, staring at the chart, feeling his sphincter crimp with fear, Robbie would've happily paid 25 grand *not* to have to go. But, this wasn't just *his* dope floating under a buoy way out in the Channel. It was Lech's dope too. And Lech was definitely counting on Robbie coming back with it. In fact he'd probably be somewhat pissed off if Robbie didn't.

Of course Robbie didn't come back with it. And that is why Lech was now helping himself to one of the most expensive cars on Robbie's inventory. Trouble was, of course, it was Robbie's inventory but *not* Robbie's car. The car was stock, for which he'd borrowed capital from the bank. And Robbie had since borrowed cash on his credit cards and from a private loan firm, to pay the interest he owed the bank. Interest on the red 'Vette – and the Maserati, and the Aston Martin. On all the cars, in fact. None of them were really his. If he sold all of them today – which was never going to happen – even if he sold them at his list price, he'd *still* owe money to the bank and to the private loan people.

Robbie never came back with the green buoy attached to the rope, attached to the crab pot, which was full of black hash, because Robbie couldn't find it. He thinks he found the spot, though he can't be sure. He was so physically sick by the time he reached the position of the lat-long numbers, his hands were shaking so hard, and he was practically hallucinating from being so dehydrated, on account of the almost continual vomiting taking place during the five-and-a-half most miserable hours of his entire life.

When he got there, Robbie could barely focus on the plotter. It had an alarm, that sounded as he reached the destination, but he found nothing. He stared at the sea. He even climbed on the roof, clutching onto both rails until his knuckles went white and looked all around the boat as far as he could see. And all he could see was big black waves and tankers the size of small industrial towns bearing down on him like they were the Death Star and he was a fucking canoe.

That day he decided to sell the boat and never set foot on any vessel that wasn't big enough to have its own dance floor, spa and casino – ever again.

Even though Robbie was pretty sure the Polish guy believed his story about heading into the centre of the shipping lanes looking for a needle in a fucking haystack, there was a principle to be settled – a principle of trust and partnership.

Which is why Lech was taking the 'Vette.

Robbie pointed the bread knife at him. Over the Polish guy's shoulder Robbie could see another guy unbolting the showroom doors. They concertinaed as they opened, folding back on each other, as they ran on a steel track. They were sticking because they hadn't been used much in the last couple of months, because Robbie hadn't sold any cars, or even given any test drives, because he'd been too busy shopping with Elsa, sleeping with Elsa, eating with Elsa, getting high with Elsa, driving Elsa to rehab, visiting Elsa *in* rehab, driving a tiny boat across a huge ugly ocean, or lying in his crib sweating like a pig with the mumps.

The other guy was probably Polish too, because he said something to Lech in a language which Robbie couldn't understand. He thought it was probably something about the bread knife, because they both looked at it at the same time.

Lech didn't say anything directly to Robbie. He just opened the door to the red Corvette, revved a couple of blips on the throttle, making the engine stutter with that classic Chevy gurgle, before slipping it into drive and easing it out onto the forecourt. He stopped to let the other guy get in and then he drove away, brake lights blinking, as he reached the junction, leaving a white muslin square on the shiny floor and a big hole in Robbie's inventory.

Robbie stood there wondering a moment, why Lech took the 'Vette. Sure it was a great example, stunning calf-skin leather, but the Aston Martin was worth way more money. Then it dawned on Robbie, they took the Chevy because it was nearest the door, the easiest to drive away, and the most practical one to remove, if you intended to empty the showroom one car at a time.

What is it about boats? Tug had never been able to see the fascination. He'd grown up amongst boats. At school other boys' dads had boats, worked on boats, helped man lifeboats, built boats, delivered boats, even drove cranes that lifted boats – in and out the water. Tug didn't do boats.

Kids at school had dinghies or rowboats or kayaks and stuff, so Tug was unique by *not* doing boats, not liking boats and dissing the kids who did. It didn't make Tug popular exactly, but then he didn't want to be popular, Tug wanted to be different.

Far as Tug could see boats were just a lot of grief. Take this morning, it wasn't even 7 am and already boats were messing up his hair. Tug had planned to go to the gym before work. Do some free weights. Do some treadmill. Maybe do 15 minutes on the cross-trainer. Hit the shower and do his hair. They had proper heavy duty hair dryers in the changing rooms, perfect for getting it just how he liked it, before work.

Only his phone rang on the way to the gym. It was one of the skippers at the harbour, 'Leaky' Caines, a cousin on his mother's side. Leaky was a top bloke; they played a lot of footie together when they were teenagers. Anyway, Leaky called because he thought Tug should know all the police tape had been ripped off the ropes of the Kitty K. He'd seen it when he was loading fish boxes off the back of his van and he knew Tug's chaps had spent hours sealing it all up yesterday. Leaky wasn't sure, but it looked to him that the seal they'd wired to the wheelhouse door was off too. Leaky reckoned Tug should come and have a look. Thought it might be important.

Tug himself wasn't too fussed. Though he knew his boss would shit a bunch of kittens if he thought a possible crime scene had been contaminated, before the crime scene lads had finished with it. Tug wasn't too fussed, because *he* didn't really think any crime had been committed. Just another stupid tragic accident. And in Tug's opinion the teenager in question was a pain in the arse. So the tragedy might not be all that tragic after all.

Seemed to Tug that if the little shit-bag fell off the roof while the boat was steaming along, then he was kind of asking for it. And yeah, of course Tug could see how the boat might probably not be fully insured and how there might be some sort of compensation claim down the line. None of which was his business. But, taking into account how windy his boss could get about inadmissible or contaminated evidence, Tug reckoned Leaky was right and he should get himself down to the Kitty K, to see what's occurring.

Which was a pisser, because when he left his flat he didn't do his hair, because he was intending to do it at the gym. Only now he doesn't have time to go to the gym because he ought to suss out the Kitty before his boss gets a whiff, which means going straight to the harbour. He could always stop in a lay-by and put a bit of gel on his hair. He's got it in his gym bag. Could do it in the rear view mirror. Wouldn't have a drier of course. Although he could put the car heater on max and point the air vents towards his head.

Tug pulled up in the lay-by by the Radipole reed beds half a mile away from the harbour and was just reaching into the rear seat to grab his Adidas bag when his mobile rang again. This time the ID said it was Sara Chin's mobile calling.

Still barely 6 am in the morning. What was she calling him about? Really, Tug should've guessed: boats. More fucking grief with boats.

"You read the night duty log?" she says. Not big on small talk. Jesus, thinks Tug, all he wants is to put some product in his hair, but everyone else seems to think he should be doing something else.

"Aah … no," he says. Slowly. Sure, he might have a quick scan at the night duty log some time during the day, see if any of the names or places that crop up, chime with any of his ongoing investigations. But he sure as shit wasn't in a hurry to read it before he'd even done the morning essentials.

"Boat was broken into in Blue Haven Marina…" she says. Like it was news. "Last night. Security guard rang it in. Wants someone to come and check it out. Give him a crime number."

"I'm sure he does," says Tug. "Not exactly high on my list of things to do today, though."

"Oh."

"No."

"We got other boat grief on the Kitty K. One the lad died on–"

"I know what the Kitty K is," she says. Tug thinking he could hear a note of 'snotty' in her voice, now, like she didn't like him reminding her of something she already knew.

"Just that the owner's name jumped out at me," she says.

"Yeah?"

"Robbie Rock," she says. "The guy with the headless cat and the broken window …" Chin says. Her voice going up at the end, like she was asking a question. Like she's saying to Tug, 'You remember who *that* is?' Like she's having a dig right back.

"Showroom broken into. Cat decapitated. Now his boat's been broken into," she says, one at a time, like she's making a shopping list. "Think we should go back and say hello?"

Tug did. Definitely. But after they've seen the Kitty. And after he's done his hair.

Matty is sitting on Rich's head. Sitting right on top of it. Crushing it sideways between his arse and the filthy truck seat. Wasn't any other way he could think of to keep Rich quiet and still. And to be fair, he isn't achieving either of those. Matty and Rich are both covered in slime and weed and stink from the crab pot. There'd been a Morrisons shopping trolley caught up in the fight too. On the pier. The trolley coated in green weed and black sediment from the harbour mouth. The sediment black from all the gearbox oil that's leaked out from the knackered crabbing boats and congealed on the seabed inside the harbour, where the current goes slack.

Matty guessing Rich must've hooked out the trolley by accident before he got his grapple into the pot. Asking himself how the fuck the scrawny little bastard knew the pot was there?

Matty shifting his weight, his two buttocks now spread evenly across the side of Rich's face. Right across his jaw. Must hurt like a bastard. Must be stopping the air getting in his face and down to his lungs. Still he's bucking and twisting like a conger on a gaff hook. Matty's own head crushed now against the roof of the truck every time Rich arches up his shoulders.

Adrian shouting at Rich now to shut the fuck up. Worst thing for Adrian is he doesn't know *where* he's driving. Plan's all messed up. It needs to be somewhere he can think. There's green slime on his hands and now it's all over the steering wheel. Green slime splattered down the inside of the door and the windscreen's misted up from the heat of the three men's adrenalin-spiked bodies warming up the stinking damp slime.

Now as they drive past the Radipole reed beds, Adrian considers stopping. Just pulling up to the kerb, opening the windows, cranking up the demister, and help Matty get Rich under control. Maybe crack him a good one in the solar plexus, shut him up until they get out of town.

Adrian can feel Matty's knees jabbing into his back through the seat, as Rich bucks again and Matty has to shift his weight, to subdue him. So, Adrian decides to pull over. It won't take a minute to get themselves sorted. Be worth it. They need to. What with Matty now needing to push his hands against the roof of the truck just to get some downward thrust, on top of Rich's head.

Adrian slowing down, hand on the indicator, when he sees a car parked on the other side of the road, next to the reed beds. Car pulled up in the lay-by, a guy inside it, fiddling with his hair.

Matty lunges down hard on Rich's head, trying to squeeze the fight out of the fucking scrawny ferret, just when Adrian's eyes meet the eyes of the hair gel cop. Fuck. Just sitting there in his car.

Tug now turning his head away from the mirror, watching the blue dirty Nissan Navarra drive past. Windows all steamy. Tug can see the big brother at the wheel and the slippery one, Matty, sitting in the back, like he's got himself a chauffeur. What's weird is he's kind of bouncing too, like some toddler, on his way to a birthday party.

Something's going on, thinks Tug as he checks his watch, and then his hair.

Max the Sikh sits in the back office of his Bristol Cash Converter transferring a digital video file from the hard drive of his CCTV computer onto a DVD disc. There were three chunks of footage he needed to transfer, so he gave them each separate file names: *'Entrance', 'Kelvin & Friend', 'Friend Offer'*.

Max really loves the techie part of his job. Many of the other guys don't, but when technology functions well, is beautifully designed and reliably efficient, it practically makes Max moist. His iPhone 6S makes him moist. He loves it. He doesn't think it's that much better than the iPhone 6. The 'S' part, the voice-activated command thing, feels like a bit of a dead-end to Max. Sure it's clever, but intrinsically wrong as far as Max is concerned. He doesn't want to be able to talk to his computers. He likes the silent interface. Just the clean sharp clicks of the keys on his keyboard. Talking to computers feels like some sci-fi hangover from *Star Trek*, where the crew of a spacecraft chat to the onboard computer like it's another crew member. None of that bakes his cake. Max doesn't want to verbally interact with his computers, he wants to control them with his long, slim, neatly-manicured fingers.

The voice-activated microphones in his BMW are a different thing entirely. Voice-activation for the purposes of recording makes perfect sense. If you're covertly recording a conversation, you *definitely* want the machine to know how to switch itself on. And, the team who fitted the surveillance kit to Max's car, at the tech-base in Farnborough, did a bang-up job. Not only are the mics voice-activated so they start recording soon as there's a conversation in the vehicle, there's also a back-up manual switch too. On Max's key

**224**

fob, there's a little red LED light on one side; looks like it all part of the central locking system, but actually it indicates when the four hidden mics are recording.

Max the Sikh has already downloaded the entire BMW conversation – with the man who identified himself as 'Matt' and says he was from Weymouth – onto an MP3 file. This file is also being copied onto the same disc.

Max labelled it in a separate file as *'Possible Purchase Conversation'* and sent it to his handler as an email attachment as well. All this copying is just belt and braces stuff. Max has done undercover work for over five years and he's seen far too many convictions go tits up or melt away because evidence had been wrongly obtained or badly collated and catalogued.

Max's handler, like Max, is a stickler for accuracy and detail. He leaves nothing to chance. The reason Max's career as an undercover police officer had been so successful and led to such a long list of solid convictions had nothing really to do with having big balls and a brass neck. It's all about knowing how to use the technology correctly, and also logging evidence clearly. Sometimes his job was more like being an accountant than a cop.

The Bristol Cash Converter was the third 'Red Herring' shop Max had run in his career as a UC. Red Herring shops being a very basic, but very effective first line of offence for gathering intelligence on the criminal community of a given area.

An old style pawnshop or a Cash Converter would be taken over, or sometimes a new one opened up, in an area known to be experiencing a volume of burglaries, home invasions, car thefts and car crimes. Normally, they had to be sanctioned by the local Borough Commander, but most of the time if the Commander was in charge of an area that was experiencing high levels of house and street crime, then he'd already be getting it in the neck from residents' associations and Neighbourhood Watch schemes.

If the rates of crime were on the increase, then the Commander would also have his local MP and the local Board of Commerce and the Rotarians giving him a hard time too. Chances are he'd be more than delighted to sanction a Red Herring shop and would even find money in his budget to help with the rent, and tech costs.

Red Herring shops had proven time and time again to be useful tools in controlling certain types of crime and criminals, if they were manned and operated properly. On a very simple operational level, Red Herring shops worked by providing a premises where it became known that you could unload a bit of knock-off gear. A Cash Converter that didn't ask too many questions, was reasonably lax about proof of ID and that paid just about the going rate for stolen goods, would soon see a steady trickle of sellers beating a path to its door.

Obviously junkies and crack-heads and cat burglars and creepers (who steal from offices and gyms) would be regular visitors. They need to convert the smaller items they've nicked into quick cash. Good backroom police work could match individuals to crimes, could establish patterns and geography and habits.

The real trick with Red Herring shops was to keep the shop and any consequent convictions very remote from each other. Good handlers and backroom officers would use the intelligence to discover who was doing what, where and when, in order to set up a series of arrests, further down the line. Well away from the shop or unconnected to any recently pawned and stolen item. Putting distance between the source of the intelligence and the conviction is known in the trade as 'dry cleaning'.

Sometimes the items, although they're nicked and therefore pertinent to a specific crime, weren't of any real police interest. Sometimes it was simply the person bringing them in who was interesting. Not interesting to nick and convict and put away, but to 'turn'. To manipulate into becoming a 'criminal informant', also known as a 'Chiz', or Criminal Human Intelligence Subject.

To have a lot of evidence on someone who's at the centre of criminal activity and in turn knows a lot of other criminals can be wonderfully fertile. Once faced with the cold hard evidence against them, and reminded just how long they could be banged up for, it's amazing how many colleagues a criminal will shop or entrap, in order to save his own skin.

As a rule Max doesn't get involved in any activity outside the running of the shop and making sure that all transactions and ensuing conversations have been perfectly documented from as many angles as possible. Any of the intelligence he gathers, or faces and names he can put in the frame, are the currency of his handler and other UC field officers who follow up and put together the game plan of manipulation or arrest.

Occasionally oddities walk into his shop; people asking for other people, bad guys trying to find other bad guys. Men asking about where to buy guns, explosives, slaves and recently a Pakistani guy asking if Max knew anyone who could kill his wife for a price.

All these exchanges were passed down the line. Like the man from Weymouth, with the very unusual but very good quality hash. Of course Max would initially talk up a deal, and exchange contact numbers, but he'd then pass it over to his handler and hope it was a ball someone else could run with. Max the Sikh being happiest when he was in the shop and working with the technology.

He was neither called Max, nor was he a Sikh.

Didn't take Tug long to decide he really needs to talk to the brothers. The crime scene officers with elasticated bags over their shoes were tut-tutting about the state of the Kitty K. One of them holding the broken tamper-proof police issue seal in one gloved hand while another held an evidence bag open for him to lower it into. Taking it away to dust for prints.

One of the other CSOs was looking away from the harbour, downstream towards the sea, talking quickly and quietly and seriously on his mobile.

Tug would love to know who was on the other end, and if the conversation they were having was going to sink him any deeper into the shit than he already was. The Kitty K being his responsibility. At least that's what his boss was going to say, as he himself carefully dodged any out-pouring of shit, to keep his own neck lily-white and free from stain. Shit-dodging being an art practised by the higher ranks. An art that goes hand-in-hand with shit-dumping. Something that was about to occur in Tug's vicinity very, very soon, unless he could find some answers to do some super-slick arse-covering of his own.

When he told Chin he saw the brothers driving away from the harbour in their truck at sparrow's fart, and how big brother was driving and Matty was sat in the back, bouncing, she just looked at him, with that blank stare. No movement of her mouth. Eyes, unblinking, like she was looking at something she didn't quite comprehend, or dealing with a retard.

She was hot. And she was cool. And she looked very cute in a stab vest. But she was beginning to piss him off a chunk too. Today was not officially Tug's Fault Day. He needed to make that absolutely clear. To everyone.

The post-mortem on dead Tim was to be carried out this morning by Tony 'Eyebrows', the Coroner from Dorchester. It was starting at 9 am. In the mortuary in Weymouth General, and Tug would really like to take Chin along. Like to show her how cool and at ease he was around mortuary assistants cutting skulls open with surgical angle-grinders and stuff.

Tug had never minded post-mortems. He'd seen plenty of detective level officers chuck their ring, or even faint, at a PM. Especially, on drowned victims, or burned ones. Burned ones were the worst – everyone said so – because of the smell. Tug didn't mind the smell, didn't mind the sights either; like when they peel the face up and curl it back from the skull. He didn't even mind the bone-sawing noise that makes some of the detective guys stick fingers in their ears and turn away. None of it made any impression on Tug whatsoever. He didn't know why. They're dead. No one is in pain. No one is suffering. To be honest he's felt worse standing in a butcher's shop watching a big fat butcher saw through loin chops. Knowing that's something you're going to eat – *that* made him feel weird. But dead bodies? Nope. He could watch them being sawn up all day long.

He wondered about Chin. She didn't strike him as the squeamish type. The headless cat hadn't freaked her one bit. But a cat is a cat. A dead body is a whole different kettle.

He quite liked the idea of taking her to the PM. Let her see how funny he was with Tony 'Eyebrows'. Tony's favourite game, trying to freak people out with his latest tales of amazing and disgusting deaths he's attended, or knows a guy, who knows a guy, who attended. Tony being a kind of collector of truly sick death stories. Old ladies who died and had their face chewed off by their cats. Roofers who impaled themselves on railings. And celebrity deaths. Tony always had some little professional coroner-nugget to share about the celebs who'd died. Michael Jackson, Whitney, Amy Winehouse, some little detail didn't never get in the papers. Something only coroners know. Didn't really matter if it was true to not, Tug just loved it.

And most of all, Tug really wanted to do something to take that humouring-a-retard look off Chin's face. Something clever. Clever *police work* would probably be best though.

He's already been on the phone to Adrian's home number. He badly wanted to talk to the brothers and also talk in person to Adrian's wife. Tug remembering her from when she used to work in the Sea Life Centre, helping with dolphins, feeding them and stuff. Wearing a swimsuit all day on account of getting wet with the dolphins splashing. A swimsuit with the naff Sea Life logo on the front. Great tits though.

So Adrian's wife, Helen, said Adrian got a call from Dougie on the Nicola B at like four-thirty in the morning, or might've been five. Dougie having trouble firing up the Nicola B, and maybe being a deckhand down, so Adrian saying he might crew for Dougie. And as she's not heard anything since, she assumes that's where he is.

And so Tug's calling the Harbour Master, the slobby drunken twat that he is, and getting Dougie's mobile number. Then Tug calls Dougie who's way out somewhere 15 miles south of the Bill, the phone signal as crap as anything, and only able to catch about every third word or so. All the same, Tug making out from these one in three, that Dougie doesn't know anything about Adrian, or Matty. And the Nicola B is running like a wet dream in Wonderland since Dougie fitted a pair of reconditioned Volvo Pentas two months ago.

So really, as far as Tug is concerned, he's already doing good police work. And let's face it, what is Chin doing that's so brilliant? Except standing on the deck of the Kitty K, getting in the way of the CSOs.

"What time's the Coroner start?" she asks Tug.

"Nine. Supposed to be. More like nine-thirty by the time he's got his cinnamon Danish and dug out the angle grinder."

"Does that come off?" she asks one of the CSOs, pointing at the Kitty K's hauling jib.

"Two bolts on the side," says the guy in the white paper romper suit and shoe covers.

"That's what he's supposed to have hit his head on?" asks Chin. The CSO nods. "Let's take it to the Coroner," says Chin to Tug. "Show it to him. Get him to match it to the skull wound."

Tug nods. Not showing any expression. But inside, in his head, he's shouting, "Aw fuck! Why didn't *I* think of that?!"

"Yeah. Uh huh... Might as well... I guess," he says evenly. "Cross the I's. Dot the T's."

As boys they'd both had their own veg patch. They could choose seeds from the packets in the shed and they could have all the manure or compost they wanted too. Both held in plywood clamps at the bottom of the plot. The manure needed digging in. So did the compost. So it was no good just barrowing over a big pile of the stuff to plop on a patch, like Matty did one year. His dad giving him the fork, the one with one broken tine, and telling him to fork it in, until it was all evenly mixed. Every time Matty stopped, his dad telling him it wasn't enough. Telling him that if the manure was left in big clumps it would 'burn' the seedlings. And, that the compost was too wet, so it needed to be dried by mixing it well with the topsoil.

Matty got blisters on his hands from all the digging with the crappy fork. Put him off gardening for good. Matty didn't even bother to choose any seeds to sow that year. Even though he'd actually done what dad said, and dug his whole bed over and over, until the soil and the compost and rotted-down horseshit was all blended together in equal measures.

Way Adrian saw it, by Matty not sowing one single seed into the now perfectly prepared veg bed he was sticking two dirty fingers up to his dad. Saying, you can make me dig it, but you can't make me plant it.

After a couple of weeks dad saying if Matty didn't want to pick some seeds to plant, then dad would pick them, and *he'd* plant the patch out instead. Sort of like a threat, bit of an arm-twist, kind of little blackmail-move to make Matty finish the job. Didn't work. Matty just shrugged, like he could give a shit. Dad's lip curling. Getting riled. But keeping control of his temper. Not wanting to make it a big issue. Not wanting to put Matty off.

He did though. With the crappy fork and the blisters and the pedantry. So Matty planted nothing. Dad planted nothing. The weeds took over, until about six weeks later Matty's veg patch was like a bit of crazy wilderness in an otherwise perfectly-tended allotment.

Adrian picked his seeds. Grew his vegetables. His mum and dad making a big fuss at Sunday lunch when they were roasting his parsnips or covering his leeks in white sauce. Matty not looking or caring what vegetables they were eating. For two or three years Adrian continued cultivating his veg patch and being the good vegetable-producing son, until it felt like the point had been made, and he too left his patch of the allotment to run wild and ragged. Their dad never using those plots again, even though he kept on running the allotment until the day he died. Like those plots, those squares that he'd given to his sons and that they'd abandoned, were somehow dead to him.

If they weren't good enough for his boys to care about and to tend, then he wasn't going to tend them either. Even though the seeds and weeds that grew up on them spilled over into the good ground, he never touched them again.

When he died, the whole allotment quickly began to turn to wasteland. Adrian and Matty still used the shed. They ripped out the shelving and the trays where he used to germinate seeds, and filled the space with crab pots and anchors, ropes and buoys, nets and traps, outboard engines and a spare hauling winch they salvaged off a decommissioned Portland crabber. It was a big shed. The biggest of all the sheds on the allotment site, perched on the southern edge of Portland Bill, overlooking the sea.

Neither Adrian nor Matty ever grew another thing in the soil after their dad died. But three years ago, when she was pregnant with Josh, Helen suddenly got the veg garden bug. She watched the hairy specky guy on TV, who grew all sorts of things to cook. She bought books. Visited garden centres. Started talking to some of the old boys who had allotments to the east of dad's. An old man who had neat rows of beans growing round hazel sticks with empty Lucozade

233

bottles stuck on the end of the sticks, and strings of ripped-up plastic bags, like bunting, hung between rows of tiny seedlings.

Gradually, Helen had reclaimed some of the huge allotment in fits and starts, but she never bothered with the shed. It was too full of fishing gear and too much of a mess.

Now Rich Tovey is lying in the middle of the shed's brown lino floor. Curled up like a cooked prawn, because Matty has tied his feet together. And tied his hands together. And then tied his feet to his hands. One stinking wet green-slimed trainer is on, the other foot bare. Matty having taken the trainer off to remove Rich's sock. One of those low-cut trainer socks with a black tick above the heel, which is now stuffed in Rich's mouth, with a length of boat rag wound round his jaw and neck and passed between his teeth, to keep the sock at the back of his tongue, stop him spitting it out.

Matty wanted to put a sack on his head too. Adrian said no. Rich's eyes huge and bulging, one of them all bloodshot and red from where Matty sat on his face for so long. Rich still growling in his throat. Fighting the ropes. Adrian the other side of the floor now, down on his haunches rocking backwards and forwards from his heels to his toes, looking like some kind of crazed Muslim praying in a mosque.

Matty talking, talking, talking. Saying what they need to do with the dope. With the pot. With the truck. With Rich. With the guy from Bristol. The Sikh who wants to buy a kilo. Who is going to ring and come and give Matty money. Or this other man is going to come instead. Man who works for Max. Probably another Sikh. Matty again now talking about Rich. Saying what it is they've got to do.

Adrian rocking. Covering his ears. Trying to get a thought clear in his head. An idea. A sniff of sense. Clarity. Anything that points to a way out of all this fucking mess.

Tug is not so happy about having to drive his car across town with the boot wide open, lid sticking up in the air. The right angle of the Kitty K's hauling jib sticking out. A great square section of steel pipe, now all wrapped in bubble wrap and bagged and sealed in two huge evidence bags. Neither big enough to fit it all in, so one on each end, joined in the middle. The crime scene guys more than happy for him and Chin to take it away, because it hadn't been swabbed on the day of the accident. This being a major fuck up on the CS team's part. And now that the original CS 'Do Not Cross' tapes and seals have been broken, there's officially no point in swabbing it. Because any evidence, even DNA, would be deemed to have been potentially contaminated, and therefore of no practical use. So they were happy for the Coroner to try and match its profile against the head wound. Least it would be of some use, confirming likely cause of death and being one less item for them to worry about.

Tug is moaning about the size and the weight and the grief of the jib. But really it's because he's bummed out that bringing it along had been Chin's idea and not his. His moaning getting cut off mid-sentence, when Chin takes a call on her mobile. And, it's a bit of a cryptic one. Sounding to Tug like it was her old boss or something. Her calling him 'Sir' on the phone.

Even worse, when they get to Weymouth Hospital, Tug backs the car all the way up to the entrance to the morgue, where the meat wagons come to deliver the stiffs. Backed right up to the loading dock so that he and Chin and hopefully the mortuary assistant – a really great girl called Viv, who used to work nights as a paramedic but gave it up to become a mortuary assistant – would all together lift the jib out the back of the car. Only when Viv opens the electric shutter to the loading dock, it clattering up with a whining noise, she tells Tug the post-mortem's been postponed. Won't happen until 11 am now, probably nearer noon. All because the Health and Safety Executive have been in touch, to say they're sending down two of their representatives from head office in London, to observe and report.

"Fuck," says Tug. Seeing this turning into a whole new brand of agony.

The fact that, after never even mentioning driving the detective pool car all the three weeks they've worked together, Chin chooses this very moment to say *she* wants to drive, is bound to bunch up Tug's panties. And to top that, now she's saying she wants to drive them to Poole Harbour and back, just to check out the thing about Robbie Rock having a boat, and it getting broke into last night. But in truth, these annoyances pale into insignificance compared to the newsflash that the Health and Safety Executive want to stick their oar in this business about the Kitty K.

It's actually a good job Chin's driving, because it means Tug can wave his hands about, a lot. He slaps the back of one of them into the dashboard several times, to punctuate and emphasise just how monumentally fucked up this is fast becoming.

He says, "Sea Fish Authority is responsible for providing licences and certificates of competency to skippers and crew, right?" She nods. "The Maritime and Coastguard Agency are responsible for licensing the boats and making sure they carry the right safety gear: life jackets, flares, life-rafts and shit. Yeah?" She shrugs and raises an eyebrow. Cute little arched thing. "Neither of them wants a licensed boat or skipper to be charged or convicted for not behaving properly, in the event of an accident. Or heaven-forbid, not carrying the right safety gear. Because that looks very bad for the sea fishing industry. And the sea fishing industry is already a political trapped fart."

Tug is clenching his jaw as he rants. Chin glancing at him out the corner of her eye as she takes the big dual carriageway out of Weymouth, the one they built for the Olympics. "So, the Sea Fish

Authority calls in the Health and Safety Executive, who just happen to be the biggest bunch of clipboard-carrying red tape-loving wankers on Planet Earth."

Tug saying Health and Safety have been sicked on the case to help prove there wasn't an accident. To suggest that instead there was foul play or criminal neglect. Criminal neglect being best for the H and S. Because that way it turns it into a crime and not an accident.

"H and S'll be as happy as pigs in shit if they can make this into a 'crime'." Tug finding himself making quote marks round the word, with two fingers on each hand – which is something he'd seen, but never knowingly done himself before. And, he kind of likes it. "A crime, for which *we* will then have a crime number, a statistic and a boss breathing down *our* necks, to solve." Tug is on a roll now. He can't stop. "A crime that might not even have a *name*. Or a suspect. But will be *our* crime, to put to bed. It'll be *our* problem, not theirs. All because the Health and fucking Safety Executive climbed up the gantry, pulled down their budgie-smugglers and took a dump on us."

By the time he's completely finished ranting about the ramifications of the whole Kitty K death thing, they're driving along the long thin causeway that leads onto Sandbanks. Poole Harbour on one side, breathtakingly expensive real estate on the other. As they turn off into Robbie's road, a steel blue Aston Martin DB4 drives past them, with two men in the front seats, one of them in a checked tweed jacket and big widow's peak growing on his forehead.

Both Chin and Tug recognising the car from Robbie's showroom. Robbie must've sold a car, thinks Tug. Maybe things are looking up for the economy at last.

When they pull up outside the showroom, the concertina glass door is wide open, and now there's gaps where yesterday there were cars. Three gaps? Is Robbie doing a sneaky runner, thinks Tug. Is he liquidating stock, preparing to suddenly disappear? Funny, because just yesterday he didn't look like he could even walk to the posh little off-license on the corner and back without having a coronary.

"We *have* to do it," says Matty. His hand moving, touching stuff in the shed. Things leaning against the wall. A broken oar. A spade. The sledge hammer dad used to knock in the posts of the fruit cage, which is now just posts and ripped netting and weeds. The fork with the broken tine. Matty picking it up now, looking at it like he's remembering that pile of dark clotted horseshit. Feeling the blisters again. His wandering hand touching stuff, like he's searching for the right thing to do it with.

"We can't," says Adrian, his voice sounding weak.

"We *got* to."

"No."

"Think we can just untie him? Say 'All right Richie, mate let's call it quits now'?"

Adrian crouching again. Feeling his heels on the back of his buttocks. Hunching his shoulders. There's something about wanting to curl up small, make himself into a tiny ball that feels instinctive in this situation.

"He doesn't even know what's in the pot," Adrian hisses, like he's half-trying to avoid Rich overhearing them. Which is ridiculous. Rich lying only feet away from them. Eyes bulging open, following their every move. Air sucking in and out around the sock, fast, like he's panting.

"He's a stupid prick. But he's not that stupid," says Matty. "He knows where we dumped the pot. Fuck knows how. He seen it's rammed full of something. He knows we jumped him cause he had the pot. Chucked him in the truck. Sat on his head. Cause he had the pot. He fucking knows *something* about that pot is worth having."

"But, he doesn't know *what*," repeats Adrian, like it matters. "What if," he says, like he's just thought of something profound, "What if we just let him go?" Even as he's saying it, he knows that is the one thing they're never going to do.

There's no such thing as a big male pike. Big pike are female. Every pike over 30 pounds is female. Fish as long as a greyhound and as vicious as a sociopathic stoat, are always female. Male pike don't ever grow big.

Female pike are the future. The carriers of generations. Female pike make pike eggs. They carry the seedpods of pike to come. For 62 million years pike have survived where other fish have failed. From Alaska to Alicante pike have endured meteor strikes, earthquakes, ice ages and glacial melts

Dinosaurs came and went. Humans evolved. The planet froze and thawed, froze and thawed, the seas rose and fell, land erupted and dissolved. Plates shifted. Volcanoes erupted and still pike prevailed. All because of females. Big fat females.

One big fecund female can carry a couple of million eggs. Enough to repopulate even the most devastated stock in one dump. Just one fat female with her precious cargo of eggs can pull the entire pike population back from the brink of collapse. One fat female pike is a living, breathing, floating mother ship. A mother lode of potential pike procreation.

As she lays down her stringy sticky threads of ripe pike eggs that cling like Nature's Velcro to weeds and fronds, all she needs to finish her epic work is a little squirt of semen. Some pike sperm to mix with and mingle and fertilise her eggs.

Pike milt. Thin and milky, washing amongst her eggs, the tiny spermatozoa piercing the thick membranes of her ovaries' crop. But one male's sperm, one pike's milky milt could never be enough. Or could never offer enough genetic diversity to ensure the robust endurance of pike down through multi-millennia. And so the big fat ugly female pike needs *many* mates. Multiple males are required to squirt their seed upon her mammoth cargo of precious eggs.

The small pike's squirt attracts the attention of other small ambitious males, who jostle and compete to sow their pike spunk amongst the big girls' carpet of sticky eggs.

Male pike never grow very big, partly because Mother Nature doesn't need them to be big. She just needs them to be many. And spunky. A few huge females and a rash of little males is the way pike have become the most long lasting fish species in the waters of our planet.

The fact that their teeth are so large and their jaws will articulate to fit in food objects almost as big as themselves helps a lot. And of course, there's nothing a big pike won't try to eat. Dead or alive. Fish, fowl or fur.

Pike have been known to eat whole geese, yappy dogs, otters and ospreys.

But, most commonly, what a big fat female pike will turn to snack upon just after she's exhausted herself and dumped her huge load of eggs, is a little male pike.

Or two.

Female pike are the only pike that grow big and grow old. They hang together in all female groups on the edge of fast water, inhabiting the back-eddies and dead zones where there is fresh oxygen, but little current to fight against. They can hang, neutral in their buoyancy, together eye to eye, tail to tail, with other big females, growing and nurturing a new stock of eggs in their primeval ovaries, while in their stomachs they slowly digest the flesh and bones of their skinny male mates.

Female pike hang together. Safe in their size. Unified in their gender. While the spunky little males idiotically compete and jostle with each other, to get their squirt over those precious sticky eggs.

And in so doing, they inadvertently provide the big ugly female pike with something easy and stupid to eat.

Female pike hang together.

And Helen's phone rings only three times, before she picks it up, to hear Dougie's wife Fiona's accusing voice.

"So," she says, as Helen finger-wipes a smear of Nutella from the arm of Jack's high chair, "What the fuck is your husband up to now?"

Sort of getting a bit of a habit. Turning up at Sandbanks Classic Cars to find everything open, but nobody at home.

Three cars less than yesterday. The office door wide open. Papers and files spread across the big office desk, like someone has been searching, looking for stuff. The top drawer of the filing cabinet open. And so is the little key locker on the wall, with the rows of ignition keys, pertaining to the cars in the showroom. Gaps between the sets of keys, with the same Sandbanks Classic Cars key fob attached to each one. Gaps, like missing teeth.

Chin calling "Hello!" again. Into the office. Up the stairs. Like it's *déjà vu*. One of those recurring dreams where the same sequence happens over and over again. Only this time there's no cat with no head.

"Hello!" she calls again. Tug looking around the showroom, nothing changed except the missing cars and the boot of a big British Alvis, a maroon one with brown leather interior, is open.

Tug looks in. The carpet's been pulled back to reveal a compartment with a little chrome handle to open it. Tug seeing it's where the scissor-jack and tyre wrench is kept. A whole breakdown kit. Little red reflective triangle thing in there too, with a fold-out wire strut, that you use to prop up in the road. Warn any cars coming along that there's a problem. Even a pair of cotton work gloves and a foot pump in there too, all fitted into compartments around the spare tyre. Tug thinking that if he dug around a bit he'd probably find a custom-made towrope in there as well. With a proper spliced-eye on each end and a red square of cloth spliced in the middle to warn other motorists that the car was under tow.

Those were the days; when cars had proper tool kits and owners' manuals and useful items stashed away in custom-built compartments, to assist you should you ever be so unfortunate as to break down. Now, drivers with a mechanical problem, just stick on their hazard warning lights and call the AA. Sit there listening to Heart FM until a big yellow van pulls up. Never even get out the car.

Chin about to shout out again, when there's a noise from upstairs: a scrape and a bump and a muffled voice. Tug looking at Chin, she's already moving towards the office door leading to the stairs. She glances back at him, her hand snaking around to the back of her hip where she keeps her auto-lock baton in a nylon case on her belt. The harsh ripping sound of the heavy duty Velcro safety strap being pulled back has a physical effect on Tug, like the tinkle bell on Pavlov's dog. A great sound. The sound of action about to happen.

Really was *déjà vu*, he thinks. God, he wishes they could carry guns. Wouldn't it be so sweet to be able to unholster your Glock 9 millimetre and pad carefully up this staircase, one on either side, like they teach you in the FBI Academy.

Instead, they only got telescopic twatting-sticks. Chin not even taking hers out, just loosening the strap. No stab vest this time. So not quite *déjà vu*. Tug now getting a really good look at Chin's arse, a perfect round gym-fit peach, as she moves up the stairs stealthily ahead of him. Cocking her head to listen for more sounds. Tug just now realising that the fact he can watch her cute bum so well, is because she is in front of him. Because she is leading the way, *again*. He is following. It's like with her wanting to drive over here. Is this the way it's going? Is she taking over the power in this relationship?

Chin stops on the stairs now. Listening again. Tug about to take the opportunity to push past, when there's a sudden horrendous, almighty crash. The sound of wood splintering. The staircase they're standing on vibrating, like there's some sort of mini earthquake.

Before Tug's even got a bearing on what just happened, Chin's thrown open the kitchenette door and stepped in towards the source of the huge noise.

Shards of glass and wood are still raining down from the ceiling, where a skylight window is hanging down. Two of the small panes are smashed and the frame of the skylight ripped off, leaving jagged ends of splintered wood. The other half of the skylight frame is lying on the kitchen floor still caught in the loop of rope.

Straight away Tug recognises the rope. Top quality old fashioned sisal. He'd bet good money it's the one would've come from the boot of the maroon Alvis. The rest of the rope now tangled across the kitchen floor in a mess of glass, wood shards and toppled over furniture. One of the John Lewis dining chairs is lying on its side. And there's a smashed Ikea photo frame, the wood of the frame knocked apart and the broken shards of glass lying in a sunburst pattern across the photo of a man and a woman in a balloon basket.

The end of the Alvis towrope is looped around Robbie Rock's neck. He's sprawled across the floor, his robe wide open, his chubby white belly and shrivelled genitals on full display. Blood oozing from cuts on his face and forehead and even from his fingers. Now he's rolling from side to side, crunching on the glass, desperately trying to slacken the noose around his neck to catch some air.

Wrestling Rich from the truck to the allotment shed had been a major feat. Even after tying him up with the rope from the back of the truck, he still fought like a greased-up Rottweiler. It took the both of them, to half-carry, half-drag and half-kick Rich along the narrow hedged path from the lane to the shed. Rich bit Matty's hand badly, teeth marks gouging into both the palm side and the skin on the back. It hurt like fuck, but while he was biting he wasn't shouting. Keeping him quiet being a big part of the battle. There's no one else around at the allotments yet, but there's houses about 70 yards away, little two-up-two-down brick and flint cottages, where most of the old boys who tend the allotments live. It was a big risk bringing him here. Someone could easily spot them dragging him to the shed. But Adrian couldn't think of anywhere else to take him. Nowhere that could be made secure. Nowhere they could lock. Where they won't get interrupted.

Thing is, what with moving Rich being such a struggle, it means they'd had to leave the crab pot in the flat bed of the truck. It was bad enough the truck being parked out on the lane, pretty much telling everyone that Adrian was visiting the allotment, but leaving a hundred-thousand quid's worth of dope in the flat bed, inside a stolen crab pot, in broad daylight, is stretching their luck way too far. Before they do anything else, they need to bring the dope in the shed and move the truck out of sight.

When Sara Chin hooked her finger under the rope wrapped around Robbie Rock's neck and eased the coil through the spliced eye, at last he could breathe. Taking huge gulps of air like a goldfish, trying to swallow it by the gallon. She brushes the glass from his face, wipes at the blood with kitchen roll, which shows the scratches are really just superficial. She even helps him close his robe, without looking down at his belly or his balls. Helping him to close it properly by tucking one side under the other and tying the belt. His hands are shaking so much he couldn't tie it himself. She stands the chair back up on its legs by the table. Then opens the loop on the rope noose that he'd put over his own head and tied so stupidly to the strut of the skylight window frame.

She helps Robbie off the floor, dusting the broken glass from his robe and eases his big frame into the shapely dining chair with the chrome steel legs. He thanks her. Sara Chin sees him looking down at the broken picture frame and she stoops to pick it up. She parts the wooden sides to let the sunburst shards of glass clatter onto the floor. Then she pushes the angle joints of the frame back together.

"Be fine with a dab of glue," she says as she hands it to him. Watching, as he turns it around to look at it. Robbie Rock then starts to cry like a baby. The sound of him choking, trying to catch his breath was even worse than when he had the rope looped around his throat. He's crying and sobbing and gasping. Huge fat tears rolling down both cheeks, splashing on the John Lewis tabletop.

Sara Chin putting her hand on his big sloping shoulders, to calm him, reassure him, offer him a little human solace. But the

**249**

touch is like a trigger, like a volume control that makes Robbie Rock cry and sob and sob and cry, even louder than before.

A good 20 minutes Robbie sobbed. Chin never once leaving his side, saying nothing. Just looking at him. Looking down at the balloon photo. Meanwhile, Tug was creeping around the bedroom, the bathroom, checking out the contents of the bathroom cabinet, even crunching his way across the kitchen floor, down the stairs to check out the office again. Tug matching the printed inventory on the desk against the number and make of cars still parked in the showroom.

All the time, Chin just standing beside Robbie as he cries. Waiting until his loud heart-wracking sobs dwindle into small quiet whimpers and the flood of tears begins to dry.

Then, and only then, when Robbie had almost literally cried his eyes out, he stops. Then he blows his nose on kitchen roll, over and over again, like he's got a gallon of snot to shift. Then with a wad of kitchen roll he wipes his eyes. Drying them. Leaving them red and puffy. With a big ball of soggy tissue paper cupped in his hand, his voice still a little hoarse and shaky, and with Sara Chin finally sitting down on the chair facing him, Robbie Rock tells her everything.

It's just like he's stepped through the doors of Clouds House rehab and treatment centre and someone's told him: "This is Sara Chin. She's your counsellor". Robbie pours his heart out. The floodgates are open. Robbie looks into Chin's deep brown almond slanting eyes and tells her all about the lap dancing, the escorting, the coke, the fun, the sex, the love, the boat, the balloon, the Poles, the widow's peak, carrots in the shape of little fish, the lat-long numbers, the dope, the deal, the sea, the rope, the cars he doesn't even own, and most of all the way he feels about beautiful, sweet, funny, gorgeous Elsa, who says his name 'Robbie' with a tiny little Slavic growl on the 'R' that makes it sound like 'Grrobbie.'

Driving back to Weymouth with Chin behind the wheel didn't feel so bad this time. What Tug likes about it is that it leaves his hands free to do stuff, like make phone calls and he can stare out the window at all the Poole Harbour yummy mummies pushing their top-of-the-range buggies across Boating Lake Green, at the bottom of Lilliput Hill.

Chin asked Robbie if he still had the A4 sheet of paper with the lat-long numbers that Lech had given him. Then she'd put it inside an evidence bag, so they could check it for prints. She was sussed enough to put in it in one of the large-size evidence bags. Big enough so the paper'd be opened right out so Tug can read the numbers through the clear plastic bag as they're bowling along towards Weymouth.

With his free hands Tug redials the mobile number he'd got from the Harbour Master earlier to get hold of Dougie out on the Nicola B again.

Dougie not sounding pleased to get two calls from the Old Bill in one day. But relieved this time when Tug says he only wants him to check out some lat-long numbers on his chart plotter, and tell him whereabouts they are located.

"Way down on Hurd's Deep," Dougie says. The signal on his phone was no better than before. "South," he says, "Way south. Down past the drop off."

"Does anyone from Weymouth put out gear around those grounds?" asks Tug. "Like crab pots and stuff?"

Now Tug hearing the laugh in Dougie's voice, like this stupid cop had just asked a stupid land-lubbing cop-like question.

"No one with any sense," said Dougie.

"No one? Definitely?" asks Tug again.

"Brothers on Kitty K might," he says. "But, like I said. No one with any sense."

OK, not exactly a boner.

Not a hard-on. Not hard, hard. Not even a semi, really. More than a tingle though. A twitch. A little throb. Like a heart beat that traveled all the way down to his knob.

Tug had felt that throb in his Calvin's before, at work. *Because* of work. His cock stirring like a sleeping mole having a dream about worms. Not, like when he caught a flash of side-boob. Or got a glimpse down a yummy mummy's cashmere top as she stooped to reposition the bottle in her baby's mouth. Not even like the rumble he felt when he got a chance to check out Chin's tight cheeks. Nothing sexual.

Well... *kind* of. But not because he was thinking about it in a sexual way. Just because it turned him on. Tweaked his thong.

Police work could do that. The right set of circumstances. Catching a break. Fitting a new piece in a crime jigsaw. Making connections. Smelling a collar. The sweet scent of culpable un-fucking-deniable guilt. Now *that* stuff is sexy.

Knowing when some little scrote is edging nearer and nearer to a bang-to-rights situation is sweet. In that delicious moment, Tug would feel himself practising the expression he was going to adopt, when he walked into the Detective Inspector's office. All cocky. Good news to impart. That moment always made his threads feel a little tighter.

So now, in the car, when Tug hung up his Samsung after talking to Dougie out on his crabber as it slammed the ebb tide across Portland Race, Tug's little dreamy mole tossed in its duvet. He was about to impart to Chin the sexy jigsaw-piece crime news he'd just gleaned. And...

She was going to fucking *love* this.

Joining the dots from Robbie Rock's snot-dripping tale of disorganised crime to the pot-pulling, bait-stinking, lying-through-their-teeth brothers, Matty and Ade, was going to truly put some damp in her panties. Of this he had no doubt.

And even though there was a vein of snotty that shone through Chin's hot oriental features, hiding way too close to the surface, he still wanted to impress her. *Fuck*, yeah.

Anyway, a little acid could be sexy. Especially if this new news meant suddenly she was a little more awed by him, and yet meantime he'd turned a tad frosty on her. Yup. That could very well be the perfect recipe for a proper full-on boner.

Sex and police work. Always got a roar from the crowd. Tug was as sure as shit Chin got a lady-boner from a nice hunk of crime-solving falling into her lap too. And what he was about to tell her, about the brothers being the only ones Dougie ever knew to voluntarily go anywhere near Robbie 'I-fucked-up-so-bad' Rock's lat-long numbers, was as close to blue-on-blue foreplay that Tug could possibly imagine.

"These numbers," says Tug, his finger tapping the A4 plastic evidence bag, "Are way the fuck across the Channel nearly."

"We know that," says Chin, her voice flat as a witch's tit. "Robbie Rock *went* there. Remember?"

"Yeah, but. It's a bad place. Big rocks and shit. No one fishes it because it's so dangerous. Except– and you are going to absolutely fucking love this. Except the–"

Tug faltering a beat as Chin's phone only goes and fucking rings. As it does she gives him that finger. That one finger. Pointing up. That one fucking International Language of Phone Etiquette finger that means: Hold your cock. Cock. 'Cos, I have got to take this one.

"Gotta take this," she says, pressing 'Accept' on her phone with the same fucking finger she just shut him up with.

"The fuck?" says Tug. As Chin goes and calls the person on the other end, 'Sir'.

Dick-swinging is a perfectly acceptable part of police work. In any nick, in any part of the country. Any country come to that. The business of holding your business, in your hand, and then thrusting it in the face of your fellow work mates, is not only permissible, it's half way to being essential. If you've pulled off a coup. Cracked a case. Opened a line of enquiry that was hitherto shut. Then you want to let your colleagues know what a big fat cock-swinging job you've done. And not just for your own good. But for *theirs* too. A little healthy competition. Gagging on the girth of another cop's job is only going to make you sharpen your pencil. Right?

Partner-on-partner is a slightly different bucket of sprats. You don't want to make the guy you got to sit next to day-long, day after day, feel like they just got bitch-slapped, because you done a nice job.

No. Partner-on-partner dick-swinging must only be done in strict moderation. Envy is something that feels better from a distance.

In the case of Chin, Tug didn't feel so sensitive. It wasn't like they'd been partners for any length of time. And he really *did* just want to show off what a well-connected, top dog cop operator he was.

Only, just when he was about to impress her, she had to go and piss all over his parade. Just when he was telling her about his call with Dougie and the fickle finger of you're-so-busted was pointing towards the crab brothers, she had to go and fucking spoil it.

"My ex-boss," she says as she ends her call, "Sending something we might be interested in."

"I'm telling you something we *are* interested in," he says. "At least I am," he adds, trying not to sound too pissy-pants. "It Dougie says the only boat thick-as-shit enough to fish the Deeps is the Kitty K, and Robbie Rock's lat-long drop is bang in the middle of the Hurds. And when he went out there, he didn't find sweet fuck–"

"Gave his name as 'Matty'," she says, interrupting his stream.

"Who?"

"Man who made contact with a UC runs a red herring in Bristol."

Oh Jesus, Tug loves a lump of police-speak. Who the fuck doesn't? When you're on the job, you want to *sound* like you're on the job, and 'UC' he can compute… But 'Red Herring' is one fucking step too far. One step that he is so not about to admit ignorance to… When Chin just smiles. Giving Mona Lisa a run for her money on 'enigmatic'.

Bitch. Tug thinks. Cutting me off and now smirking because she knows he *doesn't* know what she's talking about, and then she goes and turns her Samsung around to face him.

"Offers the UC a buy. Large amount of high grade Afghani black…"

Tug was trying to catch his brain up which he knew was going to make his face look dumb, when his eyes focused on her Galaxy.

"Identified himself as being based in Weymouth," she says.

Tug stared at a CCTV grab of Matty, wearing a jacket made him look like a Jehovah.

"Just how stupid can a man ever be?"

"Matty," says Tug. "The fuck?"

She turns the phone to glance at the grainy shot again. "Better go pay a visit," she says, swinging the car into the Harvester car park, throwing a 180 back towards Portland.

Tug sucking his teeth now, conflicted. Excited to be going to lean on a perp, definitely. But gutted to find that Chin's dick was so much bigger than his.

They watched the baby boy bounce. His little feet in tiny blue leather shoes, like ballerinas wear. Or tightrope walkers when they slide across wires with big poles.

A little boy baby bouncing in this thing, like a big pair of pants connected to a spring. Bounce. Bounce. Bounce. The spring extending and contracting as the little snot-gobbler flies up and down. His stretchy-out toes just brushing the floor enough to boing him back up. The long spring fixed to the lintel of the living room door above his head.

Fuck, that looked fun. Should make those bouncers for adults. Bounce up and down for half an hour watching *Top Gear* on the 50 inch flat screen. What could possibly be wrong with that? Thinks Tug, before tuning in to the conversation between Chin and Adrian's wife, Helen, once more.

The house a big surprise to him. Neat and warm with a smell of those sweet wood things hot yoga-bunnies like to burn, when they do all that bending. Not that Helen looked like a hot yoga-bunny. Not a moose, though. Just normal. *Really* normal. Kind. And in Tug's estimation, boringly, unhelpfully innocent.

At this part of the hunt they do not want or need innocent. They want to smell guilt. They want to sense lies. To glimpse deceitful looks. Stare into eyes that won't quite meet theirs. So they know they're on to something. Know they're in the presence of dishonesty that they can chip away at. Manipulate. Bully. Even scare the fucking crap out of, if necessary.

Guilt is great. Innocence is sweet. But absolutely no fucking use in police work.

When Tug zoned back in from the bouncing, he could tell Chin was no nearer anything of any use. Helen's face, so annoyingly open and smiley. Her offer of a cup of tea... "Or, I've got some instant?" So obviously coming from a place of syrupy innocence that isn't going to offer them any insight.

She knows nothing. With her honey-coloured hair and her happy chubby-cheeked baby and her description of her husband leaving early doors to go help out another crabber. And her, "Well that *is* odd," when she's told hubby isn't on the Nicola B pulling Dougie's ropes.

But none of it seems to phase her one iota. She's sure she'll hear the whole story when Adrian gets home. And, is there any news of that poor woman who lost her son on the Kitty K? She sent flowers, and a letter, of course. And she's thought of popping around, but wasn't sure. Felt she probably should wait a day or two.

Absolutely none of this is making Tug think they were going to get anything out of Helen, because she plainly knew nothing. Lived in a box of baby fleece. On the subject of Adrian's brother Matty, she was a little wrinkled around the eyes. She knows he's had problems with the police in the past, but she and Adrian were really pretty sure he'd managed to put all that behind him now.

So, sixty-four-thousand-dollar question: would she let them have a look around?

"For what?" she asks.

"We suspect Matty's been involved in trafficking controlled substances..." says Chin.

"Your brother-in-law is a scummo drug dealer," says Tug. Going for wing-pulling cruel. Seeing how that would sit in her butter-wouldn't-melt mouth. Her eyes just widened.

"We know he's involved in something big, which is about to blow up in his face," says Tug.

"I thought, *we* thought, Matthew was past all that..." she says, a look of concern around her brows.

"And your husband might be caught up in it too."

"Not Adrian," says Helen. "Adrian doesn't even drink alcohol anymore. Nothing. Not a drop."

Chin and Tug both look at her. Her eyes move with cow-like innocence from one to the other.

So, is she going to let them look around this place or not? asks Tug… Pushing to see if the innocence is as real as it feels.

"Of *course*," she says. Standing up. Eager to help.

Fuck and blue bollocks, thinks Tug. No way they're going to find anything useful here then. Unless Adrian is a total fucking moron, which unlike his brother, he probably isn't.

"Parsnip," said little Jack.

"It's very sweet," says Helen, "But it's not really a name, is it?"

"Parsnip."

"It's a vegetable, honey. Something you eat."

"Parsnip."

"What about calling her after one of your friends at school?"

"Parsnip!" he said, his voice getting louder.

"What about 'Peppa', after Peppa the–"

*"Parsnip!"*

And so it was. A grand daughter of Bugsy, destined to take over as Helen's father's latest sow, got named 'Parsnip'.

Bugsy had been the queen of sows. The sow of sows. Pumping out piglets like a pig-shaped Pez dispenser year after year. The bloodline leaning more and more towards the long snout and scrawny features of the wild boar-cross as years passed. She suckled them by the dozen. Never losing a piglet. No matter how runty.

Bugsy had been a queen pig.

But as the line soured with boar blood, her progeny more and more looked the part. The wild boar strain dominating. Some growing proper tusks to go with the dead black eyes and high shoulders. And they smelled weird too. Not like normal pigs. The boar babies tainted with a scent that clung to the nostrils like rotting fish.

"Couldn't even count the number of times I've pulled a body as he's walking back from the corner shop," says Chin. "Carrying a pint of milk. Or a six-pack of Magners."

Tug beginning to feel like he's being given a lesson in police work.

"Still rubbing foil off his scratch card."

"Ask *me*, they'll be down the harbour. In The Sailors," he says. "In town, not out here on the island."

"You *always* do a drive around," she says. Taking another left and another. Going round in oblongs and squares, street after street, Sweet Hill Lane, Mead Bower, Avalanche Road. Radiating out from the little terrace where Adrian's son was probably still bouncing his tiny tits off.

Sounding like she's handing out more Chicken McNuggets of Police Operational advice. Tug dragging his brain for something a bit acid to splash on her smugness. When there it fucking *is*. Christmas and birthday all rolled into one.

The truck.

The blue piece-of-shit Nissan Navara 250 diesel with the flat bed and crew cab. Scratched and dented and rusted from years of being arse-donkey to a commercial potter. Parked. Two wheels up on the kerb just at the mouth of the narrow lane leading up to the Southwell allotments.

Christmas. Birthday. Valentine and Father's Day all melted together, in one big ribbon-bowed present.

Two side windows open. Nearside rear door not shut properly. Green stinking slime dripping down the side of the back coat. Splatters of stinky green all up the inside of one door. Up as far as the roof. Crab pot lying in the flat bed. And…

"That's blood."

"Looks like it to me," says Tug, following the point of Chin's finger, with a nail so neat and curved and white underneath the overhang, it had to have been painted by some midget Korean hunched over in a back street nail bar. While wearing one of those surgeon masks.

"Call it in. Get some Plod up here," he says, following the splodges of red on the Portland stone kerb that lead to a bigger splatter, that points onwards to the rusty gateway at the end of the lane where it goes up to the allotments.

Lifting the radio out her belt, about to push the call button, Chin looks up, directly into the sweating face of Adrian Collins.

"Shit!"

Adrian now stopping his stride out the lane, so hand-brake quick, his brother Matty rear-ends him. Matty knocking Adrian another step nearer to the Chinese detective who already rattled his cage on the Kitty.

As Matty cannons into Adrian. All eyes meet.

And before anyone draws another breath, Adrian's dodged round the rear of the truck and is sprinting fast down Ripcroft Lane towards the cliffs and Tout Quarry.

Teeth clenched, legs pumping.

While Matty is backing up the lane like a polecat ferret working arse-ways down a rat hole. A heartbeat later Matty's vaulting a shiplap fence into a terraced back garden. Followed by another, and another. Flashes of Little Tikes toys and rubber-lined goldfish ponds passing the corner of his eye as he crashes into yet another fence. This one feeling like it's made of bread sticks. Pieces splintering under his boot as he tries another vault, but ends up just ploughing through.

On he goes, heading south one garden at a time.

Tug never really liked to run. At the gym he was strictly a weights man. Free weights. Proper job. Not those spastic machines that're supposed to mimic the action of free weights, but without all the wobble and clatter and the need to rack and unrack barbells.

Tug *liked* the clatter. Dropping a pair of 20kg dumbbells into the weight rack made a good beefy thunk. A heavy chunky steel sound, that told everyone around that you'd just been pumping some big-ass iron.

Tug liked the moments inbetween each weightlifting set. When he could rest his muscles, have a butcher's in the mirror at his biceps, or the deepening valley that cut across the top of his deltoids.

Or better still scope the treadmills, steppers and cross-trainers for trim Lycra-wrapped buttocks. Tug loving the rear view of a fit girl in black or pink stretchy stuff, just beginning to break out into a delicate sweat. Nice.

But not in any way liking to get on those treadmills himself. Nope. The whirring whine of the belt, the thud-thud-thud-thud of trainer against rubber tread. No thank you. Made him breathless just thinking about it. Tug preferring the muscle-burn of weights to the lung-fucking exertion of running.

Tug never really liked to run.

Which made chasing the brother, Adrian, down Ripcroft Lane such a massive haemorrhoid pain in the arse. Adrian older, heavier, wearing clumpy great work boots, and yet still accelerating fast away from Tug.

This does not look good. As Adrian climbs up a white Portland stone wall and disappears over it into the massive cave and tunnel riddled Tout Quarry, Tug well and truly fucked off to be losing such a lot of ground so soon in the chase. But all the same, pleased as freelance pie-tester that Chin isn't going to be watching him perform so badly in the perp-pursuing stakes. On account of her choosing to take off after Matty herself.

Chin *loved* to run. On the flat she was like a whippet on crack. Juiced to the max. Slender petite legs pumping a sprint-time more in keeping with some giant-legged Afro-Caribbean jock rather than a tiny oriental girl with a pony tail and black shoes sold in the 'Back To School' section of Clarks.

Chin loving to run on the flat. Not at all loving this raggedy arse steeplechase that Matty was taking her on, through the jagged detritus of booby-trapped Southwell back gardens.

Jumps and fishpond trenches, trampolines and outraged dogs withstanding, Chin was still gaining on Matty across this garden obstacle course. Chin could have easily matched Matty's pace. Exceeded it. Brought him down with a twat from her baton. Stood on his neck and cuffed his rope-gnarled hands behind his back.

Could have done. If he hadn't made a tight right as he landed on the potato bed of Number 16 Mead Bower and dodged around their Fiat-sized greenhouse.

Chin following his swift right turn, only a pace behind. Two at the most. Accelerating around the back of the greenhouse, her head down, powering fast, digging deep and running, balls up, straight into his fist.

Bosh!

Matty sure he could feel some sort of bone crunching just before the Chinese-looking detective went down like a poleaxed rag doll. Knees buckling under her in response to the brute force of his swing. Her accordion-like collapse not quite spectacular enough to dissuade Matty from stomping his Caterpillar boot on her ribcage – twice. Before he continued on towards Tout Quarry.

Matty knowing she's a tough little fucker. Anyone could see it in those cold conger eel eyes. So Matty not taking any chance she might get up again in a hurry.

Rich Tovey had a spider's web tattooed below his left ear. Stretching down his neck and under his grubby collar. To the right of centre, a spider clung to the strands of its web, looking like a mongrel-cross between a ladybird and a starfish.

"Black widow," Rich would say to anyone who asked. "Fucking kill a man with one bite."

Rich didn't say anything at the moment, what with the black wet sock still jammed into the back of his throat.

But when Helen pulled the sock out his mouth, dirty words flowed in a torrent like she'd just yanked the plug out a dam. Gushing out in a fuck-filled flood of abuse.

"Untie my hands, you fucking cunt bitch," was Rich Tovey's opening volley. "Your fucking husband and his halfwit brother are so fucking busted."

Helen flinching from the fetid stench of his breath.

"Undo. My. Fucking. *Hands!*"

Helen now watching the spider shudder in its web as the veins and sinews on the side of Rich's neck pulsed and swelled as he shouted more filth.

"They're getting done for this. End of fucking story," he spat. "Fucking jumped me. *My* pot. Finders fucking keepers. And Matty is so fucking going–"

She quickly wedged the wet black sock back into his mouth. Hard.

Rich now shaking his head like a Jack Russell trying to kill a mouthful of rat.

Then, with her knee leaning down on his throat and her left hand yanking up his greasy, slimed hair, Helen using the garden dibber that Adrian's dad made 20 years ago out of a foot of sharpened broom handle to pound the sock in between Rich Tovey's tonsils.

His eyes bulging and leaking as she rammed the sock hard against his throat. The wooden point tearing through the sock into soft flesh.

This shut up his filthy swearing, and made his eyes boggle wider with surprise and fear.

Helen took the garden dibber out of Rich's mouth. The point now red wet and dripping.

Her 'netball knee' cracking like a Ryvita, as she stood up and walked around Rich's body, to where the fork with only three tines leaned against the wall.

Tout Quarry, Bowers Quarry, Kingbarrow Excavations, Albion Jordan's Mine and Thrutch Cave are all stone-working sites located on top of the huge lump of rock that is the Island of Portland.

From these gouged and blasted and drilled and sawn and chipped workings into the lump, came the centuries-old, seemingly endless supply of Portland stone.

The Bank of England, the Cenotaph, Somerset House, St. Paul's Cathedral, Hampton Court, the British Museum and Eddystone Lighthouse, all constructed from the oolithic limestone that forms the sperm-shaped rock whose head is sniffing at the arse of Weymouth, and whose slender tail becomes Portland Bill, pointing a jagged upright fuck-you finger towards France.

Tout, Bowers, Kingbarrow, Albion and Thrutch were all historic quarry sites of Portland, they were also the illicit playgrounds of Adrian and Matty and all their dip-shit schoolmates ever since Miss Killick's class in Underhill Junior School.

As schoolboys they'd investigated every hole and cave and 'Danger Do Not Enter' shaft they could find. Lighting fires, killing rats, stealing tools and taking dumps down shafts in order to hear the sweet satisfying 'plop' of turd hitting groundwater a hundred-and-fifty foot below.

The fork with three tines instead of four was always a kack-handed tool to use. Forking soil it was 25 percent less efficient. Hefting manure it would always tip slightly to one side, making it necessary to grip the shaft tighter to stop it trying to swivel in your hand.

But having one less tine on the left side made no difference to Helen's job of pressing the far right tine against the badly-drawn black widow spider's spastic body, while lifting her cracking knee high above the fork's head and stamping down with her mock Croc, as hard as if she were breaking a layer of winter ice frozen on a pig trough.

Adrian and Matty knew every place to hide in the bowel-like innards of Tout Quarry. But an island is always an island, even if it is now joined by a long thin causeway to the mainland. There is only one way on. And one way off. One road. One exit. Unless of course you're prepared to dive into the sea and take your chances swimming around Portland Bill, all 13 miles of its coastline, against the second fastest tidal race in Great Britain.

And if you did that, you'd really just be a prick. A dead prick.

Bouncing is fun. Definitely. Sitting in your pushchair in the vegetable garden watching a cabbage-white butterfly flutter from one broad bean stalk to another in the slanting sunlight is fun. No question. Dropping your Peppa Pig beaker onto the ground and watching Ribena juice leak out the mouth holes into the earth is fun too.

But not nearly as much fun as riding in a wheelbarrow while your mummy pushes it from the allotment shed to daddy's truck and back.

Sooner or later the brothers were going to have to hold their freezing cold damp, shivering hands aloft and walk out of the workings of Tout Quarry into the eye-squinting glare of a police-issue million-candle LED flashlight beam.

The cold night air making clouds of steam curl out with each breath, as Chin, face bruised and plastered, ribs bound, pressed the button on her radio and hissed…

"We've got them."

There was only so many times Tug could say, "I don't fucking believe this," over and over again, stressing every word differently every time he said it. Shouting it. Roaring it. In the faces of the two police constables standing in front of him outside of Interview Room 2.

"I do not fucking *believe* this," he said again, slightly changing his sentence construction, but looking more and more like he was about to rip a wooden top's head off.

There was only so many times Tug could say it before Jackie, against all her instincts and desires, would have to put her shoes back on, suck in her belly and walk around the custody counter to throw some water on Tug's wrath-filled flames.

There was a lot of questions Adrian could answer as he sat, hands cuffed in front of him, in Interview Room 2. Seated on a hard orange plastic chair opposite the Chinese-looking detective, whose blackened eyes he did not want to meet. Meanwhile, her bloodshot pupils drilling holes in his face. His own eyes staring down at his hands, covered in plasters and blood-dried scratches from all the blackthorn and brambles growing down the Tout Quarry cut cliff faces.

There was a lot of questions she asked about what happened that day out on the Kitty K. Where they went. What they found. What really happened to Tim? Did he fall? Why was he up on the roof anyway? Was he really on the roof? Because, they tested the jib boom for DNA. Hairs. Blood. Anything human matched to Tim's unique human genetic code. But there was nothing.

So if he did hit his head on the steel L-shaped boom with the rope pulley, why was there no evidence of it ever having happened? Why did he and Matty take the Kitty K out at night? She knows they did. Broke the seals. Ripped the tape. Why? Where did they go?

They know all about his brother, she tells him. Bristol. Handing out samples of hash. Making deals. Talking big. Dragging Adrian deeper and deeper into a hole that he's not going to climb out of in under a ten-stretch. Minimum.

A hole that is going to swallow up his wife and his marriage and his mortgage. His two little boys. Oh, and her job. You have any idea how quickly she'll get kicked out of her teacher assistant training programme when the local education authority finds out about her husband's criminal activities?

Adrian got any idea how twitchy schools are about teaching staff and CRB checks? Know how many fingers you'd need to count up the days before she gets called into the Headmaster's office? Sent home. Eyes downcast. Teachers in the staff room wagging their tongues come break time. Eating up the delicious scandal like a plate of free nibbles at a Waitrose deli counter.

Does Adrian truly understand what a hot, bubbling jacuzzi full of shit he's lowering himself, his tiny innocent boys and his heart-of-gold wannabe primary school teacher wife, into?

All this 'cause of his dead-in-the-water brother, acting like a retard? And possibly a murderer? Huh? How's that sound?

Is that what *really* happened on the Kitty? Is that what they're all going to be looking at? Because if it goes down that particular dark alley, then Adrian better cut his bad blood loose very quickly. Like *now*, quickly. On account of the fact that you can bet the farm, the boat, the shoes off your little boys' bouncing feet, that Matty will be sat next door in Interview Room 1 – facing her colleague, gripping the handle of a big old spade – as he digs a stinking pit to bury his brother?

You think Matty's sat there saying nothing? She asks.

You think he's just sat there schtum in the face of evidence, photos, testimony, tape recordings, CCTV, prints, samples, intents and conspiracies?

You think he's not giving his version quick as he can? Signing a statement. Pointing a finger. While you watch a nice little home life collapse and crumble around your ears, as you sit staring at your hands over and over again, just saying 'no comment'.

"You think *he's* saying 'no comment'?"

"No comment."

"You think he's not giving us the Story According To Matty?"

"No comment."

"You honestly believe keeping quiet while he talks, is the best possible course of action?"

"No comment."

There were a lot of questions Detective Chin asked of Adrian over and over again, that he could answer. But, chose not to. Lots of questions he knew the answers to. Answers that filled his stomach full of acid. And fear. Shame. Pain. And guilt. Answers that threatened the innocent little lives of people he professed to love.

And yet there was one question she kept asking over and over and over again, that he really truly could not give her the answer to.

"So. Where the fuck is your truck?"

Parsnip was such a sweet name. Lovely. Childishly innocent and very original. Helen was pleased Jack had held his ground. It showed pluck. She'd tell the story at her school, to her Key Stage 1 pupils. And show them a picture of the wooden sign she and little Jack'd painted together with a flower in place of the dot of the 'i' in Parsnip.

Parsnip was a sweet name.

For a shitty sow.

Helen's father never took to her. Hard to handle. Quick to snap. Ugly. Her snout long and scarred and her temperament, pure evil. When she was in season, he'd let the boar into her sty but even he wasn't that interested. Scared almost. He'd follow her around but half-hearted. When he tried to mount her, she'd whip her head round, tear into him. A few times she'd left bloody teeth marks in the boar's cheek. Ripped the lower edge off one ear.

Parsnip was not a nice pig.

Helen was glad Parsnip turned out bad, though. Not for her father. Or for little Jack. But for herself. Because when she tipped the chunks out of the thick black industrial rubble sack onto the wet mud, Parsnip would rip into them with the rabid hunger only a slightly inbred bad pig could muster.

She'd eat anything.

Bad or not, Parsnip was more than happy today, to sink her dirty yellow teeth into the slabs of white-grey meat. Including the one with the faded blue writing across it.

Writing that just said 'Rich'.

It started with a Cup-a-Soup. Ainsley Harriott. Stilton and Broccoli. Three Cup-a-Soups to be precise. Two Stilton and Broccoli and a Chicken and Country Vegetables.

Ainsley's shiny bald black head and unfeasibly white teeth glinting from the cardboard cut-out beside the nipple-high display stand at the end of Aisle Three.

Matty only in Asda to get a pork pie or a pastie, or one of those ten-inch-long sausage rolls with the flaky pastry that blows away in any south-westerly when you bite into it out on deck. Half your fucking wrap-around blowing off towards the Isle of Wight.

Pastie, sausage roll or pork pie, didn't matter. Whatever had a red marked-down sticker stuck on it. Something galloping towards its expiry date.

A spotty teenage girl in a lime green fleece with a half-arsed smile and a wodge of Orbit Freeze on the chew, was giving out free soup sachets to lumpy, tattooed mums as they wheeled trolleys in the direction of a three-for-two White Lightning offer.

Matty liking the look of her tits. Even in the manky Asda fleece. Picking up a Stilton and Broccoli from her tray as he walked past carrying his two pasties and a Yorkie. Giving her a wink as he slips the sachet in his pocket. She looks right through him though, like he's a thin spray of rebound piss-mist. Or else she's just recently turned zombie.

So he goes around again. Cheeky grin stuck in place. And picks up a Chicken and Country Vegetables this time, with another Stilton and Broccoli just to show he's a man of appetites. Badge on her very high, very melon shapely tit says her name is 'Taylor'.

Matty asking for her phone number outright, just slightly before she stops chewing Orbit, flicks her gaze up to meet his eyes, and says, "Piss off. Perve."

So it started with a Cup-a-Soup. Three. That Matty threw across the wheelhouse, clattering into the corner by the filthy chipped mugs stuffed in a rack just below the two unused, untouched automatic life jackets.

One of the sachets disappearing down behind the toolbox full of crappy rusted Chinese spanners.

"Fucking piece-of-shit boat," says Matty accusingly. "I'm only thinking it'd be nice to dip me pastie in hot soup. Yeah? Only, of course there's *no fucking gas.*"

The other sachets landing on the two-ring burner, with the grill of sticky rusty bars and an adjustable strut to hold the kettle in place in rough seas.

*"No. Fucking. Gas."* says Matty, hissing in Adrian's face. Like it's his fault Matty's Country Vegetables are never going to know the sweet caress of boiling water.

"For about the last three *months*," says Adrian. "Not that you'd fucking know."

Last time Matty ever boiled a kettle on the Kitty K was when he was trying to expand the plastic lock on a security tag attached to a shoplifted pair of size 6 Timberland boots he bought in The Sailors, from 'Tight' Mick, and then wanted Adrian to buy off him, for Helen. On account of her being the only one he could think of who'd wear works boots in half the size of anyone who actually wore work boots to work.

Adrian pushing past Matty now, roughly. Out onto the deck, where he kicked up the lid of a brown wooden locker.

"See that," he points at a blue propane gas bottle slicked with orange rust and mackerel scales sitting in the pit of the rotted locker. "Costs 32 quid for a refill. Back of the Texaco garage," he says. "Anytime you feel like a fucking Cup-a-Soup. Be my guest."

Adrian knew chances of Matty finding the right spanner to turn the right nut, the right way, to undo the pipe linking the bottle to the burner, through a hole drilled in the wall of the wheelhouse, and dragging it up the Texaco garage, was about as likely as Portland shitehawks shitting Euros.

So, he did it himself.

That afternoon after they'd unloaded into Weyfish and Matty had stomped off up the harbour muttering about the shit price of brown crab at Brixham, and what he was going to do to that cunt Rich Tovey when he saw him again. Slippery fucking weasel would gnaw his own leg off to get out of a corner. Probably fucking swallow it too. Stealing my fucking dope and our truck was fucked up enough. But torching the truck up on the deserted MoD Bridging Camp. Now that was a low blow. Truck all gutted out like a pouting. Thing getting so hot, wheel rims melting to the break drums.

Since when did it become 'his' dope and 'our' truck? Adrian thinking, as he took the wire brush to the rust crust on the gas bottle regulator, in order to spray it with WD40 and uncouple it.

As Kitty's engine gurgled and lurched like a proper park bench alkie trying to swallow the first Special Brew of the day, Adrian tidies the corner of the wheelhouse above the gas burners. Tidies. Three mugs in the rack. Teaspoons in a mug. Jar of Spar instant coffee and a tub of dried milk, jammed down the side of the burner.

On the floor beside it stands a three-litre bottle of Morrisons spring water. In the window runner groove, a big new shiny box of matches. And pride of place, on top of the burner's heavily stained stainless steel frame, Adrian had laid out Matty's three Cup a Soup sachets.

Ainsley's smile looking a bit crumpled, but still very white.

Just because everything is shit doesn't mean they have to wallow and roll around in it. Nope. New gas bottle. New coffee jar. New matches. It's hardly a gin palace, but at least, thanks to Adrian changing the propane bottle, on board the Kitty K, they can now make a brew.

Of course, Matty didn't notice. All morning in between half-hearted hauls of worse than usual pots, Matty giving Adrian his 'expert' opinion of the police charges currently levied against them. Opinions according to Matty and his team of 'legal advisors', who were mostly toothless, tattooed men propping up the bar in The Sailors.

Fair enough, he was bang-to-rights for punching the Chinese cop. That was going to be a hard one to dodge. But there were mitigating circumstances. The other stuff. The bit of black hash and the pictures. Those sorts of busts fell apart *all* the time. Technicalities. Especially as the so-called fucking dope is now missing.

Tovey is *so* fucking dead. So dead. When Matty gets his hands on him.

In fact, all in all, to be honest, it just makes Matty look like a bit of a fantasist twat with a big mouth and a little lump of dope. Who goes and makes a complete tit of himself on CCTV. Nothing else.

"That won't never fucking stick," he says. Matty never mentioning Tim.

Not once.

Ever.

"I changed the bottle," said Adrian, now pointing a steel toecap at the rotting wooden locker.

They were out on deck together, Adrian in a thick woollen jumper. Matty in his skanky, spattered *Star Wars* t-shirt. The K drifting over a patch called 'The 34's' just to the west of the Bill. The lull after they'd pulled up a shank of pots that hadn't done any good in over three weeks, sitting and re-shooting on the same ground. Rocky seabed being too jagged and the pots sitting wrong, then getting all shagged up in the roaring spring ebbs. Adrian deciding it's now time to haul them and shift them east of the Bill. Shoot them in close to the cliff face just out of the screamer tide.

Three pots of the shank lying on the deck, needing repairs. Between the brothers, a pair of pliers and a fist full of cable ties, to fix the slices of car tyre rubber, back on to the frames.

"What bottle?" asks Matty.

"Could even have a Cup-a-Soup," suggests Adrian.

Matty now clocking the clean pipe sticking out the gas bottle locker and doing the mental calculation, that adds up to: Matty, in wheelhouse, making Cup-a-Soup, equals Matty *not* having to keep stabbing his fingers on the sharp ends of snipped cable ties, while breathing the lingering stink of over-soaked crab bait, out on deck.

"Fuck, *yeah*," says Matty. "On it, like a car bonnet".

And he drops the pliers and walks across the deck to yank open the wheelhouse door.

The 'bilge' is a boat's belly. Its guts. The deepest pocket of space which, like an abdominal trench, runs the length of the vessel on the inside of its keel.

A boat floats like a man on his back. The keel, like a spine, slightly-curved, lying deepest in the water with the air-filled belly encased above it. The bilge is the lowest internal space within any vessel and so it becomes gravity's toilet. Anything, any liquid, oil, fuel, piss, blood, ooze, grease, tea or fish jizz, that can seep through the deck, down holes, gaps, ill-fitting corners, leaking scuppers, will end up slopping around inside the belly of the bilge.

Oil that leaks from the engine mixes with seawater leaking from the cooling system, mixes with freshwater from the tank, mixes with saltwater and crab shit from the vivier.

The bilge pump is normally a battery-operated Chinese-made piece of shit that sucks up the thick gloopy soup of mechanical emissions and coughs it out of a piped hole on the outside of the hull, just above the water line.

A bilge pump's life is not a happy life. Semi-submerged in a witch's brew of scum juice all day long, kicking into electronic action when a float-regulated switch deems the depth of foul liquid detritus is deep enough to need venting out into the sea. Then the pipe vent vomits lumpy boat scurf into the sea, causing a slick of grease to trail behind as it goes.

Kitty's deepest bilge deposits are too old, too thick, too congealed to actually be sucked up by any tiny little diaphragm driven bilge pump. So they stay, year after year, growing deeper, thicker and more toxic as time passes.

In ancient sail ships and slave transporters, bilge gas was a killer. Diseased fumes, if breathed, could poison or asphyxiate. Sometimes the quantity of human waste and organic matter, would give off volatile levels of methane gas, causing explosions and unnaturally fierce combustions.

Fires on board boats are never fun.

Unlike the vast open-bellied vessels of old, modern boat design moved away from the single, huge boat-long bilge, to a multiple compartmentalised design.

Compartments are good for boats. And good for bilges to some extent. Compartments can relate to specific functions: an engine compartment, a fuel tank compartment, an anchor chain compartment. The breaking up of the belly of the boat into sections means that between each compartment, separating walls have to be erected. These walls increase structural strength as well as provide an infilling with strong buoyant material. Even if that's only wood, it all helps the thing float. A bonus in most circumstances, except in the case of fire.

In the event of fire, it actually just means there's more stuff to burn.

Without fire, compartmentalisation of the bilge makes a lot of sense. Even in a high seas collision where the external structure is stoved-in under impact, chances are water will just pour into one compartment. The other separate compartments remaining intact, water tight, inherently buoyant and therefore able to help keep the vessel afloat.

Compartments are good for water ingress. Compartments are good for overall structural integrity. What compartments *aren't* good for is that methane gas build-up. Because the smaller the compartment, the less oxygen there is to dilute the gas. The less oxygen, the more methane. The more methane, the more potentially combustible, concentrated and powerful an explosion is likely to be.

On fishing boats, compared to ancient square-rigged sail boats, the lack of hens, pigs and goats or shackled slaves on board, reduces the amount of shit, and therefore the risk of unwanted methane.

So all in all, methane is no longer a real hazard on board commercial fishing boats.

No one is worried about methane production on fishing boats. Not since the collapse of the whale fishing industry, methane hasn't been a problem.

In fact, the only gas that really worries anyone working on a boat these days is propane.

Matty looking at the clean mugs. No brown sludge around the bottom edge. And a teaspoon! Metal one. Real one. Not plastic. Jar of Spar instant coffee. His three Cup-a-Soups laid out on the top of the burner grill, with its struts that now looked like they've had some of their rust and gunk wire-brushed off.

Shit. Things are looking up. Instead of everything in their world getting worse. One thing getting better…

Matty glancing out of the wheelhouse window at Adrian, past the long untouched life jacket. Adrian shifting across the deck, this side of the busted pots in his stupid fucking woolly jumper looking like some twat off *Country File*.

All the same, Matty understanding what Adrian had done here, by attempting to make an improvement. Adding a plus. Instead of just minuses all the time. Fair play.

The smallest seed of a smile curling at the edge of Matty's mouth, as outside Adrian seems to be dragging two pots up alongside the closed wheelhouse door. And then, just that moment, Matty sees it…

A new box of Bryant and May long matches. A whole brand spanking new box. Each match nearly five inches long. Huge phosphorous heads blobbed onto matchsticks thick as drinking straws. The sort you buy if you've got some big fat fuck-off wood burner, or a tricky pilot flame that's deep in the bowels of some big gas boiler. Or else, you're lighting every single candle on a 21-year-old's birthday cake, and you've never heard of a Clipper disposable.

A box of matches so over-engineered for the job of lighting the Kitty's puny gas burner, that Matty's thinking Ade must've nicked them. Or cloe Spar'd run out of regular-sized ones.

Matty taking one out of the box, feeling its weight. Size of it. Like a joke match. Three times bigger than a normal match. Matty, in awe, strikes it against the black sandpapery stuff along the side of the box. Huge head fizzing up into a ball of chemical flame, as the head simultaneously pings off the matchstick and twangs against the steel of the burner, bouncing down towards the wheelhouse floor.

Useless fucking thing. Matty holding up the huge matchstick to see where it had snapped clean off after striking. Clean through. Like someone had already cut it half way.

Propane is an amazing invention; a really cracking piece of innovative domestic gas technology. A by-product of petrol and natural gas refining, its most significant and marketable property is its portability. Propane gas is non-toxic and odourless, but what makes it such a friendly utilitarian combustible is its co-operative willingness to liquefy under compression.

Quite simply, a very large amount of gas once compressed into a liquid, can be stored in a relatively small container. Tiny in relation to its potential energy output.

In 1910, when propane's inventor Walter O. Snelling, working at the US Bureau of Mines, first applied for its patent, the *New York Times* subsequently extolled the magical properties of this liquefied gas. Because, 'a small steel bottle will carry enough gas to light an ordinary home for three weeks.'

Propane, this miracle liquid gas, only really presents one problem in all its many widespread domestic applications. That is its propensity to sink to the floor should it ever leak from its pressurised bottle.

Propane is more than one-and-a-half times heavier than air, so when it leaks, or seeps out from where a pipe or regulator has been incorrectly fitted, the odourless gas will sink. Not just as far as the floor, but even *beneath* the floor too. Should there be any holes or gaps through which a heavy gas could pass. This being something of a nightmare in houses with cellars beneath the kitchen stove.

Or, for example, on a boat. Especially a boat with a compartmentalised bilge, where there's a small boxed-off space located beneath the wheelhouse floor. One that could fill gradually through the course of a morning, with a heavy and highly combustible explosive gas. Gas which could collect at floor-level and below and probably go undetected, because it's a gas almost devoid of odour. At least not enough odour to be noticed above the stench of putrid pot bait.

On deck, Adrian leaned one of the two crab pots he was dragging across the deck, up against the wheelhouse door. The other was then acting as a back stop, the rubber tyre tread creating practically an immovable friction between pot base and gritty deck. Then, Adrian walks towards the transom, away from the wheelhouse. As Matty, shaking his head at the stupid big matches, prepares to strike another. Almost before the previous fizzing snapped-off match head had finished falling from the cooker top, spinning in a buzz of flame to the floor.

As Adrian walks across the deck, his hand instinctively feels for the uncomfortable bulge of the uninflated 150 Newton Crewsaver automatic life jacket, hidden under his incongruously thick jumper. As Matty glances out of the rear window, his eyebrows meeting in the middle of his forehead from a frown he is pulling, in reaction to seeing Adrian, out on deck, put his foot on a crab pot, and use it as a step to get up onto the transom, at the arse-end of Kitty K.

Adrian climbing up onto the aft gunwale.

Matty would have frowned way more if he'd noticed the two life jackets that always hung untouched and unloved on the hook at the back of the wheelhouse door, were now reduced to one.

Matty would have probably said, "What... the *fuck?*" As the next match head also bust clean off, tumbling like a mini fireball to the wheelhouse floor.

But, he never did.

It's called a 'pill'.

Like so many great technological inventions, it came about because of war. Naval seamen were unable to operate efficiently at their posts wearing bulky cork life jackets. So when disaster struck, they often drowned, because they didn't have time to locate and fit their bulbous life preservers, before their crippled ships spewed them into deadly seas.

The automatic self-inflating life jacket, invented for Navy Seals and USAF pilots in 1942, was inspired by the internal swim bladders of fish. A sealed air cell that could be inflated to order, affording life-saving buoyancy.

The automatic self-inflating life jacket uses a gherkin-sized steel canister filled with highly compressed $CO_2$ gas, which when released, instantly inflates the nylon bladder inside the horseshoe-shaped life preserver.

The massively compressed $CO_2$ gas, stored at a pressure of 853 pounds per square inch, is released explosively into the jacket's bladder when the gas canister is pierced, with a firing pin. This steel spike is hammered deep into the canister's dimpled head, by a powerful spring.

The whole point of an automatic inflatable life jacket is that it should *automatically* inflate when its wearer is submerged under water. Even if the stricken seaman has been knocked unconscious from the blast of enemy shells or exploding fuel tanks, the life preserver will still automatically inflate around his neck and hold him right way up in the sea. Whether he is conscious or not. Alive or dead.

So, the powerfully sprung mechanism is designed to fire the spike into the steel canister, to release almost 900 pounds of pressurised $CO_2$ when the water-sensitive trigger device is activated.

The thing that activates the trigger is called a 'pill'.

Originally it was made of salt. A tiny, hard salt biscuit that held the firing pin locked in place. And when water flooded into the mechanism, the salt would dissolve, triggering the release of the spring, which then hammered the spike into the bottle's neck.

Nearly every time an automatic life jacket *doesn't* inflate on contact with water, the pill is to blame. The pill has a limited life span. And so automatic self-inflating life jackets need to be maintained and 're-armed' with a new pill every six months.

Adrian and Matty had never replaced the pill. Not over the last six months. Not last year. Not *any* year since the life jackets found their way onto the boat.

Even though every two years when Adrian had to fill out the Marine and Coastguard Agency's check list, for the Code of Safe Working Practices for Merchant Seamen and Commercial Fishermen, he'd always tick the box that stated the automatic life jackets had been checked and re-armed with a new gas canister and pill.

Truth is, they never bought the jackets new in the first place. When the huge 74-metre Condor Ferry had a total refit, a lot of the crew's safety equipment found its way out the back door, into The Sailors.

Most of the commercial boys in Weymouth had ex-Condor Ferry life jackets hanging on the back of their wheelhouse doors.

To be fair, even if the pill is well past its expiration date and so is fuck-all use as an automatic trigger system, it's really no big deal. So long as the wearer is still conscious when he goes over the side into the freezing, throat-rasping salty sea. It doesn't matter.

So long as they're conscious, all they got to do is pull down hard on the red nylon plastic toggle that hangs beneath the trigger mechanism to activate the manual override.

Yank the toggle hard and the pill becomes irrelevant, the cord attached to the toggle trips the firing mechanism and the sharpened steel spike gets shot by the tightly coiled spring, piercing it deep into the $CO_2$ canister.

Just as long as there's gas in the canister, everything else is peachy keen. Pull toggle. Trigger firing pin. Pierce canister. And the gas inflates the jacket's flotation bladder. Doesn't fucking matter if the pill is as old as Joanna Lumley, gas'll still flow where it's meant to go.

So when Adrian hit the sea, a mile-and-a-half south by southwest of The Bill, leaping off the gunwale into five knots of ebb tide, roaring towards Devon, he was not in the least surprised as his testicles shrivelled with the cold. Not surprised at all that the automatic mechanism on the life jacket hidden under his thick jumper didn't immediately explode into buoyant life-saving life.

The pill would be fucked. Of that he had no doubt.

As the roar of the propane explosion savaged his ears, making the frozen top of his sea-soaked head feel suddenly hot with its fiery blast, Adrian twisted his body, thrust his hand up under the jumper, and grabbed the red toggle.

As his steel-toed boots and sodden bait-stained Dickie jeans sucked him downwards, above him the roof of Kitty K's wheelhouse cartwheeled across the sky, trailing a streak of smoke and flame and fragments of Matty.

Adrian tugged down hard on the toggle.

As he closed his mouth to preserve his air and keep from guzzling a lungful of saltwater, Adrian's eyes stared up at the disappearing sky.

He yanked on the toggle. Which yanked the cord. Which pulled down the lever on the trigger mechanism. Which shot the steel firing pin, upwards in a perfect clean trajectory...

...into nothing.

The canister of $CO_2$ having long before been unscrewed from the self-inflating life jacket mechanism, to be screwed into the butt of Tim's Heckler and Koch P30.

The one with the anodized aluminium finish and the Ambrose Dexter grip.